Praise for the adventures of Ty Merrick

QUANTUM MOON

"Refreshing."

—*Locus*

"Vitola works as hard at creating an engaging mystery as she does at the science fiction, and she succeeds at both."

—*Time Out Books*

"Add Vitola to your list of names to watch for."

—*Science Fiction Chronicles*

OPALITE MOON

(A Philip K. Dick Award nominee)

"Vitola's strong suit is taking the problems of today and projecting them onto the fun-house mirror of the future."

—*Contra Costa Times*

"A cleverly intricate tale of intriguing possibilities."

—*Romantic Times*

MANJINN MOON

"The perfect blending of mystery and science fiction with a few paranormal elements sprinkled on top of the exciting story line."

—*Midwest Review of Books*

"A neat mystery wrapped up in intriguing speculation—just the kind of reading in which connoisseurs delight."

—*Romantic Times*

Ace Books by Denise Vitola

QUANTUM MOON
OPALITE MOON
MANJINN MOON
THE RED SKY FILE
THE RADON FILE

THE RADON FILE

DENISE VITOLA

THE RADON FILE

An Ace Book / published by arrangement with
the author

PRINTING HISTORY
Ace edition / October 1999

Cover art by Cliff Nielsen.

For information address: The Berkley Publishing Group,
a division of Penguin Putnam Inc.,
375 Hudson Street, New York, New York 10014.

The Penguin Putnam Inc. World Wide Web site address is
http://www.penguinputnam.com

ISBN: 0-441-00670-1

ACE®
Ace Books are published
by The Berkley Publishing Group,
a division of Penguin Putnam Inc.,
375 Hudson Street, New York, New York 10014.
ACE and the "A" design are trademarks
belonging to Penguin Putnam Inc.

PRINTED IN THE UNITED STATES OF AMERICA

10 9 8 7 6 5 4 3 2 1

For my friends and students at
The Idea Factory

THE RADON FILE

ONE

Criticism gone unrecognized settles in the bones, causing arthritis. This wisdom came straight from the mouth of Bernard Horn's maestro, Silvio Valinari, and if anyone knew about criticism, he did. Every day it had been the same with him: "When Hakeem Nigan was your age he was singing at the San Carlo Opera House. And you! Look at you. Hoping to perform *St. Ophelia's Requiem* for a bunch of politicos who are too stupid to know the opera is intended to mock them. You're a saint of a singer, Bernardo. Use your gift. Stop wasting it on the idle and rich. Sing! Sing for the masses. This is immortality."

Horn tried to give the thoughts of his musical mentor a hardy shove from his mind by carefully focusing on the shiny points of crystals embedded in the stone walls and ceiling of the PHO Rejuvenation Facility. The flickering light of the storm lamp picked up their glitter, but unfortunately, he couldn't dislodge the image of Silvio's scowling face and that spoiled everything. He was the reason Horn had this debilitating disease. Silvio's constant berating had a way of inflaming a person, and if the person wasn't strong enough, this fire would burn up the inspiration instead of stoking the creativity. In Horn's case, this flame had possessed him at a cellular level, and when the world didn't respond according to expectations, it had nowhere to blossom except in his joints.

Horn turned over on his hospital bed, and this slight movement made the springs scream out. The noise was magnified in his underground chamber, reminding him of the acoustics of the Sunrise Concert Hall in District 179. Shaped like a lotus flower, the temple opened onto an immense water park that reflected the colors of dawn each day. He'd sung there just once, and then only as a minor voice in a big production, but he'd fallen in love with the majesty and the beauty of the place. Sadly, the government had not permitted him to sing there again. Silvio was still incensed with the disrespect they'd shown him, and though Horn kept silent, he had grudgingly agreed with the old man. He had done everything for the government, right down to giving over his life and liberty, and yet they would not grant him these simple, creative opportunities.

Silvio was the last of the idealists, but his big talk wasn't based on one bit of reality. The masses didn't pay to hear the opera. Horn's job was to sing where he was told to sing, and like it or not, he owed his success to the bureaucrats. Their appreciation had been limited, but they'd finally designated him as a humanitarian treasure.

Silvio simply didn't understand this, and even if he did, it wasn't enough for him. He thought Horn had definite talent, but after all was said and done, it didn't really matter. His spine was so twisted from the arthritis that he couldn't stand straight enough to practice singing scales much less sing an entire opera.

He was forty-five years old and all washed up. Would he crawl to the day of judgment pushing his regrets in front of him? Would he ever be confident that his was truly an awesome, though unrecognized talent, or would he be forever plagued with his insecurities, content to scuffle for crumbs, because he was afraid the truth might reveal his dismal identity?

Silvio understood none of this.

Horn turned over once more, coughing against the agony this movement brought to bear upon his body. Clutching the pillow, he waited for the spasm to run its course and when he could breathe again, he began humming a few bars of an aria from *La Traviata*. It helped to calm the pain, but it did nothing to ease the burden carried by his soul. *Sing! Sing for the masses! Rely upon the magic of your creative soul.* Silvio was the stupid one. There was no magic.

After being diagnosed with rheumatoid arthritis, his doctor at the Planetary Health Organization had recommended that he take the rarefied air at the mine. The physician had explained that the PHO Rejuvenation Facility was a natural source of radon, a gas emitted from uranium. For years, folks with bad bones had been coming there to breathe in the colorless, odorless fumes, and many had undergone remarkable cures. Though radon also caused lung cancer, no one he'd talked to was concerned about it. After all, living with arthritis was a hideous existence, too.

The pain eased somewhat, but by that time, the nurse had arrived. She tut-tutted him for being so secretive about his suffering as she raised his bed and helped him to adjust his blankets.

''I need to take a sample of spinal fluid,'' she said.

Horn winced. It didn't hurt when she took the goo, but afterward he would get a giant headache that would last for hours. ''Can't we put that off until tomorrow morning?''

She shook her head solemnly. ''We need to gauge the effects of the radon, Mr. Horn. We can only do that by tracking the rise and fall of lymphocytes present in the fluid.''

He was doing penance for his sins. Clearly, his base chakra was opening, for when that happened all manner of physical pain befell a person. Because it was the first supernatural energy center to be unlocked in his body, it was analogous to opening the gates of hell and releasing the demons, but instead of this evil invading the living world, it corrupted the living cells of the host organism. He'd prayed and fasted during the hot months, hoping this simple routine would allow him access to the power of the second chakra. It was said that wild energy surged from this source, and if he could just concentrate hard enough and meditate long enough, he could tap into the well of unrestrained force, using it to expand his consciousness so far from his arthritis that he wouldn't feel the agony anymore.

He was sure he could do it, but for some reason, he was too tired to try anymore. It was either that, or he was bored with the possibilities that the science of metaphysics promised.

"The lady in the next cubicle keeps complaining about seeing little people who claim to be from the center of the earth," he said.

The nurse nodded. "Mrs. Johnson, the poor dear. She suffers from dementia. If she's bothering you, I'll ask the staff to move her. We've had a cubicle open on an upper level."

Horn understood the necessity for self-delusion. "No," he answered softly. "Please don't do that."

The nurse puckered her lips and nodded. She snapped on a pair of latex gloves, and when her fingers were comfortable, she helped him turn over. Each movement brought new electricity to his nerve endings. When he finally lay on his side and faced toward the wall, the attendant had to push his legs toward his groin because he couldn't draw his knees up without help. He heard her pop open the cellophane package that held the large, hollow epidural needle and then he felt her swab down the skin above his lower spine with the cold anesthetic. Horn closed his eyes, waiting to feel the stab of the needle as it punctured the space between his vertebrae and entered the spinal canal. While he anticipated the discomfort, his mind leaped off to replay other tortures enacted by Silvio.

His mentor had wanted to know why, after all these years of accepting the mental beatings, he was finally finding the backbone to push him away. Silvio was the true phantom for the opera—part demon, part angel. On one hand—the liberator, on the other the jailer. Still, it did no good blaming the source of the torment. It was a matter of taking responsibility for one's own existence. Silvio had tried to help him, even if his concern had a motivation borne in false hopes of fame and wealth. The maestro was simply out of his time, stuck in a degenerate society.

Horn's shrink maintained that to release the arthritis, he must first release his spirit from Silvio's domination, and for that he would need to identify the patterns comprising his fear. Once he could separate the guilt, the sorrow, and the harsh self-judgment, then, yes, he would get better and his disease might just go into remission. Rehabilitating those dark emotions would be like losing old friends that he'd spent years suckling. He'd come to rely upon them. He'd used his pain and reprisal like swords and mallets—cutting, shaping, and beating until he had formed himself into the very image of pathos. It was a mask that fit the persona of an opera singer who could not find the depth of his creativity.

He felt the nurse's fingers on the small of his back, and despite the anesthetic, he felt the jab of the needle before it entered his spine. The pressure of her hand disappeared and Horn closed his eyes, trying to hear past the rush in his ears. His doctor had told him the strange noise occasionally accompanied the procedure, but this day it was so loud, he barely heard the nurse curse gently. How long he stayed like that he didn't know. He drifted, the sound slowly diminishing until he heard a sliding footstep.

Opening his eyes, he was surprised to see a tiny, bald person—perhaps three-feet-five from the top of her silver head to the bottom of her silver feet. She stood in the space between his bed and the wall, studying him intently.

"Nurse?" he whispered.

There was no reply. Horn tried to move his legs, but unfortunately, he couldn't feel his extremities. In fact, he couldn't move at all.

The odd little being studied him, and in the dull light, she seemed more inhuman than human. Her head was pointy, her eyes were too small, and the glittering of her cloak made his eyes weep and his vision double. The strange visitor touched him on the forehead. When she did, he felt her lament, and this silent keening slammed into his brain. It was then Horn saw the bright light of the great beyond, and knew for a fact that he was dying.

TWO

In this case, the term ''irradiating a melon'' didn't pertain to charging up grocery-store vegetables. It referred to my melon, the one that sits on top of my neck, because the moment I entered the PHO Rejuvenation Facility, I got a headache that hurt down to my eyelids. The mine was the center of a crime scene, so I reluctantly ordered my migraine to take a backseat to the investigation and sought out my partner, Andy LaRue.

I found him by his hair. He was the only one in the area wearing the black uniform of the Marshals Office and his sepia tresses were long enough to flow over his utility belt. As usual, he wore the spatters and stains of lunch down the front of his cammies and that hair, as impressive as it was, needed combing.

Rolling up to him, I interrupted a discussion he was having with our medical examiner, Frank Wilson. Both men turned toward me, and LaRue, always one to table his current discourse, dropped the subject to greet me. ''Ty,'' he said. ''What kept you?''

Being a lycanthrope had kept me. That's right, I'm a werewolf—not the kind that made Lon Chaney, Jr., famous, but the type who changes subtly in thought and form. I was as normal as the next man until a stakeout spent with a faulty furnace ended up with me nearly dying from carbon monoxide poisoning. Luckily, a ward cop pulled my butt to safety, but he'd been too late to prevent my gray matter from being affected. From that time on, I've spent each round of the lunar month dealing with the various alterations that follow the onset of the wolf. Now it seemed I was not only fighting a battle with my illness, but I was again battling the District One government.

"The watch commander called me into her office for a brief moment, Andy," I answered. "It seems that she received the test results on our annual mental health review."

"We beat the game with flying colors, right?" he asked.

"Wrong. We flunked. The both of us."

Wilson suddenly started laughing. He dabbed at the sweat runnels on his forehead with one hand and clasped his middle-aged gut with the other. A minute followed where he shook with pleasure.

"I'm glad you think this is so funny," I snapped.

He tried to talk around his guffaws. "Why do they bother to test you two, Merrick? You're both crazier than Duvalier's fifth wife. Nothing is going to change there."

Duvalier. He had been the esteemed dictator who had overthrown the UN forces and turned the world into a huge toilet of humanitarian values that didn't have a chance to work from the very beginning. His ideas of equality and compassion had played into greed and corruption. The government bootlickers cleaned up while the rest of us floundered in poverty and the bungled science that had been reborn into forms of superstition and invisible magic. It took a hard person not to give in to the easy metaphysical answers provided by properly stuffed charm sacks, specially blended love potions, or eloquently spoken good luck spells. Despite having one foot in the paranormal doorway with the uniqueness of my lycanthropy, I still looked at society from a skeptical angle and I didn't like butthole-sucking bureaucrats telling me I was part of the problem.

"Did Julie explain what's going to happen since we failed the quiz?" LaRue demanded.

"No," I said quietly. "We're to meet with her after we're

done here at the crime scene. What do we have?''

Wilson finally regained his composure and explained. ''We have Bernard Horn.''

''The singer?''

''The humanitarian treasure.''

''Well, I guess that's a matter of opinion. What happened?''

Wilson stepped back and held his hand out, indicating the narrow slice of a stone corridor. ''After you.''

I'll admit, I do have claustrophobia. I don't like caves and had a feeling I wouldn't care for being deep in a uranium mine, but since I've got less common sense than courage, I headed down the hall. It led to an elevator shaft, and after a short trip into the earth, we stopped at rejuvenation level three, met there by a battery of forensic techs and crime scene photographers. We traced the antlike activity until we came to Mr. Horn's private chambers. Here, we were shown the remains of a man who'd had his pajama pants pulled down and a big, hollow needle jabbed into his lower back. Milky white liquid had run from the man into a bedpan sitting on the floor by the bed.

''Saint Ophelia,'' I whispered.

A lone technician busily filled a specimen baggie and Wilson dismissed him before replying. ''The killer drained his cerebrospinal fluid. You see, the spine and the brain are a closed system that function as a unit. The gray matter literally floats in this goo, and when the juice leaked out, Horn's brain collapsed.'' He paused for dramatic effect and then added: ''Yep. It's laying there on the inside of his skull turning black.''

''It looks like he didn't put up a struggle,'' I said.

''No. I checked his records. Horn was undergoing a therapy regime that demanded regular examinations.'' Using his chin, he pointed to the horse needle. ''Spinal taps were part of that.''

''I take it someone is interviewing the nursing staff?''

''Yes,'' LaRue said. ''But there is one person missing. A woman named Jenna York.''

''Did anyone see or hear anything?''

''No. But some of the elderly patients here are talking about people from the center of the earth.''

I glanced at him. "People from the center of the earth?"

My partner smiled, warming to the subject immediately. "Stories of a forgotten race of humans have been going around for years. Late last century, the myth was grandly embellished by the addition of UFOs."

"Unidentified flying objects?"

"That's right. There were theorists who believed that aliens were entering hollow portions of the earth by accessing openings found miles below the surface of the oceans."

"That's the hypothesis I favor," Wilson added. "Hell, I'm pretty sure Charlotte's sister is from the center of the earth. It's like Mars versus Venus."

I ignored the reference to his wife and her sibling. "Who found Horn?"

"An intern by the name of Purceval Walker," he said. "He's gone, too."

"Of course," I answered sarcastically, scanning the room. It was a twenty-foot-square cubicle carved from bare rock. The ceiling glistened with quartz crystal and flecks of fool's gold. There was a wooden cabinet parked against the far wall and several wind chimes. Seeing those, I thought of LaRue's uncle Carl, a charming, rotund man who claimed the title of feng shui priest. He would say that the wind bells promoted the wafting of chi or life energy through the mine. I pointed to the tinklers. "To better circulate the radon?"

"Actually, I noticed them and asked," LaRue said. "Horn brought them with him."

"Why?"

"He believed they contained the essence of his music."

I did my best to hide an expression of impatience but it escaped, nonetheless. "He thought he stored the tones of his voice within the wind chimes?"

"As far as I can tell."

Wilson jumped back into the conversation. "Yeah, these creative types are usually pretty warped. I guess that goes double for folks with a bucketful of talent."

"According to the head nurse in this place, Horn was here because his creativity was failing him." LaRue paused to scrape a look over me. "You know, failing him like our mental health apparently is."

I grunted. "What was the medical reason for his visit?"

"Rheumatoid arthritis," Wilson said. "Horn was almost a cripple. That's why he hadn't had any public performances in the last several months. As soon as we go through an autopsy, I can give you more of a handle on his condition previous to his demise."

"Have we come up with any wild motives about why someone would want to cash out the humanitarian cash cow?" I asked, stepping to the wooden cabinet. I pulled it open and picked through a locker of fashionable clothes while waiting for LaRue to come up with the right response. It didn't take him long.

"Well, he's got a triple-A-Class designation, which means he gets paid whether he can sing or not. I have a feeling someone had to find a way to slash the budget."

It was always likely that the government was behind the current atrocity. A person couldn't take a leak without the dung eaters barging the door down to find out if his pee was as yellow as it was supposed to be. There were more and more laws on the books, rules and regulations designed to contain the growing unrest circulating through the population. If murder was necessary to maintain the political status quo, then murder was an acceptable act, even though the subsequent cover-up drained manpower and resources because the Marshals Office was called in to investigate.

Instead of stating the evident, I pulled out a linen shirt. It was exceptionally tailored and nicely pressed. I showed it off to LaRue. "This will fit you."

My partner grinned and joined me at the cabinet as Wilson stomped away to talk to a tech. We spent a couple minutes browsing through the clothes, and before we knew it, LaRue had the basis of a whole new wardrobe.

You may think it unprofessional to steal the victim's belongings, but our society is based on the scam, and what meat you don't pick off the bone, you lose to the powerful vultures who already have full craws. It's a sad reality, but a necessary one. A marshal's pay, though Class-A designation, doesn't bring in enough to keep a parakeet alive. Luckily, LaRue and I both had some credits stashed away through fortunes found in another case. Normally, it would have contented us, yet the rumblings of civil disobedience put a premium on supplies and those who would horde them. Clothes, food, fuel—all these things were limited, and many times unavailable. So who could fault us for walking away with some scatty duds?

While LaRue unzipped his cammies and slipped on two of the shirts, I crammed socks and underwear into the deep pockets of my own uniform. We might have been procuring in a less than ethical manner, and yes, everyone did it, but there was no reason to be obvious about it.

As my partner complained about closing up the front of his uniform, I continued my search, going from drawer to drawer, finding silk handkerchiefs, a stash of handwoven ties, and one very interesting carnival mask.

THREE

LaRue and I took the mask and returned to the office, forgetting about the thing after we were immediately called into a meeting with Julie, our watch commander. She was a coarse, old broad, used to beating the bushes instead of slapping the ground around them and her expression was so dark that it instantly put us on our guard. Pointing to the hard-back chairs positioned before her cluttered desk, she ordered us to sit down. My butt had just hit the seat when she kicked the door shut and announced our current dilemma.

''The Marshals Office is reshuffling personnel,'' she said. ''New bureaucrats are coming in upstairs and new regulations and standards are being put into place. It's a policy-writing nightmare.'' Julie paused to slide in behind her desk. ''These new government weenies are downsizing the force, and you two are right in the way.''

''The mental health evaluation?'' LaRue asked.

''That's part of it.''

''What did the tester say?''

She stared at him. ''That you run your life by meaningless metaphysical principles which impact your decisions during investigations.'' Turning toward me, she added, ''You, Merrick, are deemed overboard on all counts.''

Well, you can't fight the truth. "Why us?" I asked, leaning forward. "We've got a good track record. Andy and I pulled in more murderers in the last year than anyone in the office."

Julie nodded. "I know, I know. Someone obviously has it in for you."

Her words struck up familiar paranoia in me. The list of our enemies grew longer every day.

"According to the brass, your methods don't measure up to current investigational procedures," she explained. "The new boys want to get rid of as much of the magical hokem as they can. They've already axed twelve psychic consultants on the payroll."

"How can you get rid of the superstition when that's the only way you can relate to the community?" I asked.

"Personally, I don't think you can. If the investigator doesn't operate with an eye toward society's mind-set, then he's a useless piece of twaddle. But there's a movement afoot that's trying to shift the citizen's viewpoint and the bureaucrats want it to start right here."

I sat back. The rumors had been flying for months about changes in far-off districts. Known as the Spark of Creation Movement, these people were rebuilding the world in their image and they needed strong backs and shallow minds to accomplish it. We were being herded into service like slaves of the ancient Egyptians—worked like pack animals, and for our trouble, we were fed a daily ration of raw onions, vodka, and bullshit. I suppose it was only a matter of time. Duvalier's great humanitarian dream had floundered on the morning of its inaugural day. Our society, with its lofty aspirations of creative freedom and equality, was done before breakfast was over.

"You're talking about the Sparkers, aren't you?" LaRue asked. "They've infiltrated the highest ranks of government here in the district."

Julie scowled. "I never mentioned them by name." She turned her expression onto a stack of papers sitting on her desk. "Goddamn bastards," she muttered.

"Jobs, food, housing, health care, and transportation will win the day," LaRue said.

Julie sighed, raising her gaze. "It doesn't matter. They'll be starting a full-scale propaganda campaign during the upcoming Autumn Carnival. Five days of revelry, free alcohol, new thought, looting, riots. There's nothing official, mind you, but the leaders have their heads up the same butt."

"Riots and civil disobedience can't solve anything," I said.

"Well, the ward cops are on alert. We're expecting trouble. Problem is we don't know what side it's going to be coming from."

"That's not going to make our jobs any easier," LaRue muttered.

"You won't have to worry about it if you don't solve this current case."

"What does that mean?" I asked.

"That means that the brass is giving you a chance to fit into the new government. If you find the murderer and apprehend him, then the big boys will grant you another evaluation, and this time you'll have the privilege of picking the shrink to blow through your brains. If not, you'll be stripped of your Class-A designations and someone new will be brought in to fill your shoes and your jobs."

Upon hearing this ultimatum, I turned to stare at LaRue, finding him sitting there with a strange, thoughtful look. I dismissed his expression as belonging to some arcane principle involving karma or curses and asked the question Julie expected. "What happens to us if they take away our designations? Without a labor category, we can't work."

"Precisely." She shook her head. "You'll be placed on the public work dole and forced to assume whatever duties they require of you." She stopped speaking again and seemed to calculate the moment our surprise had reached its peak. "There's more. This case is being handled jointly. You will have to share your case findings with a couple of agents from the Environmental Tax Agency."

The ETA was the most hated agency in the government, because it was responsible for gouging the citizens for their quarterly taxes.

"Why them?" I asked.

"How the hell do I know, Merrick? I get my orders the

same as you, but unlike you I know when to stop asking nosy questions.'' Her lips moved for a second before she put any noise behind them. ''My unofficial recommendation to you is to find the killer and keep as much info off the books as you can, especially if you use your usual methods to nab him. And whatever you do, don't talk openly about any forms of superstition or magic.''

FOUR

I suppose one of the things that got LaRue in trouble with the mental health examiner was his obsessive love for the old Soviet Union. Though he hails from hearty French-Canadian stock, he carries around the soul of a Russian. To this end, he eats beet soup, drinks vodka, and drives a commie car—his beloved Trabant. The Trabi has always been a wreck, an antique held over from this era of Soviet self-denial, but it had four wheels and a two-barrel engine that smoked along on a combination of oil and dirty fuel. We were grateful for this ride, though. Automobiles were a thing that belonged to the past. Most of the manufacturing plants were closed, and not even the Marshals Office had any new cars to spare for their investigators. The Trabi, then, might be the thing that helped us keep our jobs.

We took the carnival mask we'd found at the crime scene and moved our office to LaRue's Soviet sedan. Then, having such a suspicious nature, we decided to turn the car inside out to make sure we'd not been bugged with listening devices by devious bureaucrats who were busy following our every move. Not that these kinds of electronic devices were any more available than an auto, but it set our minds to rest, nonetheless.

"So, did you tell the shrink about your mother's vinegar-

and-hot-sauce love potion?'' I asked as I checked the liner above the visor.

LaRue had his head under the seat and his response was muffled. ''I told him about a lot of things. What about you? Cue him in on your lycanthropic episodes this time?''

''That's what I can't figure. Gibson told me not to mention it and I didn't. Still, he grades me as loony as you. We've been had, partner.''

LaRue's head popped up, barely stopping short of whacking the steering wheel. ''No doubt. Who have we pissed off lately?''

As far as I could tell, just about everyone. ''We are the model of sweetness and light. How could we have done anything to annoy anyone?''

He grunted, but didn't build on my attempt at humor. I could tell he wasn't in any mood to joke about the situation, so I bent to the job of scraping out the contents of the glove box.

When we'd completed the chore, we'd discovered no bugs, but did find a one-credit note that had floated beneath the front seat, a forgotten charm sack stuffed inside the ashtray, and some gooey stuff on the back floorboard. Satisfied we were alone, we sat in the muddy parking lot and studied the mask.

It was beautiful, handcrafted from blond leather and struck through with tiny, paste gems that glittered and sparkled when held to the light. The mask was fashioned to be tied around the head and worn across the eyes and nose only. Like a psychometrist hoping to get vibes off an object, I put on the carnival gear.

''This leather will make you sweat,'' I said, admiring myself in the rearview mirror.

''It'll give you a case of acne, too,'' LaRue answered. ''Not to mention a variety of diseases.'' Sitting back, he stretched his arms, using the steering wheel to balance them. I thought I was in for a lecture about hygiene, but he hauled the subject back to our current dilemma. ''Did you see any investigators at the crime scene whom you didn't know?''

I shook my head. ''No, but then why should we have? Do

you think these ETA twits are going to do any of the dirty work? That's up to us, as usual."

"So, how are we going to keep info off the books and still work the backdoor market?"

Good question. The backdoor market was the district's underground network, where a person could buy magic and superstition as well as organically grown vegetables. It was illegal, but ignored by everyone, because the shortages on goods and services made it the only place a person could go to find the things needed to survive.

I pulled off the mask and ran a fingernail under the stitched edging, snapping delicate threads as I did. When I finally had the facing pulled away, I found the mask maker's initials carved delicately into the leather. "T.C.," I announced. "That would be Tom Cullen, I'll bet."

LaRue started the Trabi and pointed us down the street. "Let's see if that old weasel is in his usual hole."

I stuffed the mask into my pocket, settling back for the ride while allowing my indignation to boil and churn. Things were just getting good for me and this intrusion into my peace of mind by government reorganizing pissed me off. I finally had food, clothes, and fuel. I also had the devotion of Dr. Lane Gibson.

My lycanthropy is the reason we are together in the first place. Gibson is a talented neurologist, who is trying to cure or control my strange disease. I don't fool myself that he's out to help me for the warm, fuzzy feelings that compassion brings. Gibson has his own agenda, which includes turning a buck on the information he garners from studying me, but while this problem pierces our relationship, our feelings for each other have kept this splinter from infecting the soft tissue surrounding it.

The truth is, I don't care how much money Gibson makes off my lycanthropy. I can't keep my hands off him and want him around all the time. Perhaps it's the flush of romance; my experience with love being a big, fat zero until he showed up. Whatever it was, I knew I didn't appreciate anything that might alter the status quo. Life, with all its hard knocks, owed me that much.

We reached Tom Cullen's apartment twenty minutes later. Cullen lived on the third floor of a decrepit high-rise in a ward known as Liberation Alley. This neighborhood got its name not because it celebrated freedom, but because the pickpockets would liberate you from your wallet if you weren't careful.

Cullen answered his door after a couple of knocks and took a moment to paste a surprised look across his hangdog face before inviting us in. He ran a hand through his scrub of black hair and pointed to a park bench situated in the middle of the one-room flat. I sat down, but LaRue decided to take a swing around the cluttered space, pausing here and there to admire a latex mask or the turn of a pink ostrich feather. While he coaxed in the view, I began the interview.

''From the looks of this workshop of yours, I take it your District Merchandising License is in order,'' I said.

Cullen nodded, swallowed hard, and sat down in a bentwood rocker. ''Yes, Marshal Merrick. My papers are registered. I'm on the carnival list this year; just check. My name is there. I paid a good price for that spot and I haven't done anything wrong. I ain't been hustling nobody, either.''

''We aren't here to prosecute you, Tom,'' I said pleasantly. ''We were simply going to remind you in case you forgot to submit your forms this year.''

He snorted. ''How the hell could I forget? The district don't let anyone forget. If you pay your environmental taxes, you get these gentle little reminders about your other obligations.'' Cullen paused to stare at me before adding: ''But then you work for the government. I guess you don't have to pay taxes at all.''

How I wished that were so. ''No, we get gouged like everyone else.'' Reaching into my pocket, I pulled out the mask. ''Do you remember who you made this for?''

Cullen studied it before fessing up. ''Yeah. The opera singer.''

''Bernard Horn?''

''Yes, ma'am.''

''When?''

''He came to pick it up about a week ago.'' Cullen stopped

in his explanation, played with a question, and then decided to ask it. "He died, didn't he?"

"Yes. He was murdered."

Cullen went on the offensive immediately. "Well, it weren't because of the mask. It was clean—no evil hexes, voodoo spit, nor demon scum. No poisons that might get soaked up by the skin, neither. That leather came from a district-approved supplier, too. I ain't done nothin' wrong."

"We just want to ask you some questions, Cullen," LaRue barked.

The man nodded and rooted through his hair like he was looking for something stuck to his scalp. "I don't know what I can tell you."

"Did he have anyone with him when he visited you?" I asked.

"Yes. A big, fat woman."

"Who was she?"

"He introduced her as his fiancée."

"Did she have a name?"

"Betty." He screwed up his lips while he thought hard about her. "Sorry, but I can't remember these fancy-schmancy names. It was a long one. She was a real talker; I can tell you that. She wouldn't let him get a word in edgewise. Kept talking about how excited she was about the carnival. He didn't seem none too enthused, though."

"Why not?"

He shrugged. "I got the feeling she was doing the buying and he was doing the paying. You know how that goes."

"Why did they buy this mask?"

"Masks. They ordered ten of them." He pointed to his handiwork. "I figured they wanted them for their friends during the carnival, but then she wanted them slopped with a spell."

"What kind of spell?"

"Creativity spell," he answered. "Well, I told her that I didn't have the whomping power to put on something like that. The most I could give her was a storage whammy."

"The mask stores creativity?" I asked.

"Yep." Cullen leaned forward. "I'll tell you folks a little

secret if you walk out of here and leave me be.''

''What's that?''

''Them creativity spells are right popular amongst the Sparkers.''

FIVE

As for creativity and the growing sentiment toward free expression, our mask maker obviously didn't agree, because in the end, Cullen clammed up tight. He'd never made a mask for Horn before and he'd had no long, urbane conversations with him. So we returned to the office to find out the whereabouts of the fiancée named Betty, and to schedule interviews with the staff of PHO Rejuvenation Mine, but when we arrived, we discovered that our ETA counterparts were blatantly burning a trail before us. The goose steppers stood in our greasy interrogation room, a blond man and a dark-haired woman, each sporting spit and polish and unconcerned about stepping into the middle of our interrogation. They grilled an old woman as if they had gestapo blood circulating in those rock-hard veins of theirs. Since they were so unconcerned about us, LaRue and I stormed in.

The female agent glared at us. "Who do you think you are?"

She had a deep voice, and in the course of that short sentence I formed an ugly opinion about her. "We think we're Marshals LaRue and Merrick. Who do you think you are?"

The man snorted. "Of course. The werewolf and her trained human escort."

LaRue and I are used to the snubs and insults, but that doesn't mean we have to take them. Upon hearing this guy's observation, my partner exploded. LaRue is not a big man, yet he is fast and powerful. Provoked, he moves like a panther. In the next moment he proved his abilities by grabbing the agent's neck with one hand while he slammed him against the wall with the other. The commotion caused the woman to draw her service revolver.

It had been a long time since a fellow officer had drawn a gun on us and it riled me immediately. In the span of a second I could tell she held the weapon like a girl who didn't want to screw up her manicure. I kicked it from her fingers and it clattered to the floor, spinning toward the frightened witness cowering at the table.

Our commotion called down Julie's attention and she rushed into the melee to separate us like rutting sheep. It took another couple of minutes of grunting, pushing, and accusing before we all shut up. When she finally had order, she picked up the gun and slapped it back into the female agent's hands. "Nichols," she said, "You and Carver better get one thing straight. You're here to observe and provide routine support to the investigators assigned to this case. Beyond that, you are to stay out of the way and obey the rules, which include never drawing your weapon on a fellow law enforcement official. If you do it again, I will set you out to dry the hard way. Is that clear?"

"Why the hell are they here anyway?" I demanded fiercely. "Is there something about Bernard Horn you'd like to share?"

"Shut up, Merrick!" Julie roared. We locked stares and antlers for a full minute before I disentangled and took a chair at the table, climbing upon it like a Pony Express rider ready to take off across the range. Julie turned back to the ETA agents.

Nichols sneered and Carver mumbled, but in the end they agreed to be good little pigs and stay on the far side of the stage lights. Julie faced LaRue and me and then pointed to the old lady. "Take over the interview."

Carver started to protest, spit flying from his fat lips. "This isn't right, Commander. We were in the midst of a fact-finding interrogation.''

''Merrick and LaRue will take care of it,'' Julie snapped. ''Now clear out before I change my mind and let my marshals loose.''

The dark duo conceded the day and retreated from the room, slamming the door behind them.

I, of course, couldn't let the situation lie without kicking it a few times. ''You said we were supposed to share our findings with the ETA. Now they're dogging our steps. Can we still trust you, Julie?''

She scowled at me. ''About as much as I can trust you. I was hoping to avoid complications, but with you two, I can see I was grasping at twigs when I really needed a branch.''

''You should know by now that you need the whole tree with us,'' LaRue answered. He sighed. ''I don't appreciate all this.''

''I understand, but there is nothing I can do. My hands are tied and I can't cut you any slack. If it happens again, you'll be brought up on disciplinary charges, regardless of who started it. I told you the brass is watching you through the keyhole, so do me a favor. No more fuckups. Stay away from Nichols and Carver, and when you are forced to communicate your reports, be pleasant and professional. Understand?''

I hate getting a wedgy that's pulled all the way from upstairs, and as usual, I was helpless when my underwear was yanked. I nodded. ''We'll do our best to steer clear of them.''

Before she stomped from the room, Julie glared at LaRue, who reluctantly agreed to be a good boy by nodding. After she was gone, I glanced at my partner. He stared at the invisible trail she'd left behind, and taking a deep breath, he changed the air in the room by turning his focus onto the old lady.

''You would be Mrs. Trisha Neal,'' he said.

''Yes, sir, I would be.''

Sliding into the chair next to me, he jumped into the questions. ''You are employed by the PHO at their rejuvenation facility. Is that correct?''

''Yes, sir. I'm in charge of housekeeping.''

"Did you meet Bernard Horn?"

"Oh, yes. I talked to him every day when I'd drop off his fresh linens. He was a gentleman. Real nice and all."

"What did you talk about?"

"Mostly about opera." She touched her face, her fingertips lingering on the deep crevice of a winkle. "I went to the opera when I was younger. My husband sang in District One Choir. Free tickets, you know."

"Did you hear Mr. Horn sing during a live performance?"

"No. It was before his time. Besides, he never made it real big. I've been hearing that recently he was showing considerable strength of voice, like he had some miracle hit his vocal cords or something, but to be honest, I've listened to the recordings and I don't hear a change at all."

"Why do you figure there was all this hoopla over his voice?" LaRue asked.

She shrugged and then leaned close to speak conspiratorially. "If you ask me, it has nothing to do with talent, but a whole heck of a lot to do with propaganda."

"What do you mean by that?" LaRue whispered.

Neal sat back. "I don't know. I just know that talk is talk whether it comes over the district array or over the telephone." She spent a moment rubbing her tongue along her front teeth as though she was trying to dislodge food or a new idea. Come to find out, it was an opinion she wrestled with. "If you ask me, Horn probably had the talent. He just didn't have the might."

"The might?"

"Sure. He wasn't courageous enough to go against the conservative stream. Every one knows that the government don't want you thinking for yourself. Mr. Horn was a good, little citizen. He made no bones about it."

LaRue rubbed at the dark stubble sweeping across his jaw. "It sounds like you don't agree with the good-little-citizen act."

"I've never agreed with the government on anything. When you live your life cleaning other people's toilets, you lose most of your objectivity and all of your thoughts about the equality of the humanitarian way."

"Did you talk to Bernard Horn the day he died?" I asked abruptly, tired of hearing the same old line of self-pity.

"Yes, Marshal. He was in a right bit of pain, too. Spinal problems."

"What did he say to you?"

"That he couldn't wait until carnival. He was going to change the world and be part of the new abundant, creative future. I always figured being a humanitarian treasure paid enough, but I guess what we have is never what we dream of getting."

"Did he tell you what his big play was?" LaRue asked.

"No, he didn't, and I didn't ask. It isn't polite."

I pulled the mask from my pocket and flapped it at her. "Did he ever talk to you about this?"

Mrs. Neal studied it. "Pretty, ain't it?"

"It stores creativity," I said flatly.

She nodded, touching it gingerly. "He didn't talk to me about it."

"Do you believe it can store creativity and then deliver it to the wearer?"

"I don't know. Never had the opportunity to try such a thing. I suspect it wouldn't work for me."

"Why?"

Neal stopped speaking to pat at her curls. "Creativity will get you in trouble. Imagining things will, too. I've never trusted the artsy-fartsy types. They're all way too rebellious for their own good. It's best to do what you're told and to live in the reality, no matter how dismal it is."

Part of my job is to read past the remarks and her last answer pushed my suspicions over the transom. "You're telling us that you don't agree with anything the Spark of Creation Movement is saying?"

She glanced around nervously before replying. "I'm not a Sparker and I never will be one. I'm a loyal citizen. I've been a humanitarian all my life. Sparkers are dangerous. You can't talk sense to a freethinker."

LaRue obviously zeroed in on her narrow-minded appreciation of life on earth by asking an unexpected question. "Tell us, Mrs. Neal. Have you ever seen any of the little people in the mine—the ones who are supposedly from the center of the earth?''

The old woman studied us for a minute, and when she answered, I could tell he'd stolen her thunder. ''I've been told they're hallucinations, that the gas in the mine has made me stupid, but I know I'm not imagining it. Hallucinations don't wear burn blankets.''

''Burn blankets?'' I asked.

''Yes. The facility has a big storage unit just crammed with supplies. Amongst this stuff are a bunch of burn blankets; you know, the kind they roll fire victims in. One side is real shiny silver.''

''What have you seen?'' I demanded.

''The linen room is on the bottom levels of the facility,'' she murmured. ''I was working down there the day Mr. Horn came up dead.'' She paused, and wrung her hands as she wrung out her confession. ''I was coming up with a clean load of towels when I saw a little person go rushing through a hole in the wall. The being was wearing a burn blanket like it was a cape.''

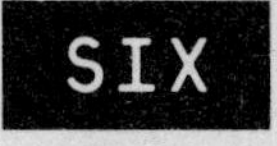

LaRue and I were still stinging over our encounter with our competition, and so we decided to take it out on Gibson. When we arrived in the neighborhood clinic he operates, we found him leaning against the reception counter writing a prescription for someone.

The thing about Gibson that keeps me coming back is his intensity. He wears it like a uniform, and today he appeared to be in full dress. He glanced up as we pushed through the doors and flashed me a wild-eyed squint. Dropping the pen, Gibson paused to run a hand across his long, sandy-blond hair before checking the security of the leather thong holding his ponytail. Satisfied, he came around the desk to greet us.

The clinic was jammed as usual with people staring at us like we were going to jump in front of their appointments. ‘‘We can come back later, if it's more convenient,’’ I said.

He shook his head. ‘‘I have help today. Let's go into my office.’’

We followed him down the short hall into the cracked cubbyhole where he did his paperwork. The place was a wreck: patient files spread across the floor, stacks of medical histories in one corner, a carton of thermometers open and the contents piled on a cot.

"What happened, Doc?" LaRue asked as he righted an overturned chair.

Gibson grunted, shut the door, locked it, and then leaned against it. "The Planetary Health Organization is investigating me."

"What?" I said. "Why?"

"Because of allegations that I'm defrauding the government of funds by using equipment and medical supplies in my efforts to provide you with a cure for your lycanthropy."

I sat down heavily in the chair that LaRue had picked up. "Does it look like they're going to get you?"

He sighed and walked over to his desk, parking his butt on the edge of it. "I had the permission of the governing council of the PHO, but now the members of that esteemed group have been replaced. Who knows how well I'll fare?" Pausing, he studded me with a look. "I suppose I'll do about as well as the two of you."

"So, you heard, huh?" LaRue said.

"Yeah. Your watch commander called. I couldn't believe what she was telling me. When we left those interviews, I was certain you'd score high on the qualifications meter." He shook his head sadly. "You two are getting the butthole shafting of a lifetime. There was no reason for the examiner to flunk you. Not with your hit records."

"We're under close scrutiny right now," I answered quietly. "In fact, we're under observation from the ETA. When we met the agents this morning, we formed an instant friendship."

Gibson chuckled darkly. "Did you kill anyone?"

"Almost. Andy, my ever-faithful monkey boy, didn't like their attitudes." I made a fist and beat lightly on the arm of the chair. "Do you know the bastards won't turn over the official list of names connected to the investigation? How are we supposed to do any kind of flatfoot work without being clued in?"

Gibson ignored my whining. "Julie mentioned there had been an unpleasant episode. She wanted me to remind you to watch what you say and do, Merrick. Whoever is behind this whole matter is going try his hardest to have you both removed from your positions. If they can't do it legally, they won't hesitate calling in their shadows.''

I nodded. ''They provoked us and we turned the nickel on them, just like expected, I'll bet.''

LaRue began picking up books that had been dumped from the shelf. ''I take it there was more to Julie's call than to tell you we failed to live up to society's standards for prime mental health.''

''There was. She wants me to help you with any information I can regarding the case of Bernard Horn.''

I smiled to myself. Julie was doing everything she could to give us an upper paw on Nichols and Carver. It was true: nobody liked tax collectors.

''So, what can you tell us?'' LaRue asked as he continued his housecleaning.

''I can tell you what a waste of funds the PHO Rejuvenation Facility is.''

Gibson's announcement made my partner stop fanning the crinkled pages of a medical journal. He stared at him. ''Now I'm interested. Why is it a waste of funds?''

''Arthritis responds favorably to drug treatment. Researchers had a chemical compound to control the advance of rheumatoid arthritis by the year 2020, and it works. But radon? It smacks of invisible magic and the holistic, feel-good movement.''

''I thought radon was good for the aches and pains.''

''Radon will give you lung cancer, Andy. It will give you hallucinations, and over the long run it will kill you. But cure arthritis? There's been no definitive studies suggesting that it cures anything.''

''What is radon?'' I asked.

''Radon is a radioactive gas,'' he explained. ''Radon 222 is formed from radium isotopes, and the rejuvenation facility is supposed to be constantly flooded with it.''

''How could that help arthritis?''

''Radon gives off alpha particles. After a while the gas begins to decay and these radioactive substances can be absorbed by the body.'' He paused, rubbing his lips with the tips of his fingers. ''Scientists discovered that rheumatoid arthritis, a crippling version of the disease, was in fact, infectious. It had been debated for decades until Dr. Rupert Tompkins discovered the proof. There was a general consensus at the time that radon therapy could relieve the symptoms and arrest the infection, but this announcement was a bit premature. The idea was an outflow of research done on radiation treatment for cancer patients.'' He stopped, inserted a deep breath and a long exhale. ''You know how our society is. It's impossible to separate the wheat from the chaff. Someone at the PHO got hold of the idea years ago and bingo! Disinformation, disappointment, and death.''

''You said something about hallucinations,'' I said.

He nodded. ''Radon affects the gray matter, specifically the temporal lobes. It strikes up colorful, dynamic visions.''

I tossed a long look my partner's way and he met my gaze with a frown. Turning back to Gibson, I filled him in. ''We've interviewed one party so far who believes she saw a person from the center of the earth.''

''That's a good one,'' Gibson said.

I was about to ask him another question, but was interrupted by a vigorous knocking on the door. The good doctor winced at the noise and then slowly slid to a stand. He stepped by me to fling it open, and standing there, wearing a white blazer and a cross expression, was a young woman. She glared at Gibson after satisfying her curiosity with us.

''You were supposed to introduce me to all your patients, Doctor,'' she snarled.

''They aren't patients,'' he snapped. ''They're my friends, and I have no intention of introducing you.'' With that, he slammed the door in the woman's face.

''Who was that?'' I asked, after a minute.

Gibson scowled and his response was husky. ''That is the doctor who will replace me if I'm found guilty of fraud.''

SEVEN

It looked like the three of us were hip-deep in bureaucratic crap, and since we could do nothing but commiserate, we left Gibson and headed up-district to see a lady by the name of Conchita Reuben. According to LaRue, she was a tarot-reader and a woman who might know a few intimate facts about the Spark of Creation Movement. I expected an old crone with an attitude but was pleasantly surprised to meet a fashionable young gal wearing a bright red skirt and a hand-knit halter top. She was endowed with more than a fortune-telling ability and I could see why my partner wanted to come here. When we arrived, she gave him a full-blown kiss.

"Andy, it's been too long," she cooed. "What? A whole week?"

LaRue smiled, glanced at me with an embarrassed expression, and then pointed toward a nicely upholstered chair. At least he'd found a fancy who had a few bucks of her own.

"Nice apartment you have here, Ms. Reuben," I said.

She spun away from LaRue and danced toward the kitchenette. "Thanks, Marshal Merrick. I've scrounged the back-door market for years looking for just the right stuff. It's comfortable, anyway." She paused before entering the galley. "How does espresso sound?"

"Sound's fine," LaRue said, joining me by sitting on a well-appointed sofa. He stared at me, but continued speaking to his girlfriend. "Conchita, our visit isn't a social one."

She stopped fiddling with her coffeepot long enough to shoot him a frown. "Are you on an investigation?"

"Yes. We're looking into the murder of Bernard Horn, the opera singer."

Reuben continued her chores while she shook her head. "He was very good. Never made it big, though. I wonder why."

"We thought you might be able to tell us," LaRue said.

"Through the cards?"

"Through what you might know about the Sparkers," I said.

"I know what everyone else knows," she said guardedly.

"You can be open and honest with us," LaRue murmured. "You know I didn't come to haul you off to the office. We're up against the brick wall of the bureaucracy. The ETA is claiming judicial authority for some reason, and right now they're carefully perusing the witness sheets and withholding names connected with this case. We have to get a leg up, Chita, or we're out of our jobs."

"The ETA?" she asked. "Why didn't you say so in the first place?"

She remained silent until she'd served the small beverage cups. The espresso smelled so good that I wished I could take the odor home. Sipping it, I revised my desire to include the coffee and the coffeepot.

"What do you know about the Sparkers?" LaRue asked quietly.

"They believe that every man has the right to cultivate his own creativity and, therefore, his own life," she answered. "People are tired of sneaking around in the shadows, Andy. They're tired of living in this squalor because the government won't allow them the space to breathe and create. The regulations on freedom of thought are becoming more and more oppressive as the years wear on." She paused, and when she spoke again it sounded like she was pleading a case. "We're humans. Humans create. If we do not, then our species will find itself heading toward extinction."

"Is this what the Sparkers want—more space for people to invent and create?"

"Yes. Look at this district. Don't you think it's fondling its destruction, even as we speak?"

I had to hand it to LaRue—he knew what he wanted from his bed lays—intelligent, erudite, and beautiful. "Still, all that is empty rhetoric, isn't it?"

She shrugged. "I think that the idea is sound."

"I think it sounds like revolution," I said. "Do you know anyone actively involved in this movement?"

Reuben hid her expression behind her tiny cup. Then, following a delicate sip, she spoke. "I don't know anyone who is participating actively. Most people I talk to have heard the rumbles and agree with the Sparkers, but no one admits it openly. With the changes in power, it's hard to know who to trust, and it seems that the government will use any cause to further its own corruption and greed. People want to join; they're dying to join; they're just not sure who they're giving their loyalties to."

It was the same old bureaucratic toilet paper, smeared with the half-truths and secrets. I watched as Reuben sat there for a minute like she might be soaking up some invisible power held in the coffee cup. "I have an idea," she announced.

Rising, she stepped to a small, cherrywood cabinet sitting in the corner. She pulled open the top drawer, slid out a set of tarot cards, and turning, she explained her idea. "I can tell you through the cards who your killer is."

My patience for this metaphysical bullshit was so short that I couldn't apply the brakes on my mouth. "I don't believe in fortune-telling."

LaRue was a little more open than I. "How can you tell who it is?"

"Well, I can't give you any names, but I can give you a profile on your murderer. Are you ready?"

Despite my outburst, he commanded her into action. "Show us this person, then."

She sat down and pushed away the demitasse cups, making

room to cast the cards. Reuben inserted another delay as she took a deep breath and lipped a prayer. Then: "This drawing will indicate the personality of the killer." She laid down the first card. "The seven of cups. Debauch."

I leaned forward. "It's an interesting card, but what does it mean?"

"The suit of cups represents emotions," she explained, "and the seven of cups represents a personality who indulges in his or her desires to the point that he or she lives in a state of depravity. This is not good. It already fits the scenario for a killer."

"What relationship did this person have with Bernard Horn?" LaRue asked.

Reuben shuffled the cards and drew again. "Three of cups—abundance." She took a sip of espresso and launched into her metaphysical lecture. "Again the suit of cups represents our emotional selves, and in this case, abundance applies to a wealth of feelings and the riches of the heart."

"So, the person cared about him," I said flatly. "Pardon me for making this obvious point, but that goes without saying. Most killers are intimate with those they plug."

Reuben didn't flinch at my accusation. Instead, she continued with her explanation. "Not only does the three of cups represent the abundance of emotion, but also the ability to nurture. From a zodiac perspective, this energy is Mercury in Cancer. The person you're looking for had a nurturing relationship with the singer. One he tried to communicate daily."

"Go on," LaRue urged.

The next card she pulled made her smile. "The four of wands—completion. The suit of wands represents our intuition and spiritual aspirations. Whoever this person is, he wanted to achieve something that in his mind signified an ending."

I shook my head but kept my claptrap shut. What she told us was generic information. We were still no closer to a firm ID.

Reuben stared at me. "Would you like to know more?"

It was my turn to jump into this insanity. "Yeah. Tell us why Bernard Horn was murdered."

She scowled, but then nodded. Saying another short prayer,

she let me have it. ‘‘Arcanum 21—the universe.’’ She smiled. ‘‘The major arcanum are cards which signify archetypes and divine principles. This card signifies the All-of-All. The attainment of a lifetime. If you ask me, the reason Bernard Horn came up dead was because he was going after the whole shooting match, and someone needed to stop him.’’

EIGHT

As far as I was concerned, Miss Conchita Reuben had an impressive body and talked a good line, but the tarot cards pushed her information past credible boundaries. The reason I say this is because her psychic abilities didn't include warning us about upcoming trouble, and if they couldn't do that, what good were they?

Satan let the dark angels loose the moment LaRue and I stepped onto the street and headed toward the Trabi. A battered, navy-blue sedan swerved around the corner, squalling tires and gunning a loud engine. As it raced up the street, we got a good look at it and saw that there were three occupants, each wearing a black hood. The person in the front passenger seat leaned out of the window and sprayed us with the business end of a dredge gun while his counterpart in the back of the car loaded the broad-mouthed weapon with assorted shrapnel. It was a bulky homemade job, but armed with nails, rivets, rocks, glass, and wood, it became a launcher of death.

LaRue saw the glint of tin first, and pushed me to the sidewalk, where I kissed a crack filled with scum and mud. My partner rolled toward me and we both crawled for the fragile protection afforded by the Trabi. With every bang and clink of shrapnel hitting his beloved commie car, LaRue winced and died a little, but worse than that was the fact that there were a lot of people on the street who were caught in the fire.

A woman screamed just before her head was cracked open by a large rock; an old man collapsed nearby, clawing at the jagged knife blade puncturing his leg, and a child, playing ball at the curb called out for his mama when a hailstorm of metal spikes passed through him.

We drew our own weapons, but buried our heads. It was a quick kill, a drive-by shooting that played out so fast we never got a bullet off in return.

''Was that intended for us?'' LaRue husked.

I shook my head and pulled to my knees before answering, suddenly aware of my anger. ''Who else would it have been intended for?''

These exhibits of violence were on the increase, and more and more the assaults were aimed at marshals and ward cops who just happened to be out in the open. It was a crying shame. If the Sparkers were behind these attacks, as everybody seemed to think, then they were nothing more than wolves crowding around the scraps thrown out by the humanitarian government. Creativity, freedom—these were all nice words and big-sounding talk. Unfortunately, the death rattles wrought by the new thought came even louder.

I tapped the stud in my com-node and nearly made my eyes bleed from the volume. Reaching into my ear, I used my thumbnail to delete the sound to a reasonable level. Dispatch finally responded to my signal, just as I was busy wrestling the link from under my uniform. Communications on the district array had been bad ever since a hurricane had nearly wiped the locality off the map, and transmissions were continually stomped on while the static concealed most other broadcasts. The whole point of calling in for emergency assistance was lost on this miracle of technology. To prove myself right, I spent the next five minutes trying to inform the dispatcher that we had a street full of civilian casualties.

When my call got through, I helped LaRue give aid and comfort to the fallen bystanders. I have to admit that while my hands held shut a gaping wound, my mind was unable to contain a stinging gash of suspicious thoughts. Was the government part of this growing problem? As corrupt and greedy as it was, this made more sense than I wanted it to.

An hour passed before a team of paramedics lumbered up in a decrepit ambulance to help the victims on their way to the hospital or the morgue. We used a public drinking fountain to wash off the blood and then returned to investigate the damage on the Trabi. LaRue was in a whine mode about the nails poking through the driver's-side door and along the back fender.

"I spent a year's salary scrounging the parts I needed to get this car together," he wailed. "Look at it, Ty. Just look at it."

I did, and he was right without saying it—the Bolshevik beauty of his life was pretty messed up. "You better fill out a claim voucher when we get back to the office."

He nodded curtly and yanked open the car door, cursing as he found more damage in the interior. "Watch yourself. There's shattered glass in your seat."

I joined him, scraping out the explosion before climbing inside. Sitting there, we stared off into space for a few minutes. I waited until I felt LaRue relax slightly and then hit him with my thoughts. "We're trudging through a minefield, Andy."

"Yeah," he growled. "It's going to be a challenge to survive, no matter who wins the revolution."

NINE

We decided to go back to my fifth-floor flat to change our uniforms and wipe off the remains of human crud. It was noon when we arrived at my walk-up to find my roommate, Baba, busily stirring a pot of beans over the tiny flame of the propane stove. Approaching her, I smelled the sweet odor of the gas burning off and the powerful scent of some of LaRue's home-made vodka. He swears the booze takes on an added luster with the addition of a head of garlic. Baba, retired from the waste treatment plant, has the iron stomach and plenty of time to sample his concoctions, and as it goes, she starts nipping early, portioning out the alcohol-soaked garlic cloves to last as long as a bottle.

I peered into the bean pot, and standing there, I knew without raising my head that she was feeling no pain.

She noticed the blood on my cammies. "What happened to you?"

"Someone tried to kill us, Baba."

"It looks like they almost did, too, my dear."

I nodded, and stepped away from the beans. LaRue searched through the front closet, trying to scrounge up the extra uniform he kept there. He found it on the bottom of the pile, wrinkled and dusty. Shaking the cammies out, he glanced at me. "I'm going to buy you some clothes hangers." With that, he retreated into the bedroom and shut the door behind him.

Clothes hangers were about all I didn't have. I'd laid in a supply of propane as well as batteries, blankets, and nonperishable foods, just in case the world flipped upside down and Duvalier's Dream turned into our worst nightmare. My apartment was starting to resemble Gibson's digs, but where his place held a doctor's idea of essential items, my treasure items included books, pirated vids, recycled paper, and stubby lead pencils. In my head, I helped society by preserving bits and pieces of it in the midst of galloping anarchy.

To make matters more cluttered, Baba had her one possession—an oversized weaving loom—stuffed in between the boxes and stacks. There she would sit for hours at a time, creating trash blankets, coverlets that were made with the scraps the world provided her—old aluminum foil, cardboard, plastic, and odd lengths of thread and string.

I paced around the flat, trying to work off some of my nervous energy. My walk eventually brought me to Baba's loom, and I sat down in the rickety chair to admire her latest endeavor. I had to hand it to the old, crotchety lush. She had talent. There was creativity in her hands and her brain. Instead of bellyaching about not being able to fully express herself as a human being, she was doing everything she could to pack the world with her own personal vision.

Baba finished stirring the beans and ate a vodka garlic clove before turning to address me. "Who's got it in for you?"

"Sparkers, ETA, concerned citizens," I answered.

"In other words, anybody who walks and breathes."

I chuckled. "That's about the size of it." I forgot to talk for a moment as I traced my fingers along the blanket. Baba's weaving was precise. How she accomplished a perfect knit-and-tuck after taking a nip or two was amazing. Did it mean that alcohol unleashed her creativity and manual dexterity? Was it true that those great artists who did not suffer from madness needed the bottle to produce masterpieces?

From what Gibson tells me, the brain has a way of locking down our talents by keeping the access ways to them a secret. Something as simple as an amino acid can prevent a person from realizing his highest potential, and according to the good doctor, there is no medical procedure known that will stimulate the gray matter enough to make it open this passage. Either you have the right chemicals from birth, or you don't.

"We've been ordered to report to a couple of tax collectors on our current investigation," I said. "If we fail to find the killer, then the ETA will bring proceedings against us and strip us of our class designations. If they do, Andy and I are out the whole shabang." I sighed, suddenly weary, and barely able to fight an attack of defeat.

"It's not right what these goddamned gangsters are doing to this world," Baba stormed. "It's going to end in a big explosion. Mark my word." Turning back to her beans, she continued to fume. "How can they do that to you, Ty? You've been a good citizen."

The ETA has gained a lot of power, Baba. Do you know that they have a force of agents as large as the one for the Marshals Office?"

"Don't I know? You see the goose steppers everywhere. Mrs. Tuccio was complaining just the other day because they raided her son's apartment while his kids were home from school."

"What were they looking for?"

"Evidence of backdoor dealing. The bastards wanted to make sure they got their fair share of nothing."

"Does her son do a lot of under-the-table business?"

She shrugged. "Probably. Who doesn't?"

I certainly couldn't disagree with her on that. "Baba, have you heard much muttering about the Sparkers?"

She sat down on our tattered, lumpy couch and situated her cotton housecoat before answering. "I've heard it—lots of it. They aren't any better than the crooks we got in the government now. Blood runs red no matter who stabs the knife into your back."

"Do you think they've infiltrated the current government?"

"Yes. At least the propaganda outfits. They've been at it a long time and now are finally beginning to get their wacky message out."

I glanced at her. "How long have they been around?"

She thought a moment, frowning slightly. "As far as I can remember, the Sparkers have been around in one form or the other for at least thirty years."

"In one form or the other? What does that mean?"

"The SoC has gone by different names and followed slightly different schools of thought, but at some point you find out it's all the same philosophy. I recall when I turned twenty-five, my husband asked me if I wanted to join the Daughters of the Sun."

"I've never heard of that one."

"It was the Sparkers with the slogan Spirit, Cooperation, Creativity." She paused to stand up. As she did, I heard her bones crack.

"Did you join the Daughters of the Sun?"

Baba grinned. "Hell, no. I wouldn't do anything that ugly old man asked me to do." With that, she scuffed over to her stash of garlic and popped another clove.

LaRue walked into the living room and flopped down in a beat-up chair. "I heard your story," he said. "Do you know who the SoC leaders are?"

"No," she answered. "But I do know what kind of magic they use."

Not again. I took a deep breath and a moment to let my gaze cut over the myriad wealth of charm sacks, tin bangers, air fresheners, dream nets, and spell jars situated around the flat. Baba had undertaken her own crusade—that of finding a magical relish that would taste good and cure me of my lycanthropy, and until the time that she found one, she made do with her fluff of superstition and a small budget allotted to the occult.

"What kind of magic?" LaRue prodded.

Baba leaned forward and blew garlic stink in his direction. "Kundalini power," she said. "They use the energy of the chakras."

TEN

Kundalini is a form of invisible magic that is popular on the backdoor market because it makes the claim that every person in the world is born with the ability to summon great, supernatural strength through the body's chakras or energy points. According to practitioners, these invisible power centers are the sense organs of the astral body and provide an adept means of crossing into the ethereal dimensions. There are seven chakras ranging from the crown of the head to the pelvis, and from what LaRue says, those who know how to bring up this power can use the lower energy centers in the pursuit of villainy.

I really didn't care to hear the lecture and so ended the discussion by having my partner call in to see if we'd been granted a peek at the investigation list. As it turned out, the squad secretary had the goods and gave us some leads to run down. We paused long enough to fortify with beans and garlic before leaving the flat, but I couldn't help pausing in the shadows of my apartment building's front stoop to scan for dark sedans.

When it looked like the coast was clear, I took the top step and stopped again. The sun had started its drop behind the dilapidated skyscrapers, but the rays still lanced through the district, picking up the sparkle of broken glass and rusting tin. Litter fluttered down the street; the neighborhood coking plant spewed a special brew of poison from its stacks; and the breeze sliding in off the Black River had the ripe scent of decay. People made homes amid this trash, either by setting up digs in collapsing buildings or by constructing cardboard-and-canvas houses in the crowded alleys. Wherever they could light a can of Sterno was their place of refuge. We had turned into a society of grubbing expatriates who reflected upon the value of life the same way dogs and pigs did.

Unfortunately, once out in the open, my partner started talking again.

"It's been said the yogis in old India used to practice the kundalini," he said, pulling up beside me. "They called it the rise of the serpent." When I didn't answer, he continued. "It's said that the kundalini force comes from the center of our being and it's the energy contained within the spark of creation. Once awakened, it rises from the spark through the chakra areas until it reaches liberation and the person has a union with the universe. It's basically a transformative power." LaRue stopped speaking to train his gaze upon me. Then: "Maybe your lycanthropy is a form of kundalini."

I nodded. Gibson and a score of specialists had proclaimed my malady to be the result of many things, both physiological and psychological. What was another label? I appreciated LaRue's supernatural attempt to explain my condition, but I'd as soon not have anything to do with metaphysical serpent crap, so I changed the subject. "Let's go back to the mine and see what we can scrape up. I believe less in people from the center of the earth than I do in kundalini."

Off we went, rattling over to the crime scene in his beloved Trabi. With every creak and groan, LaRue shivered and whined about the mincemeat made of his car. I felt for him every inch of the way, not because I was that upset about the damage, but because another attack could happen again at any time.

We arrived at the facility and walked inside the sprawling, single-story concrete complex that topped the mine. Upon showing our IDs to the cute, little receptionist, we were forced to wait for over an hour before the physician in charge was able to talk to us. It was then that we found out he'd already granted an interview to the two ETA agents.

Dr. Elbert Derry invited us into his plush office filled with memorabilia of a successful career, and using jerky movements, he pointed to a leather couch. We sat down while he joined us in a nearby chair. The minute the doctor opened his mouth, he sprayed us with spit and indignation.

"How many more interrogations must I endure?" he asked petulantly.

"How many have you endured?" LaRue asked in return.

"Your counterparts kept me down in the hole for over two hours. Now you. I do have duties, Marshals, and I'm falling behind. Don't you people ever share your data?"

"Not this time, Dr. Derry," LaRue answered. "In fact, we would like to know what the agents questioned you about."

He sat back, wiped a hand across his brow and then through his thinning, brown hair. "Well, the unfortunate death of Mr. Horn, of course."

"What did you tell them?"

"What could I tell them? The man died. I was up here, attending to business. I didn't see a thing."

"What specific questions did they ask you?" LaRue demanded.

"For one thing, they wanted to know all about the mine," he said. "They were insistent on getting a detailed tour that included information about the facility."

"Did you give them what they wanted?" I asked.

He swiveled his gaze to consider me. "If I hadn't, I would be down at the ETA being subjected to a surprise tax audit or something equally torturous. Besides, it's no skin off my nose. If they can make out the medical and scientific jargon, they can have the info."

"We would like disk copies of everything you passed to them, please," I said.

He nodded. "See my secretary before you leave."

LaRue pushed the interview onward. "Did they ask about a nurse by the name of Jenna York?"

"Yes, yes, what about her?"

"We understand she gave medication to Mr. Horn shortly before his death."

"Yes, so?"

LaRue leaned forward. "Where is she?"

"I haven't got the foggiest idea."

"She wasn't here during the initial investigation of the crime scene, though many of the patients claimed to have seen her as she delivered pills and shots that morning. The Marshals Office hasn't been able to locate her. We've even sent a couple of ward cops by her home and she wasn't there, either. What happened to her?"

He sat back and frowned. "I don't know. I assumed she was down at the Marshals Office."

"You look surprised. Didn't Agents Nichols and Carver ask this question?"

"No, they didn't." Derry rose and paced off the length of a nice, plush carpet. "This distresses me."

"Why?"

He held up a finger and walked woodenly to his desk, where he stabbed at the button on the intercom. His secretary finally answered, but he blasted over her response. "Did Jenna York check out today?"

"One moment, sir," she said. A minute of silence followed before she returned to the intercom. "The computer log indicates that she checked in yesterday. No checkout listed."

"Thank you," he said, glancing at us. He terminated the link and returned to his chair, sighing.

"What's the problem?" LaRue barked.

Dr. Derry's jitters escalated. His hands swept over his head again and then he shook his fingers as though he was slinging invisible sweat. "No one can leave this facility unless they go by the front desk and physically log out."

"Then she's still in the mine. Is that unusual?"

"Our staff members work short shifts, Marshal LaRue. Most people volunteer for a few hours of duty during their days off. That way they can make sure to get in their quota of humanitarian service during the year."

"We still don't have a complete package on Ms. York. Can you tell us where she works when not in the mine?"

"She's a psychiatric nurse. I don't have that information immediately available, but if you're concerned, all our volunteers are PHO board–certified."

The mask I carried in my pocket must have indeed sparked my creativity, because I couldn't help asking an off-the-wall question. "Is it possible that York has received notice from the government that she must meet new criteria to keep her position at the hospital?"

Derry blinked and then stared at the carpet. It took him a second to answer. "We all have."

ELEVEN

In the end, we left Dr. Derry to his duties and rode the elevator down into the hole to have a look around ourselves. Once in the mine, we found several ward cops still doing the legwork on the crime scene by interviewing the facility's patients taking in the radiation. They were all seniors, an observation that didn't get by LaRue.

''It doesn't seem like any of these dinosaurs could have committed the crime,'' he whispered. ''You might actually need a bit of forward locomotion to get clear before anyone discovers you.''

I smiled. ''Old people hear things, Andy. God knows, Baba can hear the cap coming off a vodka bottle over on the next street. I hope the ward cops might come up with something we can use.''

''If Nichols and Carver don't get to it first.''

''You know, I'd really like to know who's behind this government reshuffling and what those two might know about the Spark of Creation Movement.''

The moment I said it, I received an answer—not from LaRue, but from an old fellow sitting on an overturned bucket in the hall outside his cubicle. Upon glancing in his direction, I realized he was as broken and as crippled as any man could be. I also noticed that he was blind, and when we approached, he lanced my belly button with his sightless stare.

"Did you say something?" I asked.

"I said, utopias cannot exist without enforcers," he answered. "You were talking about those two animals who came through here an hour ago, weren't you?"

"Yes," I said. "What's your name?"

"Ellie MacGregor. You two are marshals, aren't you?"

LaRue leaned against the wall. "Yes. How'd you know that?"

"Got a great sniffer. Marshals are cleaner smelling than ETA agents. Them bastards smell like poop. My wife says I can smell right down to people's shorts, so I guess that's what it is, then." He laughed, coughed, and grunted.

"I assume when you refer to utopias, you're really talking about the SoC?" LaRue asked.

"Could be. It applies to any of the totalitarian regimes, you see."

"What about the SoC?"

"What about it? It'll breed contempt, loathing, and violence in its own time. Before you know it, they'll have the Creativity Cops tracking down killers."

I grinned. The old boy was probably right. "You're assuming that the Sparkers will take over in a big way."

"Don't bother fooling yourself, Marshal."

"Did you know Bernard Horn?" LaRue asked abruptly.

MacGregor nodded. "Yes. I'm an opera lover. We talked many times. I told him blue stories and he sang Neapolitan love songs for me. I was upset to hear that his voice has been silenced. Yes, very sorry. Horn had the magic in his throat."

"Magic?" LaRue said. "What do you mean? His talent?"

"No. He had the thing that the Sparkers talk about—that rare gem of supernatural power. Horn had the ability to plant the seed of wonderment in a person's brain by singing certain notes. He had the power to stimulate the crown chakra. By increasing the frequency of this energy center, he could help a person to open up to his true self. His sounds touched the core of the person and in this core can be found the creativity." MacGregor paused to massage his crooked fingers. "You know the amazing thing? Horn never suspected a thing. He had no idea how special he really was.''

''Surely, he understood at some level how many people appreciated his voice,'' I said.

''Of course. But hearing people tell you how skilled you are doesn't do anything if you don't feel the magic occurring on the inside.''

''And Horn didn't?''

''Not at all. He felt beaten. Well, that's the general lot of most of us, isn't it? That's why the SoC is taking over. They make promises of utopia; arm it with force; and give us a new set of lies to play with.''

''Did Horn strike you as a person who would be affiliated with the Sparkers?'' I asked.

He shook his head. ''I doubt it. He cursed a blue streak every time someone mentioned them. Nope. He didn't care a thing about the SoC.''

''Do you think the SoC is responsible for Bernard Horn's murder?''

''Yes.''

''Why? If he was so talented, then he would have been a perfect candidate for a Sparker poster child. They could have retrained him to think any way they wanted him to.''

MacGregor laughed. ''They don't want to retrain anyone,'' he said. ''If you don't fit the mold, they simply destroy you.''

TWELVE

Nurse Florence Addison stared at us through the bottom of her bifocals like this would help her read us better. She let LaRue and me linger in the dark passage off from the main facility before inviting us inside the windowless, whitewashed room she called her office. By the time we actually were seated in this cramped hole, my claustrophobia was on ultra-max and my nerves were frizzing. It made me feel crawly from the start.

"Why do you have an office so far from the main facility?" I asked.

Addison gazed at me with a hard expression. "I prefer the quiet, Marshal."

From the steely clank of her tone, I could tell this old woman used her weight to push people around much the same way that Julie did. I wasn't crazy about her attitude already, and normally being weary of getting shoved, I hammered in an immediate threat. "Let's get this straight from the get-go, Ms. Addison," I growled. "We're not in a pissing contest here. You're the head nurse of this creeptorium and there's been a murder in your jurisdiction. If we can't find the killer, we'll have to pin the wrap on someone. Be difficult and you'll become convenient."

She pulled at a flopping curl of her stringy, gray hair, and then, after a moment, she nodded. "What do you want to know, Marshals?"

LaRue glued his question into the conversation. "Were you here when Bernard Horn's body was discovered?"

"Yes. I was busy in my office."

"Alone?"

"Yes."

"Were you alerted immediately when Horn was found?"

"Yes."

"Did you go have a look for yourself?"

Her answer was so flat, it splatted. "No."

LaRue leaned forward and his white, metal chair squeaked. "Why didn't you go to the crime scene? This matter concerned you in the most important way."

"I told you I was busy," she answered crisply. "Paperwork." It was her turn to lean forward. "Besides, I've seen dead bodies before."

I broke the headlock by crossing my ankles and stretching. "I'll bet you have."

Addison glanced at me. "What's that supposed to mean?"

"According to your labor files, you're a triage nurse who spent years in the emergency unit of the PHO Hospital. You must have seen the results of many an attempted murder and bungled suicide."

She relaxed, slid back in her seat, and sighed. "I spent too many years in that emergency unit, Marshal. One more hideous death did not need my attention. And when I read the report, I was just as glad I stayed right here while everyone else had a good look."

"Did you know Mr. Horn?" I asked.

"Not personally. We were introduced, of course."

"Who introduced you?"

"Dr. Derry."

"But you never actually attended to Mr. Horn's needs while he was here."

"No, Marshal Merrick. I'm basically an administrator now. I occasionally help in teaching situations, but beyond that, I do not interact with the patients."

"Teaching situations?"

"Yes. The PHO sends its med students here. It's a chance for them to have experience with illness and patients who require long-term rehabilitation."

"How many students do you have here at any one time?"

"Usually four or five. This time, though, we only have one. Budget constraints."

"That would be Purceval Walker?" LaRue asked.

She shook her head and aimed her pop-bottle lenses toward her desk. Taking a moment, she flipped through several sheets of paper before coming up with a name. "Yes, that's right. Young Purceval. Just like the knight of the Round Table. He acts that way, too."

"What way?"

"You know—gallant, chivalrous, innocent, open, and trusting."

"What's wrong with that?" I asked.

"Nothing, I suppose," she answered. "I guess after so many years of being a nurse, I don't have any of those qualities left, so I guess I notice them." Addison paused to whip up thoughts of the past. Then: "He was an orphan."

"Does that make a difference?" I said.

"Well, it's a known fact that orphans are rarely capable of displaying such enlightened attitudes. They usually end up being homeless boozehounds who spend their days climbing through Dumpsters in search of scraps. If they don't do that, then they've managed to step into a life of crime." She stopped to insert a hard stare in my direction. "It's a problem within the system, Marshal. The Public Welfare Administration is low on money, low on provisions, and low on social workers. What can you expect of these children? They grow into misinformed adults because their psyche has been stunted by their experiences in the shelters where they spent their childhoods."

I felt LaRue squirm, but I didn't react with indignation like he thought I would. Instead, I let her prejudiced opinions slide off my lizard scales. "Did Walker communicate on a regular basis with Horn?"

"Yes, I believe so," she answered. "I recall he was excited when he found out Mr. Horn was coming to the facility. Apparently, he was a big fan of the opera. In fact, I heard he was practically inconsolable when Horn turned up murdered.''

''From the tone of your voice, I get the feeling that you find such behavior odd,'' LaRue said. ''A lot of people become unhinged at the sight of violent death. Orphans may have more problems than most.''

Addison chuckled darkly. ''Yes, they do.''

''What happened?'' LaRue demanded.

''Young Purceval Walker met his dragon along the way and the beast cremated him.'' When we didn't respond, she dropped her obliqueness to explain. ''Once in a while you'll get a very gifted person who wants to become a doctor. He or she wants to help heal the world. They're searching for the Holy Grail of Hippocrates, you might say. The only problem is they don't have the stomach for the game of medicine. They are knights who die on the quest.''

''So, Walker had a hard time dealing with Horn's death,'' I said.

Addison nodded. ''From what I understand, he had a nervous breakdown.''

THIRTEEN

Our conversation was rudely interrupted by someone screaming about little silver people. LaRue and I rushed toward the screeching to find a middle-aged woman in a wheelchair furiously pushing her way toward the elevator shaft. ''It went down there! I saw it!''

We cruised on by the patient, and pulling our sidearms, we closed in on the tube. From our vantage point, we could see the elevator cables swaying, but beyond that, our look into the shaft showed us nothing but darkness. LaRue punched savagely at the button to recall the car while I turned on the woman.

''What did you see?'' I snapped.

''It was a space alien,'' she said. ''Dressed all in sparkles and wearing a silver cape.''

''Are you sure it wasn't just a human wearing a burn blanket?'' LaRue asked.

The woman's expression displayed her mounting terror. ''No, no! It was an alien.'' She glanced about frantically and practically did a wheelie in an effort to get the chair turned around and headed for the entrance.

LaRue did his best to take advantage of her fright. ''Where were you when you saw it?''

"Right where I shouldn't have been—wheeling by the medicine chest. It was in there stealing stuff. Probably got sick aliens with some awful disease living right below us." With that, the woman finally managed to reverse her cart and skidded down the hallway.

Thankfully, the elevator arrived and we jumped on, pulling the gate shut behind us as we began the slow descent to the bottom of the mine. We traveled for a full minute before touching down in the basement. It was a poorly lit repository of junk, boxes, papers, castoff plastic, and used rags. The single lightbulb did nothing to point out the additional hazards of broken glass, tacks, and loose gravel, so we were forced to use our service lanterns in an effort to find our way toward Trisha Neal's linen room.

"That lady could have been seeing things," I whispered. "Between the drugs they shoot them up with and the radon, we might be following a make-believe bogey."

LaRue didn't reply until he played his flashlight beam over a pile of moldy pillows and onto the uneven stone floor. "Muddy footprints," he said, pointing.

I squatted down for a closer look. "They look like boots." Laying my hand against one of the prints, I added: "Whoever wore these had little feet. They could be kid's shoes."

A small noise from the shadows brought our attention around. I stood, and clipped my flashlight to my utility belt so I could grip my pistol with both hands. We stepped lightly toward the noise and after several feet found ourselves at a juncture. Pausing, we listened again, and decided to explore the passage to the right.

It was a narrow, dark corridor with a low-slung ceiling. Water ran in fat streams down the wall, making the floor slick in places. We slapped through the puddles and stubbed our toes on uneven rocks. My composure was slowly being molested by my claustrophobia until we saw a dim light up ahead and heard the strains of tinny music. I sighed, grateful to push this neurotic beast from my mind. We'd found Trisha Neal's linen room.

In fact, she appeared from an adjacent chamber, carrying a

load of laundry in her arms. Our appearance startled her and she dropped all the towels.

LaRue lowered his lantern. "It's Marshals Merrick and LaRue," he announced. "I'm sorry if we frightened you."

Neal exhaled loudly and patted her breast before drawing a deep breath. "Land sakes! With all the talk of men from the center of the earth, I've been right jumpy lately." She bent to pick up her towels.

We helped her, and while we grabbed the rags I asked her the pressing question of the moment. "A lady upstairs swears she saw someone come down this way via the elevator shaft."

She shook her head. "I never saw anyone. The ETA agents were here with Dr. Derry a little while ago. Maybe that's who she meant."

"Did you tell them about the hole in the wall?" I asked.

"Yes. Do you want to see it?"

I nodded. "Please."

We followed her into a long, sweaty space fitted with storm lanterns and aluminum washtubs. I'll admit it—I thought a government organization could have at least provided electrical service to the linen room and given Mrs. Neal a washing machine, but no. Instead, she was forced to use a scrub board.

LaRue wiped his hand through the cloud of steam rising off the tubs. "This is hot water. Where do you get it?"

"There's a steam spring that runs through the mine at this level. It was one of the reasons they didn't cut any deeper, you see."

"Where's the hole?" I asked.

She jabbed toward the far wall. "Right there underneath that counter."

I let LaRue precede me with the flashlight and then hunkered down to join him beneath the rickety workbench. The fissure was a two-by-two-foot, jagged passageway. A yard beyond this entrance, we saw what looked like a man-made object partially obscured by a large rock.

"Can you make out what that thing is?" I said.

LaRue shrugged. "I'm not sure." Glancing back at Mrs. Neal, he said: "Is there another way into this room?"

"Not that I know of," she answered.

He turned to stare at me. "You might be able to reach it."

Great. Not only was I in jeopardy of losing my job, but now I was being forced to turn into a mole. I reluctantly stowed my weapon and removed my shoulder holster and belt. Saying a quick prayer that my lycanthropy wouldn't compromise me by attacking the moment I squeezed into the cut, I pushed the lantern ahead of me and wiggled through behind it. Once I pushed up to my hips, I found I could go no farther. I scrabbled for the object with my flashlight, but it sat at an odd angle by the rock.

It was hot in the hole and I had to stop my excavation to take a deep breath and calm my galloping fear of tight spaces. Unfortunately, I was still swigging air when a sudden breeze blew down the shaft and kicked dust into my face. Here I was wedged in a hole in a dark cave and sneezing my brains out.

"Are you okay, Ty?" LaRue called.

I started to answer but instead, my attention played on the steady breeze wafting through the space. I raised up, balancing on my hands as far as the constricting hole would allow me and shone my lantern light down the rabbit run. It sloped at a sharp angle.

After a moment of trying to see movement in obscuring shadows, I heard LaRue's muffled voice. "Are you all right? Do you have the object?"

"I'm okay," I replied, and returned to my poking and prodding. Finally, inch by inch, I knocked the object free of its hiding place, but just as I dislodged it, a sound came up the shaft and the cool breeze abruptly stopped.

My lycanthropy affects all my senses, and where my ears are concerned, I often hear at a one-second delay. This feature of my supernatural illness allows me to interpret the backdrop of sounds. It's like listening to an aria, sung at a different level, and now I was sure that what I heard had a mechanical precision to it. Cocking my head slightly, I listened for confirmation. Yes, a man-made hum.

I grabbed the object and called out to LaRue. "Give me a pull, Andy. I'm stuck."

A second later I felt his strong hands curl around my ankles and then he yanked me backward. I rolled on loose gravel, popping through the hole like a pickle out of a jar.

"What did you find?" he asked.

It was a white, soft-soled shoe, of the type worn by nurses and doctors. Whoever it had belonged to had boats for feet.

Trisha Neal was the first to comment on the shoe. "Now, how did that get in there? You reckon the little people stole it?"

"Only if they were going to use it as a soup bowl," I answered. Pulling the tongue back on the shoe, I found an identity tag and wasn't surprised when the name read JENNA YORK. I glanced at LaRue and then at Neal. "Are you sure this is the basement? Could there be another level below us?"

Neal shrugged. "I ain't sure of anything, Marshal. I do know that the elevator stops here. There ain't no more buttons to push."

"Why?" LaRue asked me.

"I heard machinery, Andy. There might be a mechanical service corridor underneath us." I let my gaze trace over the slipper. "Still, it doesn't explain why there was a big shoe in a tiny crevice."

"The moles got Nurse York," Neal said flatly. "That would explain the shoe."

LaRue helped me stand up and took the sneaker while I brushed the dust off my cammies.

"The moles?" he asked. "You're talking about the supposed creatures from the center of the earth?"

"Yes," she said.

"Why do you think they got York?"

"I don't know the what-fors, but the stories say that the moles always leave behind an article of clothing. It's like a calling card."

The shoe was in a deep, dark hole; not a convenient place for discovery. Thinking about it, my suspicious nature zoomed in to mold the angle of my thoughts. "Did you stay in the room with Agents Nichols and Carver while they made their inspection?"

Neal harrumphed before answering. "No, indeed. Like I

told you—they frost my chops. I don't want to be nowhere around them."

I stole a look toward LaRue and read my thoughts in his expression. Once more it seemed, we were on the wrong end of a boondoggle.

FOURTEEN

Like some cartoon character, steam practically squirted from LaRue's ears when he'd realized we'd probably been hoodwinked by Nichols and Carver. By the time we reached the Trabi, he'd talked through his surprise, letting it boil over into the investigation until he pieced together the fragments of an elegant conspiracy theory—one that involved all the government agencies and extraterrestrial aliens. I, on the other hand, was more concerned about watching our backs, and in the short span it took to reach the car, I suspected everyone. Before opening the Trabi door, I paused to interrupt my partner as he compared our society's situation to that which arose in the old Soviet Union previous to its demise.

"We need to see Casper Conrad," I said.

My statement was enough to swing LaRue's attention directly onto me. "Do you think the Office of Intelligence is behind this hostile takeover and not the Spark of Creation Movement?"

I shook my head. "Maybe they're one and the same."

Conrad was the OI's chief of public accountability. He was also the biggest SOB that we'd had the pleasure of coming across. Conrad controlled telepaths, psychics, and remote viewers, and thereby he controlled the population through delusion and well-placed interference. Gibson had unwittingly offered up medical information concerning my lycanthropy to Conrad in hopes he would be paid for his efforts, but it was tough luck for the good doctor. Conrad didn't deal in scraps. He wanted the whole bolt of fabric.

Since our run-in with this nefarious bureaucrat, I'd been walking softly, praying he would forget about me and my paranormal partnership, but the more I thought about it, the more this investigation seemed custom-made.

"We need to get this clear with him," I said. "At least we need to face him when he lies to us."

"We might have better luck getting the truth if we shoot him in the leg first," LaRue answered.

"Yeah, I know. He'd probably lie his way through a broken neck, but it's worth a try."

We climbed inside the Trabi and LaRue spent the next half hour working the choke. Finally, the hussy roared to life and we were off to the gray, oppressive building that housed the employees of the Office of Intelligence.

Conrad invited us into his sterile office, smoothing the wrinkles in the same paper suit he'd worn when we'd dealt with him before. He seemed surprised by our visit, but his expression didn't fool me. We were probably on the appointments list.

We sat down in the straight-backed chairs positioned precisely in front of his desk, and stalling, he paused to align his pen set and nameplate. I didn't wait for him to dispense with the customary pleasantries.

"We want to know if you're behind the Spark of Creation Movement," I demanded.

Conrad wiggled an eyebrow at me and then smiled. "Now, why would you ask that?"

"Because you have the ability to change people's thoughts," I barked. "Don't bullshit us, Conrad. I'm still as dangerous as I ever was, but now, thanks to you and your wackos, I have less patience."

He sat back in his squeaky, cheap office chair to study me. Then: "If I tell you what you want to know, what will you do for me in return?"

Like I said—no patience. Before he could get his next breath, I drew my gun and pointed it at him. "I'll shoot your face off, Conrad. How about that?"

"You don't scare me, Merrick," he answered. "You wouldn't get out of this building."

"Do you want to take that chance? After all, we are marshals and we still have influence."

He stared at me for a few more moments. "We're not behind the SoC," he finally said. "In fact, we're doing what we can to maintain the status quo."

"Why don't I believe you?"

"Think about it. These people want to abolish agencies like ours. They want freedom of choice for the citizenry. The Sparkers find ways to pass our secrets along, and now they've made it so we have to monitor our public image at every turn, because if we don't, then we risk becoming part of the problem for the current district government."

"Why can't you just hinder a few freethinkers?" LaRue asked. "We saw what your remote viewers could do with their telepathic smoke and mirrors. Why not make the members of the SoC regret the day they ever struck out on this path?"

He snorted. "Budget restraints. I don't have the manpower. The District Council has effectively stripped us of many of our resources."

"And besides," I said, "you don't know who the ringleaders are. Why is that?"

"You were always a perceptive one, Marshal Merrick." Conrad leaned forward, counted his fingers, and finally spoke. "We are the eyes of justice. The OI sees all; unfortunately, we are as helpless as if we were blind. The people who are behind this movement are extremely powerful mentally. They don't fall easily to everyday trickery."

"Who do you think is behind the SoC?" LaRue asked.

"Genius is behind it," he answered. When we didn't look satisfied with the answer, he went on. "We don't know exactly who is the inspiration for the SoC. Whoever it is, he or she is well shielded. We do know that there is a legion of followers, but those we've tested are adept at defying our best efforts."

I didn't believe him, but I didn't feel like shooting him, so

I replaced my service revolver. "You're saying that the OI got caught with its pants down."

"I beg your pardon?"

"While you were running scams on innocent people, you obviously had competition out there, working quietly. There's someone else who knows a thing or two about brainwashing and mental retuning."

He shrugged. "It's what happens when the old is replaced by the new. Some go, some stay. I'm sure you understand how that is."

I ignored his assertion. "What do you know about the opera singer Bernard Horn?"

"Oh, yes. His death was reported by the media. I should have figured you two would be put on that case. To answer your question, the only thing I knew about him was that he couldn't sing that well."

"We were told that he had the ability to implant the seed of wonderment in a person's brain by singing certain notes."

Conrad blinked and paused to readjust his nameplate. "Sounds like an OI ploy, doesn't it? If Horn had this power, then he didn't use it."

"Why do you say that?"

"He just wasn't that popular. The arts and humanities are based on critical choice by the government. Your success is in their hands. Horn was passed over. He played bit parts in operas; did the occasional party booking, but for the most part, he was unknown."

"Then why would someone go to the trouble of killing him?" LaRue asked.

"Perhaps he was a threat to someone in the SoC."

"Or perhaps someone found out he was working for you."

"Not on our payroll, I can guarantee it."

"I still don't believe you, Conrad," I said.

He sighed, pursed his lips, and studied me. At some point he obviously made a decision of some sort, because it showed up in his face as an expression of surrender. "Okay, I don't need you breathing down my back right now, so I'll give you a tidbit to chew on. We once tested Horn's mentor, a man by the name of Silvio Valinari. The man proved inadequate for our needs, but he might be able to give you a reason why someone would want to kill his protégé. That's about all I can help you with.''

Conrad stood, ending our meeting as though he was the pope done with mass. ''You'll have to excuse me. I have duties to attend to.''

We rose and stepped to the door, but before we could leave, Conrad called out to me. ''You know, Marshal Merrick, the OI will get through this rough spot, but I wonder about you.''

''What's that supposed to mean?'' I snapped.

''You just might need a place to call home in this new order and I might be the one you'll have to turn to.'' He glanced beyond me to LaRue and added: ''I'll even make room for your partner. Anything to keep the lycanthrope happy.''

FIFTEEN

The next morning LaRue and I decided to do another quick check on the whereabouts of Purceval Walker. He was not to be found at his one-room basement flat; in fact, all of his stuff was gone and his landlord was spitting bullets about how he had vamoosed without paying the month's rent. The old boy who owned the building knew little about Walker except that he was a student at the university, but unfortunately, student records were closed to us, and so we had to start digging dirt by sifting through the district database.

When we returned to the office, we found the bullpen full of excitement, because the ETA agents had done some legwork and had dragged Silvio Valinari in for questioning. He sat cuffed to the table in the interrogation room like a common criminal while Nichols and Carver banged around him. We watched this carnival act for a time before we turned back to the matters at hand and patiently waited for our turn to interrogate Horn's mentor. While we cooled our jets, my partner reached into his desk drawer and dug out a charm sack he'd hidden away there.

I couldn't help smiling. LaRue had as much trouble with authority as I did. ''What's that for, Andy?'' I asked, sliding into my seat beside him.

"It's a mixture of cardamom seed, salt, and glass beads," he answered. "It's suppose to amplify the power of the throat chakra and enhance communication." With that, he ceremoniously placed the string around his head and tucked his prize under his collar. "I asked my mom a few questions about kundalini last night."

"And to demonstrate the power and versatility of an all-purpose occult practitioner, she whipped up a batch of chakra chutney," I said.

"You know how she is, Ty. She prides herself on her knowledge."

That was the problem with the world, wasn't it? Everybody prided themselves on being able to handle the secrets of magic. Unfortunately, this wealth of bogus knowledge was the very reason we'd been thrown into the Second Dark Ages.

Rather than add fuel to a possible lecture centering on the techniques to override universal polarities and chakra vortices, I pulled up the files on my computer to look for information on Purceval Walker. It was only a moment more before I yanked LaRue's attention away from the magic bag.

According to the personal data, Walker had been orphaned soon after birth. He had been sent to the District One Facility for Infants and Children, where he remained until the age of fifteen. At that point young Purceval was placed in a public training program operated by the Agricultural Office. Having been a ward of the district, I could read between the lines of this report. The public training program was no more than legally condoned, forced labor. If Walker worked for the AO, then it meant he'd spent his teen years struggling under the weight of a vegetable basket as he walked through fields, picking his own personal ton of beans and corn.

It is during these days of servitude that the government takes time to evaluate the new crop of unattached people. There are no family units, no friends outside those you grow up with, no knowledge of the world beyond that which the district council deems appropriate. Orphans fill in the jagged spaces of society, usually happy to bag the jobs nobody else wants. The government rarely looks for talent among our kind, and I count myself lucky because I wangled myself into a

Class-A designation. It could have gone the other way just as easily, and at that moment I could have been behind a brush, busy washing out a sewer instead of reading about someone else's story of fate and fortune.

Walker had almost received the brush, himself, had not fate intervened. His files were loaded with juvenile delinquency—first, there was work truancy; second, there were planned revolts. Some days Walker came to the field and left the moment he could to return to the quiet of the orphanage; other days, he would pick and prune and then purposely destroy the fruits and veggies of his labor. He was also fond of fighting, drinking, and doing drugs. He had been picked up several times by ward cops as he tried to sell packets of quantum, a controlled substance that alters the mind before it melts the brain.

Upon reading the arrest record, LaRue sat back in his chair with a grunt. "With the demerits this fellow has, he should be in a labor camp instead of the university."

I leaned back in my chair, popped a look over the top of our cubicle walls, and saw Nichols prancing around in the interrogation room like a goose-stepping Amazon. Satisfied that they hadn't accidentally shot Valinari, I returned to the file to see why Walker hadn't ended up in the slammer while LaRue extrapolated about reorganizing the surrounding cosmic dust before destiny could come into play.

As far as I could tell, there was not one speck of cosmic dust on any of it. The only thing I noticed was the presence of a scam, because buried deep in the information was a confession by Walker claiming that he'd been abducted by space aliens at the tender age of six.

SIXTEEN

I had just finished reading this piece of interesting information when Frank Wilson slid into our messy, cardamom-smelling hole.

He sat down in the broken chair by my desk, picked his teeth with the end of a matchstick, and studied us. I thought he was going to get right into a report about Horn's deceased condition, but instead, he started in on Carver and Nichols. "What do you make of those two?" he whispered.

"LaRue thinks Carver is kind of cute," I said. "He reminds him of cinema heartthrob, Presley Steele."

Wilson craned his neck and glanced toward the interrogation room, taking a moment to watch the goose steppers through the window. "Yeah, he does look a little like him at that. Charlotte is crazy over that fellow Steele." Angling his gaze back to us, he grunted, and then made himself comfortable in the chair. "Watch yourself around those tax collectors."

"Besides stating the obvious," I asked, "why?"

He leaned close to us and I smelled dill pickle on his breath. "They stepped out of a silk-lined sewer somewhere."

"What do you mean by that?" LaRue said.

"They've been scratched from district records," he said. "I

ran a check on them when they came into my lab demanding the forensic material, and except for closed ETA documents, I came away empty-handed.''

''Did you give them what they wanted?''

''No. I told them we were still running our tests.'' He paused to blow more pickle breath on me. ''Julie told me to give you the heads-up first. She's pissed, you know. They come stomping in here making demands and the old lady is forced to bow down to them. But I can tell just from looking at her, Julie wants to turn them into cracker meal.'' Wilson stopped his monologue yet again, and shot a look toward the tax creeps. Frowning, he finally swiveled his attention back to us. ''Horn's official cause of death is brain failure. I examined all the organs and found him to have a variety of problems—one of which was alcoholism.''

''He was a drunk?''

''His liver was shot; it was as hard as a rock. He must have sucked down gallons of homemade hooch, and from what I saw not all of it underwent proper distillation before it was consumed. No wonder he couldn't sing. Whatever he was drinking acted like battery acid to chew up his throat and stomach lining. His intestines were a mess, too. If he hadn't been murdered, he'd have been dead in a few months.''

''Was there anything else?'' I asked.

Wilson nodded. ''There was something unusual, yes. He didn't have arthritis. As far as I can tell, he suffered from myositis, an inflammation of muscle tissues. It causes pain, tenderness, and weakness, but it doesn't cripple the bones.''

''What?'' LaRue said. ''Why was he at the PHO facility?''

''Misdiagnosis, maybe?'' Wilson offered.

I sat back and stared at the medical examiner before glancing at LaRue to make my pronouncement. ''I don't think it was a misdiagnosis. I think someone wanted Horn there to make killing him more convenient.''

''Well, that wouldn't be a first,'' LaRue answered.

I hit Wilson with a hard stare. ''Who was Horn's doctor?''

''Now, that's the other interesting thing. He didn't seem to have one; at least he wasn't indicated in the records.''

I shook my head and took a moment to prop my feet on my desk. ''What else did I expect?''

Wilson burped. ''Yeah, I know. There is one thing, though. We found a latex glove in the trash can in Horn's cubicle. Jenna York's fingerprints were all over them.''

SEVENTEEN

Wilson crept away after giving us his report, muttering something about stalling Carver and Nichols with some trumped-up bullshit. By that time the agents had finished grilling Silvio Valinari and we were allowed to do our interrogation.

He was in his late fifties, short, stocky, and boldly wearing his thick, white hair in dreadlocks, having neatly tied off the ends of his braids with ribbons and beads. Valinari stared at us suspiciously and burst out into accusation as though he was singing a sweeping operatic aria.

"Well, aren't you going to ask me how much in taxes I paid last year?" he demanded.

We made ourselves comfortable at the table before I opened the game. "Why should we?"

"Because those other goons did. They kept asking and asking, like I would tell them if I had any hidden away. Stupido!" He turned to me and I saw actual pain in his blue eyes. "Please find out who killed Bernard."

"This is very important to you, isn't it?" I said quietly.

He nodded. "Bernard was the reason for my existence. He was my passion."

I'll admit, sometimes I'm slow. "Were you two lovers?"

Valinari grinned. "In spirit, Marshal, not in flesh. When I

speak of my passion, I talk about the ecstasy of creativity. Have you never felt it?''

Again, I was a step behind him. ''I'm not sure. Can you describe it?''

''If I have to describe it, then you've never entered into this realm of amazing magic. I feel pity for you.''

I didn't want this grunt's sympathy and hearing his thoughts on my life immediately fired up my mood. ''Speaking of magic, Mr. Valinari, are you a believer?''

He licked his cracked lips before replying. ''I was referring to the miracle of creativity.''

''I know you were. Now please answer my question. Do you believe in invisible magic?''

''I believe in some things only because I have seen and experienced the power and the truth of the occult.''

He hemmed and hawed, obviously afraid of being in violation of some code against superstitious practices, so I helped him along by playing on his fear. ''The cops down in the lockup don't take to people who break the blue laws.''

''Blue laws?''

''Yeah, the ones that say: there will be no laundry hung on outdoor lines on Sundays; no open displays of alcohol on front stoops of homes on any day of the week, and finally, no magical spells will be cast during the full moon.''

Valinari frowned. ''There is no such law.''

''We can throw you in the slammer until your hair turns brown if we suspect you of breaking any of these regulations. Would you like a quick tour of our facilities?''

He stared at me, but after a minute he nodded, sighing heavily in his defeat. ''I believe in astrology and the tarot cards. My wife and I practice the arcane arts. So now that you've got the truth out of me, what will you do?''

''Ask you another question,'' I answered.

''What, then?''

''Horn's voice. Did you believe he could plant the seed of wonderment into people's brains and open up the chakra centers of the astral body?''

''I don't believe in any of that.''

"Why not? What makes that magic different from what you already believe in?"

Valinari yanked at his chains and when he responded his voice held a touch of fire. "You're trying to get me to admit to magic practiced by the goddamned Sparkers. I won't do that. You can put me in jail or cut off my fingers. It doesn't matter. I'm a loyal humanitarian citizen. I always have been."

LaRue brushed a hand through his snarled, sepia mane and took the interview down a new line. "Were the ETA agents worried that you were making money on your relationship with Horn and not reporting the income?"

Valinari shrugged. "They didn't come out and say that."

"Were you?"

"No. Bernard was emphatic. He wouldn't work under the table. I could have gotten him many, many bookings, but he refused. He was afraid."

"Of what?"

"Of losing his class designation and his status as a humanitarian treasure." Valinari snorted. "Humanitarian treasure. That's a laugh. They give that title to people who have no ambition but a lot of talent. It's like a cocoon of safety. Pays a small stipends, and not much in benefits."

"Horn had a Class A-3 designation," I said.

"Yes. Which meant he paid more in environmental taxes than the average man. The ETA charged him thirty-five percent when everyone else pays ten percent, so in the long run the government recovered the credits they gave him for his HT status."

"How long have you known Horn?" I asked.

"Since he was sent to me for private lessons."

I took a moment to consult the file that Nichols and Carver had so thoughtfully provided. "It says here you work at the District Distillery."

"Yes. I'm a maintenance foreman in charge of the keg crews."

"Keg crews?"

"We clean the beer vats," he answered flatly. "I have musical ability but was never fortunate enough to go to the university. My family was poor and our labor designations have traditionally been in the dirt. I'm a Class-C designation and I barely earn enough to feed myself after taxes. If it weren't for my work with special children, I would not be able to feed my wife and six kids. Even with it, I have a hard time." He sucked in a deep breath. "Look, I'm legal. I have all the paperwork. I have permission from the district."

LaRue slid from the chair and took a turn around the room. He stopped to stare out the window and I glanced in his direction to see him watching Nichols swish her butt around the homicide pen. "What kind of special children do you help?" I asked.

"Gifted, talented kids," he said.

"I imagine it pays well."

"No," Valinari said, "it doesn't."

LaRue spun away from the tax collector to frown at him. "Why not?"

"Because they're not children from wealthy families. I take in the strays."

"Orphans?" I asked.

Valinari nodded and then, despite the restraints of the cuffs, he reached out to touch my hand with his fingertips. "You're an orphan, aren't you?"

Did I wear my past as openly as I might wear a black armband? I pulled my hand back. "How did you know that?"

"I have taken in waifs for thirty years, Marshal," he said quietly. "I can tell by the eyes. Every orphan I have ever met has that same emptiness. Bernard had it. In fact, when he came to me it was because he had incredible singing talent, but was so traumatized by the loss of his parents that he refused to speak."

"Orphans are ignored," I snapped. "How did Horn rate a look?"

"For a short time the government decided to take a second look at abandoned children. They set up a program whereby they kicked back funds to these ailing facilities if they could prove they harbored gifted kids. Bernard was sent to me for lessons in the hope that he would open up, communicate, and be a real treasure for the orphans' fund."

"I take it he opened up," LaRue said.

"He blossomed," Valinari answered, with a small, satisfied smile. "When he got excited about music, you couldn't shut him up. After he became of legal age, he continued working with me, and when tested for his talent, he managed to win a scholarship to the District Humanities School. Still, even there, in the midst of academia, he always returned to his maestro." His words slowed until they faded away.

"Did you know Horn was an alcoholic?" I asked.

"Yes. We all are. Aren't you?"

I blew off his question. "Why was Horn at the PHO facility?"

"Doctor's orders. He said it would help his arthritis."

"Who was his doctor?"

He shook his head. "Bernard never mentioned his name."

"According to our medical examiner, Horn didn't have arthritis, a fact that would have been clear to anyone examining him."

Valinari offered surrender with outstretched arms. "I thought he did. He was so crippled." He shook his head sadly. "Crippled in body and spirit."

"Would you say he was depressed?"

"Oh, yes. Being a prisoner to the whims of society will do that to you, especially if you lack strength."

I heard a lot more in the noise behind this man's words. "You sure do talk well for someone who has a Class-C labor designation."

He glared at me before spitting out his indignation. "What does my class designation have to do with my intelligence? Even children destined for the toilet jobs are taught to read, if for nothing else than to know how to flush away their lives in the end."

"Do you have books, Mr. Valinari? Censored books?"

"No," he answered in a husky voice. "Of course, not."

I leaned toward the man, and grabbing him by a couple of braids, I yanked his head my way. This close, he stank like the beer vat he was in charge of scrubbing. "We all have illegal books and vids. Since you lied about owning something that you shouldn't, it gives me the idea that you may do a little dealing in seditious material. What say you, maestro?"

"No," he murmured. "Not me. Honest." Swallowing, he pleaded. "Please. I have a bad back and you're hurting me. I've done nothing wrong. Surely you can't deny a person a little education."

I let him go, falling in a weak moment for the abandoned ideal of the inalienable rights granted by Duvalier. "What did Horn have to do with the Spark of Creation Movement?"

Valinari blinked at the question. "Nothing."

"Are you sure?" I said as I snatched his hair again.

He balked, but in the end he confessed. "Bernard may have played a few gigs—mostly fund-raisers at homes in nice neighborhoods. Nothing more. But just because he did doesn't mean he was involved with them."

"Names," LaRue barked. "We want names."

Valinari jumped at my partner's gruffness, but the attitude worked and he coughed up the information. "About three weeks ago Bernard sang for a man named Ralph Kane."

"And who would Ralph Kane be?"

"He's an auditor for the Environmental Tax Agency."

Oh, purge my numbers. Now we were getting somewhere. I was about to say something, but Julie stopped into the interrogation room to interrupt us. "I just came through reception. The squad secretary says Baba is on the phone for you and she sounds upset."

I jumped up, glanced at LaRue, and stomped to the nearest extension. Picking up the receiver, I set it against my ear and heard my roommate's wheezing breath. It wasn't like her to call me at work. "Baba? What's wrong?"

"Ty, my dear," she said with a trembling voice, "we've been robbed."

EIGHTEEN

When LaRue and I arrived at my flat, we found beans and blood on the floor as well as Baba nursing a gash on the back of her head. She dripped red into a white towel I'd swiped from Gibson's medical stash. I rushed to her while LaRue got on the horn and ran up the meter trying to contact the good doctor.

"What happened?" I asked, helping her with the rag.

"The goddamned bastards ambushed me, my dear," she wailed. "Oh, my head hurts."

I'll bet it did. I carefully held the towel against her noggin, trying to stanch the blood flow while not making matters worse for her poor, battered skull.

"I was doing the beans." She sniffled. "I had the vid machine turned on and the sound was way up. They banged me in the noggin when I was looking the other way."

I tried my best to coo my sympathy. "It's okay. Just relax. Gibson will be here in a little bit."

"But, Ty!" she cried. "They wiped us out!"

That they had. My supplies, so tenderly hoarded and bought with my one and only windfall, were all gone. Every box of blankets, every shred of dried noodles, every can of packed corn—gone. I wanted to be more responsive to Baba's needs, but I'm ashamed to say, I was so enraged by this affront that I was silenced for fear I would slobber and growl instead of speaking like a human being. Thankfully, my partner is never at a loss for words and he took over my meager ministrations as he relayed Gibson's message.

"Lane said the head has lots of blood vessels, Baba. That's why there's so much blood." He sat on the floor and cradled her against him, all the while pressing the rag gently against her head. "Lane thinks it would be a good idea if you would lie on the sofa with your feet elevated."

At least the thieves had left us the ratty furniture, even though they stole my old TV and vid machine. I rose to find a pillow to place under her feet, but soon discovered that the invaders had taken our bed linens. I was forced to roll up a couple of sets of soiled cammies from the wash basket.

"Who would do this?" Baba demanded. "Who have you made mad?"

Me? I've irritated the whole world on occasion. It could have been anyone, but my mind kept leaping to assumptions that Nichols and Carver were somehow behind this latest intrusion into my life. "Did you see anything?"

"No," she blubbered. "I fainted, I guess."

LaRue decided to hush Baba by talking about UFO abductions, after which traumatic events, the people were returned to a rifled house with their memory confused.

I wandered around the apartment, trying to walk off a dazed, dizzy feeling and was grateful when Gibson stepped through the door to shut LaRue up about alien supply routes from Earth to Yumpin-Yimini, a planet lurking in the shadows of the triple star system of Alpha Centauri.

Gibson glanced at me, saw I was fine, and kept heading toward Baba. He dropped his medical satchel on the floor with a clunk and fell to his knees to have a look at the old woman's wound. I sat down in a kitchen chair to watch from a safe distance. For several minutes I wrestled tangy thoughts heavily spiced with paranoia, but soon the movement of the good doctor's hands drew my attention and I fell into a trance.

My lycanthropy manifests in strange ways. Following a stretch, I can tell whether my eyes have changed from the diurnal shape classic to humans into that of the nocturnal arrhythmic shape so common in bears, lions, and wolves. My sight changes and I see things with a glow that reminds me of the painter van Gogh and his famous picture of a smeary, sparkly, starry night sky. Not only can I see like a rat in the dark, but I'm susceptible to the enticement of shiny objects and the mesmeric state they produce in me.

Gibson wore a gold pinkie ring, and as he worked it flashed with an alluring brightness. Perhaps the glitter turned on some comforting synapse in my brain. Whatever it was, I felt the slow return of my emotional integrity, gripped though I was by this act of simple kindness—something that I seemed to have a hard time expressing.

"You're going to have a headache for a few days, Baba," Gibson finally reported. "Let's get you to bed."

He stood and knocked me from my reverie by shooting his scrutiny toward me. "Are you all right, Merrick? You look pale."

"I'm fine," I husked.

I let my gaze skid toward the floor as they passed me for fear they would think my true concern was for the stolen goods and not my friend. At that point I wasn't sure myself.

When Gibson and Baba were in the other room, LaRue tossed the bloody towel into the trash can and then washed his hands at the tap before turning back to me. "I feel sorry for you, Ty. Whatever you and Baba need, you just ask. I'll find a way to get it for you." With that, he stepped toward the door.

"Where are you going?" I asked.

"I'm going to have my mom make up a healing charm for Baba," he announced.

NINETEEN

Gibson appeared several minutes later, shutting the bedroom door behind him. I had not moved from the chair; in fact, I had not moved much beyond my surging thoughts. He stepped around my seat and placed his hands on my shoulders. Slowly, lovingly, he began to fill me with his strength by kneading me into relaxation and backing it up with an old hypnosis trick. I fell right into the groove, predictable to the end. When he said the magic words—vata, pitta, kapha—he took me completely into his power. I woke up a few minutes later feeling a bit lighter of spirit, and knowing in my heart it was due to nothing more than a hypnogogic suggestion.

He was busy at the propane stove heating water in the kettle.

"Do you mean they left us some tea bags?" I asked.

"A little coffee, too," he said without turning.

"Will Baba be all right?"

"She was hit hard, Merrick. At her age, it's difficult to say. She has a concussion and a few minor lacerations."

I didn't like what I was hearing, but managed to keep the shake out of my voice. "How might it affect her thinking?"

He shook his head and spun around with the kettle in hand. "As the brain gets older, it breaks down on its own accord. It lacks the vitality it once had. Lots of things can happen."

Pouring the water, he added softly: ''Let's wait to see. There's no sense second-guessing the process.''

I nodded and joined him on the couch, grateful for the steaming cup of liquid. Not one to whine about crappy circumstances, I nevertheless remarked upon it. ''The lot of us are in trouble, Gibson. The worst part is we don't know who's sending the shots over the deck.''

''I know,'' he answered. ''We're not the only ones, Ty. This reshuffling has displaced folks since the beginning of the year. More and more of my patients have to pay in day-old bread.''

Rather than replying, I sipped the tea, luxuriating in the calming effect it had on me. Was that my own strength returning, or the artificial fuel Gibson had given me while I visited la-la land? I decided it didn't matter and spent a moment more sucking up the quiet. Evening had settled and the electricity had been rotated off the grid in our ward. We sat in the growing gloom, silent until I couldn't bear to be alone any longer with my self-critical review. ''Will you tell me something from a neurological standpoint?''

Gibson stalled to swig his own drink and then drew me close. ''What do you want to know?''

''I was wondering if my lycanthropy changes my overall ability to make intuitive leaps. Am I running the show or am I bound to physiological limitations?''

He didn't answer right away and it made me crawl from his embrace. When I looked at his face, I saw that wild-eyed regard that didn't exactly fill me with peace and hope.

''Tell me,'' I croaked.

He slugged his drink, placed it on the creaky coffee table, and then walked to his medical bag to pull out several stubby white candles. From there, he spent a minute more carefully placing the candles along the kitchen table and coaxing them to flame with a silver flint knicker. Only after he had established a halo of soft light did he turn back to face me. ''Yes, your thinking does change following a seizure.''

''Is it noticeable to everyone but me?''

''No. In fact, I don't think anyone realizes it. I know it because I've tracked the size of your brain at given times during your lunar cycle. It's the reason I set up the neuroscan over at the PHO Hospital tomorrow morning. I wanted to complete the data as much as possible in case the plug is pulled on me.'' He sighed and shook his head. ''I was really hoping for more time so I could set up an entire yearly record. Guess that won't happen anytime soon.''

I set my cup on the coffee table as he returned to the couch. ''What does the size of my brain have to do with anything?''

''Without going into the deep science of it, the human brain is a dissipative structure,'' he said. ''This means that it's an open system which collects stimuli and then it reorganizes this energy into something it can use. In this way, the brain evolves and transforms. If there is too little stimulus or the structure remains in a static state, then the system faces entropy. Do you understand so far?''

''Yes. If the brain doesn't get to chew on new experiences, it will eventually lose its muscle tone.''

He stared at me for a moment before smiling. ''Essentially that's it. Without stimuli, it can't grow, can't form new neural and synaptic connections. The cells will eventually die and so will the person. In the short analysis, though, if the structure is unstable even a small fluctuation in stimulus can bring about dissolution and reorganization, but if the system is stable, then it would take a strong stimulus to force the structure to destabilize, especially if the brain is characteristically able to resist various fluctuations. So, out of disorder and chaos can emerge complexity and wisdom.''

''And you can map these changes?''

''Would you believe wisdom and creativity have mass?''

I stared at him before shaking my head. ''Do they?''

''In a manner of speaking. People who are rigid in their thinking, who don't try new experiences, are essentially closed systems and their brains reflect it. Their gray matter has fewer neural connections and the cortical layers are less dense. Scientists have found that those people considered 'creative' are mentally fine-tuned to the flow of stimuli. Their dissipative structures work better, though they may have so much going on that they act a little nuts sometimes. We call it the artist's syndrome.''

''What happens to my brain?''

He reached out and took my hand. "Are you sure you want to know?"

A split second of panic nearly did me in, but I'm a glutton for punishment, so I nodded.

"With every seizure you have, you gain a little more mass in the brain," he announced. "I tracked you for three months in a row and your numbers were pretty predictable. At the full moon, you gain more connections in the temporal lobes and lose some higher processes in the frontal. When that last stretch is done, your brain settles into what I assume is your normal dissipative structure." He paused to gauge his explanation by studying my expression.

It was another uncomfortable idea heaped onto the growing mountain of uncomfortable ideas. "You are saying that toward the middle of the month, I'm more capable of utilizing my imagination and creativity than I am at the end and the beginning?"

"Depending on how many seizures you've had, the answer is yes. Like it or not, the wolf brings an added dimension to your thinking."

TWENTY

Gibson stayed with me that night and tried to push away my woes by pushing sex on me. Admittedly, his plan did work; at least until I woke up the next morning to see the empty space where my treasure trove had once been. My anger growled as loud as my belly and Gibson was caught all over again trying to calm me down. I wanted justice; I wanted accountability; and most of all, I wanted to see someone whom I didn't love doing the bleeding.

When Baba's friend Craia arrived to stay with her, the good doctor helped me to some more torment by taking me to the PHO Hospital to get the blasted brain scan done. I worked three ways to Sunday attempting to weasel out of it, but he was more insistent than usual, and being that he was under the gun the same as I, his stubbornness outweighed mine. Yet the minute the scan was completed, I bolted out the door and ran down my partner's location.

LaRue was at the office huddled over a partial set of dog-earred blueprints for the mine. He grunted the moment I slid into my seat, glanced over the top of our cubical wall, and then back to me. In a low voice, he said: ''There are six more levels beneath the laundry room.''

I joined him in the clinches so he could point them out. "How do you get to them?"

"There looks like an entrance from the elevator shaft."

"But the elevator wouldn't descend any farther."

He smiled. "That's because you have to climb out of the top of the car and take the service stairs."

"That doesn't sound very convenient," I said. "Are you sure?"

"It's the only entrance I can find."

I sat back and studied him. "Damn. I was hoping we wouldn't have to be monkeys to get in."

He wrapped up the paper in a tight scroll. "Well, we do. I'm going to get a couple of ward cops to come along and hold the elevator for us." Fighting a rubber band, he added: "How's Baba?"

"Bitching," I answered. "It's a good sign, anyway. This morning it was a loud lament for hot oatmeal."

"Did the bastards get your cereal?"

"Andy, they even stole my torn underwear."

He shook his head and reached into his desk drawer to pull out a large, grease-stained paper bag. "I figured you wouldn't have breakfast."

LaRue was right. My stomach was still roaring and I dove into the package like it was a gift from the soup-kitchen god. I found a feast of cracked olives and pickled onions; hard, black bread; a tin of sour applesauce; and a charm sack that smelled of cloves and ginger. Snagging the little crocheted sachet, I presented it to my partner.

"I appreciate the food, but you know I don't believe in this stuff."

He grinned, snatching the sack from my hand. "Sorry, that's for Baba. My mom packed the picnic basket."

"What's it supposed to do?"

"It will give her vitality." He paused to unwind the string. "I don't know if it will work, but she'll smell like a pumpkin pie."

"I suppose it's better than smelling like a garlic clove," I answered as I tore into the small loaf of bread and stuffed my mouth. Once this chore was done, I thought about talking instead of swallowing. "What about Nichols and Carver?"

"According to the logs, they've tried to interview everyone intimately connected to the case. Unfortunately, they've been stonewalled. Some folks are just impossible to track down with conventional methods."

I grinned. "What a shame." Swallowing, I reinforced the bite with another one while LaRue laid on the dessert.

"I had to call in a marker down in records," he whispered. "The truth on those two? They used to be part of an ETA sweeper team. Their claim to fame was busting down front doors to harass old ladies into paying their quarterly tax payments."

It suddenly didn't matter that I was talking instead of swallowing, because hearing that, I couldn't make my throat work. LaRue saw my difficulty and nodded. "I know what you're thinking. How did a couple of hoodlums like them get placed in a position of oversight and review at the Marshals Office?"

I finally found some spit and dispatched the hunk of bread down my throat. "Why do I have the bad feeling that they're watching our every move both professionally and personally?"

"Because paranoia runs deep," he said. "If it makes you feel any better, I figure the same thing."

I was about to come up with a spellbinding question, but was rudely interrupted by the phone. It was Gibson.

"What's the matter?" I asked, between sucks of applesauce.

"The hospital did a rush job on your scan, Merrick. Can you come over to the clinic? There's something you need to know and I'd like to see you face-to-face to tell you."

TWENTY-ONE

Despite my concern over Gibson's ominous call, I decided to put him off until after we checked out the mine. The Trabi was acting up as usual, and the Baltic Hussy stopped running in the middle of Ward 39. LaRue fiddled with the junk under the hood while I leaned on the fender.

The place was starting to gear up for the carnival and the streets were draped in plastic streamers, gaudy prayer flags, and banners. Ward 39 was normally a quiet neighborhood, but this morning the street hawkers were hoping to get a jump on the district stores by selling everything from fertility soap to old, shriveled-up pistachios. It was not so many months ago when this kind of public gathering would have been discouraged. This new laxity was just one of many freedoms that had been granted in dribs and drabs, and while it all seemed genuine and harmless, it was enough of a change to make me worry.

LaRue slammed the hood, jarring me back to our transportation problem. "Get it fixed?" I asked.

He shrugged and walked around to the driver's side. "Do you know what the problem with machinery today is?"

"What?"

"There isn't any. How can a person keep a car running on

parts that have been chipped from bones and rocks?''

I joined him inside the Trabi, saying nothing, because there was nothing to say that would change the truth. LaRue grabbed the hook of my silence, dropped the subject, and broached a new one. His lecture mode was thoroughly activated within the minute, and as we drove to the facility he held a one-sided discussion about his theories on the people from the center of the earth and how they were supposed to have a special relationship to gravity. Once he started talking about how these elusive beings controlled the balance between the core and mantle layers in the planet, I tuned him out with the occasional grunt. By the time we reached the mine, he'd moved from gravity to antigravity and made the subterranean folks responsible for earthquakes and the El Niño weather patterns.

The Marshals Office assigned us a single ward cop to help us with our task and we met him at the facility's front desk, where he busily flirted with the cutie fielding telephone calls and visitors. We dragged the cop away from the receptionist and then the three of us took off for the basement.

The elevator creaked as it descended slowly into the hole. We were forced to stop three times to admit facility personnel, two of whom talked about the miraculous cures the radon was having on Mrs. North's atrophying leg. Everyone jumped off before we reached the laundry level, and halting the car, we locked it down.

It was an old-fashioned elevator, complete with a front gate and exposed cables. The ceiling was at least nine feet high and the trapdoor was set in the right-hand corner.

Since I was the lightest, LaRue intertwined his fingers to give me a boost up. I rapped on the access panel with my knuckles, and finding it to be loose, I pushed it up and away before climbing through. When I reached the other side, I discovered that there were no emergency lights to guide my way, so I sat on the car's roof and paused to turn on my service lantern, shining the beam along the wall.

''Do you see the service entrance?'' LaRue called.

''Yeah. It's not much of one, though. A couple of steps cut into a hole in the wall.'' I reached down to offer him a hand as the ward cop gave him a push from behind. After he joined me on the top of the elevator, I pointed toward the hallway leading off from the shaft. "We'll have to make a jump for it."

LaRue glanced around, and in the shine from his lamp, I saw him smile. "No, we won't. This thing carries its own ramp." He stood, and prying up a short piece of corrugated aluminum, he used it to bridge the span between us and the entrance. Once done, he boldly stomped across.

I scampered behind him, glad when my feet touched solid ground. My partner waited for me in the shadows, his head cocked toward the darkness beyond. I stopped to listen and picked out the same thrumming sound of machinery that I heard in the laundry-room hole. It was muffled, but with my aural sensitivity, I could hear the nuances behind it. There was the noise of running water, a hiss of steam pipes, and tiny, feather-sounding voices. We both drew our weapons and stepped cautiously along the sloping corridor.

The hallway cut to the right as it continued to descend and there were no signs or identifying markers to tell the traveler what he was heading toward. At one point we arrived at a three-way juncture, stalled to listen, and then picked up the trail to the left. LaRue aimed his light at the floor.

"Notice the trash?" he said.

The farther we walked the worse it got—old foam cups, newspaper, food debris. A few steps more and we found ourselves stumbling around piles of human feces.

My lycanthropy adds a supercharge to my sniffer, and my ability to smell is so acute that I occasionally suffer from a rare neurological condition called synesthesia, or blended senses. When an odor is particularly strong, it reveals itself by tickling my optic nerve and clogging my vision with riotous color and wild patterns. Knowing this, I hated having to stop to examine molehills of shit, but I did, finding that some of the droppings were fresh. Every breath I took in this sewer added a sting to my nostrils and tan squares into my sight.

"Doesn't look like a corridor the service personnel might want to use with any regularity," LaRue said.

I pointed my light toward the floor, picking up the hints of footprints. "It looks like it was used a short while ago."

We pushed on ahead. I was grateful to leave this subterranean bathroom and glad to have my vision clear up. We rounded another bend, walking slowly. Our trip had gone on for a hundred steps when we were forced to halt because the corridor dead-ended into a stone wall. This was not to be the finale of our trip, though, for lying in the deepest corner of this recess was a female body wearing a white, nurse's uniform.

TWENTY-TWO

We called Frank Wilson and asked him to bring in a forensics unit on the q.t. For once, he didn't burp, fart, or snort, and while we checked out the other corridors, he arrived with a couple of trusted techs.

The other hallways were filled with trash and debris and each ended abruptly. LaRue kept muttering about the plans of the mine being wrong, and I kept thinking he just plain couldn't read them. Still, there had to be a way down to that sound.

We gave up our hunt when Wilson's voice blasted over our com-links. As usual, my unit was set too loud and nearly popped my eyeballs out of their sockets. I staggered from the noise, and before I knew it, I was on my butt—quite close, I might add, to a pile of dried-up poop.

LaRue offered his hand, pulling me to my feet. "What happened? Did you trip?"

I shook my head. "No, the noise. Wilson's voice."

"Oh, that explains it. You've got to learn to check the volume on your link, Ty."

I took a moment to shake off a creeping dizziness. "I'm with you. Let's go see what Wilson has to say."

Our return trip went uphill, and by the time we arrived at

this newest crime scene, we were both puffing like we were carrying beer kegs on our backs. We walked in on Wilson, who cursed the garish glow of a klieg lamp as he got face-to-face with the body. "Jenna York," he announced.

LaRue and I joined him corpseside. "How do you know that?" I asked.

He grinned, but still didn't look at us. "She was wearing medic tags. You should really remember to look for those things. Every doctor or nurse is required to wear them when on duty."

"Gibson doesn't."

This time Wilson skipped his gaze to me. "Gibson is a rogue. Great doctor, but no goddamned common sense at all. It's shit like that which will get you into dry ice pretty fast."

I had to agree with him, but kept my opinion to myself. "What killed her?"

"Broken neck."

"Do you see any indication that she was beaten?" LaRue said.

"No." Wilson sat back and blew a hard blast of breath through his nose. "You know, if I had my wild guesses, I'd say she was killed by a chiropractor."

"Excuse me?"

"That's right," he answered. "Help me flip her over."

"Ah, come on, Frank," LaRue whined.

"She's dead, LaRue. Ain't like you're going to be touching unmentionable parts without her permission. Stop being a candy-ass and lend me a hand."

I helped the men turn Nurse York onto her stomach. It was true that deadweight weighed more than regular weight, and for a second I had thoughts of people from the center of the earth and their supposed ability to manipulate gravity. When we finished situating her, Wilson pushed her bloody mat of brown hair away to run his finger over her neck. The purplish hue associated with lividity colored her skin and there were several bruises at the base of her head. Her spine had been so injured that the vertebrae bulged out by a good two inches.

Wilson generously offered the play-by-play on this grisly

murder. ''These bruises are caused from the pressure made by fingers.''

''You said you thought a chiropractor had killed her,'' LaRue said. ''What do you mean?''

''She died from severe force, Merrick. In this case—a longitudinal compression with hinging—her spine was squeezed and then bent at an extreme angle. It snapped the spinal cord and crushed the vertebrae. Normally, an injury like this would occur after a fall from a pretty good height.''

''But this is something a chiropractor can do?''

''They're mighty strong folks and well versed in compression techniques. It's a sound bet that the killer knew exactly what vertebrae to pop.''

TWENTY-THREE

We left Wilson to his examination and minutes later we pulled up to Gibson's neighborhood clinic to find him alone. He stood by the glass doors, peering mournfully at the street. When we entered, his baleful look recreated itself into a severe expression, transforming with the building measure of his ire.

"Where is everyone?" I asked, stepping inside.

"I've been shut down," he answered. "My watchdog decided that I wasn't giving the patients my full attention."

"That sucks, Doc," LaRue said, in his most compassionate tone.

"Thanks, Andy." Gibson turned to study me. "What took you so long to get here?"

"We're working," I said. "What's so important, anyway?"

Gibson layered an additional frown into his face, but instead of replying, he sighed, spun on his heel, and motioned us to follow. He marched into his office and slammed the door behind us, locking it as though he expected to be interrupted. "Sit down," he ordered gruffly.

Watching him, I saw his intensity spill out into his purposeful movements, and I'll admit, it gave me the willies. Gibson doesn't usually make a big stink about things, but this time his obvious concern was demonstrated by his stiff body language. He leaned woodenly against the desk and swiped his hand over his beard stubble, searing me with that wild-eyed squint until I couldn't stand it anymore.

"What the hell is wrong?" I blurted.

"Your brain scan is what's wrong," he husked. "How many stretches have you had this cycle?"

"Five. Why?"

"I told you I was tracking increases and decreases in your brain's mass. You've stayed right in a certain percentile, even when you have those months where your synesthesia is kicked up or you fall prey to a bout of aphasia."

"What's happened now?" I asked quietly.

"Your brain is bigger than it should be, Merrick."

"This is something I need to worry about?"

"Not worry; to study." He paused, crossed his legs at the ankles, and went on to let the medical bomb drop. "Since your scans have been predictable, I can only ascribe this increase to environmental factors. We need to find out what's causing this change."

Upon hearing his medical advice, I abruptly lost my fear, harboring annoyance instead, because I knew what was coming.

"Do you feel all right?" Gibson asked.

"Yes."

"Are you sure?" he snapped.

"Yes," I growled. "How am I supposed to be feeling?"

"Headaches, blurred vision, ringing in your ears."

"No. I feel fine."

He grunted. "I want to find out everything we can about this phenomenon. I want to know what's caused it."

"Could it be the effects of radon?" LaRue asked.

Gibson turned his fierce look onto my partner. "How many times have you been down in the mine?"

"A couple," he said. "We just got back from there."

The good doctor stood up and reached for his telephone.

"What are you doing?" I asked.

"Scheduling tests for you."

I couldn't believe my ears. "Are you crazy? We're under the gun here; all three of us. Scheduling tests will only make it look like you're abusing the system even more.''

''Who cares?'' he snarled. ''As far as I'm concerned, we're dead in the water. We better get some information we can bargain with, Merrick, or we're going to find ourselves trying to live on Baba's pension when the hammer falls.''

TWENTY-FOUR

Sometimes, I give myself away. When things get intense, I often retreat into the wolf by allowing it to overcome me. I can't stop it once my emotional discord is announced and I do find it embarrassing—a sign of weakness that's impossible to conquer. My self-cruelty has a moment of a gay abandon and so I ride myself hard in a vain attempt to stifle an incoherent cry for comfort. It never works. Gibson knows the moment he's pushed the supernatural button. Thankfully, he is just as fierce in berating himself about the mistakes he makes. Because of this, going down usually ends with me up on top of the situation.

I fell into a stretch on the hind end of a curse. We were still locked in the confines of his office, wedged between chairs and tables, books and worn-out computer junk. I hit the deck so fast I practically gave myself a nosebleed. As it was, I curled into a fetal position and grabbed onto the sturdy support of LaRue's leg.

The wolf bursts through my solar plexus, singeing my nerve endings as it harvests the power found there. I am completely lost in agony, both mental and physical. While my bones grow by painful millimeters, my thoughts are turned into crusty pillars of salt, and if I try to analyze the hurt away, my brain blows these crumbling supports out from under me. It's this breakdown and ultimate restructuring of my awareness which I find so offensive. Though my lycanthropy gives me speed, endurance, muscle, and musky BO, it also feeds on my humanity, and in the end I sacrifice my authenticity.

I can usually chart the course of my stretches, even if I don't know what changes will befall me, but this episode immediately set my internal navi-computer on alert. Instead of the pain blossoming in my stomach, it found an outlet in my chest with such crushing force, I was sure I was having a coronary.

Gibson jumped on me and held me down so I wouldn't thrash around and hurt myself. I groaned, moaned, coughed, cried, growled, and howled. Finally, after five or six minutes of submitting to an exploding supernova, I was sent rocketing into the clear, unable to speak, move, or breathe.

The good doctor saw my difficulty and pushed upward on my diaphragm, his easy massage bringing the blood back into my torso before kick-starting my lungs. He continued to tenderly touch me as if he used his own life force to supply the juice for my body. It was all I could do to hide my embarrassment, but I managed by pushing up on my elbows.

"Lie still, Merrick," Gibson whispered. "You had a bad one."

No kidding. My skeletal structure had lengthened a good three inches and now my cammies felt like I was wearing a chastity belt. On top of that, my muscles had popped and strained against my uniform sleeves. As if this were not enough, I received a kisser full of sharp smells. Thankfully, the sensitivity in my nose hadn't gotten my optic nerve involved.

Gibson grabbed his stethoscope and plugged it into his ears, pushing away my thrashing hands to listen to my heart. It seemed like a waste of energy, so I submitted to his ministrations, taking deep inhales whenever he commanded me to. After several minutes he satisfied himself that I was going to live.

"You had pain in your heart area, didn't you?" he demanded.

At first I thought of lying, but rejected the idea, knowing it would do no good to turn off the bulldog in Gibson. "Yes. But I feel fine now."

"Merrick," he said, "tell me the truth."

I was. Except for a strange, rather pleasant fluttering around my heart, I felt energized and peaceful. I was about to convey my unusual vitality when I abruptly had a new phenomenon to deal with. My hearing picked up a series of lovely tones that I could have sworn had come from right beside me. I glanced at LaRue like he could have possibly made the sound, and then to Gibson. My surprised expression turned on the good doctor's curiosity and I was immediately forced to fess up in his homestyle inquisition.

"What is it?" he growled.

"I heard sounds," I murmured. "Faint sounds. They sounded like crystal bells."

Gibson frowned and tossed a concerned look toward my partner. LaRue fielded his trepidation and used it to formulate and deliver a theory. "Maybe you heard something from outside."

I cocked my head toward the floor, hoping I could ferret out the series of exquisite musical notes, but whatever aria I'd picked up on was gone. Shaking my head, I crawled to a stand and held on to the desk for a wobbly minute. "I'm sorry," I husked. "Maybe my huge brain is dishing up the noise."

It's a blessing, indeed, to have two good friends. They both blew me off with smiles and waves. Of course Gibson spun me around, pushed me into the chair, and then stuck the sharp end of a lighted instrument into my ears.

"See any sound?" LaRue asked, with a grin.

Gibson snorted before speaking. "I see darkness. Lots of darkness."

He pushed a little harder and I dragged my head away from him, complaining. "You don't have to dig for gold. All the stuff is in there."

He backed off. "Yeah, it's in there. But is there something new?"

I honestly didn't want to know. Of course, that was until I heard the crystalline tones again.

TWENTY-FIVE

I stomped out of the office the minute Gibson started scheduling appointments for me. LaRue followed, but paused when the good doctor yelled at him to make sure I showed up at the appropriate time. My partner nodded and flew from the clinic behind me.

"Let's get our visit with Ralph Kane over," I ordered as he climbed into the Trabi beside me.

LaRue obeyed me silently, and after a fitful moment trying to start the car, we were on our way. It was not until we entered the next ward that he spoke. "There's a spare set of cammies on the back floorboard."

I nodded, snagging his drift. Rifling under a couple of Baba's trash blankets, I found a wrinkled uniform of my very own. I glanced at him, sizing up the rumples in his clothes. "We're a matching pair of raggedy dolls." I chuckled.

He shook his head. "I still look better. I spilled cherry pie down myself this morning."

"Ah, yes, the montage of stains. You win, partner." With that, I performed the moves of a contortionist by stripping down to my underwear and then redressing myself in a space designed for a midget. When I was done, I made sure our conversation centered around the investigation and not some gestation of metaphysical ideas. "Did you get a chance to find out anything on this guy?"

"Ralph Kane is, indeed, an auditor for the Environmental Tax Agency. He's only twenty-one and recently graduated from tax school. The ETA hired him on an as-needed basis. He's listed as a Class-B designation, so he ain't rolling in the guano."

"A ready-made patsy?"

"Could be." He paused to negotiate a corner, and when he did, he skidded into the curb.

My partner has creativity in his hands, but I'm afraid it doesn't extend to his driving abilities. To prove the point, LaRue ground the gears as he gunned the engine.

"It's going to take everything I have to be civil to this bastard," he growled.

I knew the feeling, but didn't comment. The ETA auditors were the burr in every backside in the district.

I settled in for the short trip without another word, thinking instead of ways we could reverse some of the tax collector's annual abuse so Kane would suffer a little. It was not so much that I wanted to see the score evened as it was my need for a bit of evil enjoyment.

When we pulled up in front of Kane's dilapidated high-rise, LaRue broke the silence by pointing at the building before saying: "This place is haunted. I read it in the newspaper recently. It's supposed to be filled with giant ghost rats that chew on furniture. One of the tenants was complaining about the teeth marks in the legs of her baby's crib."

Ghost rats. "Sounds like a termite problem."

"It just sounds ridiculous to me," LaRue answered.

That was my partner. One minute he was going on about supernatural light beings, and the next he was pooh-poohing invisible rodents. Sometimes I wondered what his metaphysical meter was set on. Was there a cutoff point in feasibility? I'd asked him before and he'd just shrugged, so I kept my question quiet as I stalked through the lobby with a fearless swagger. Unfortunately, I lost my cocksure attitude after I found out Kane lived on the fifteenth floor and the elevator was out of service. For some reason, I chewed most of the energy oats before we reached his apartment and was left puffing and light-headed. I leaned against the wall while LaRue summoned the man with a loud knock.

When he answered and he saw it was two marshals, Mr. Kane panicked. He tried to slam the door in our faces, but my partner saw the shock in his expression and shoved his foot in the way before muscling inside.

LaRue not only uses his mouth as a weapon, but he uses surprise, too, and before I knew it, I heard the familiar thump when he laid the blade of his hand against Kane's chest. His strike was not enough to crack the man's sternum, but instead, it set the kinetic energy into motion, giving LaRue the advantage. He pushed Kane against the far wall, growling his dissatisfaction. "That is not a nice way to treat a law enforcement officer."

Kane was one of those ferret-faced fellows with thin, wavy tan hair; a long, pencil neck; and an Adam's apple that was half the size of a red delicious. "You people said you wouldn't bother me again," he wheezed.

"What people?" LaRue demanded.

"The other two—Nichols and Carver. They said no one else would interview me."

Damn! We couldn't seem to squeeze by those two.

LaRue ground Kane into the wall before releasing him. His power dissipated in a flash and he forgot about the rude reception to wander around the large studio apartment. Pausing, he picked up a delicate Chinese vase. "Looks like you do quite well on your salary," he said. "Better than I do, in fact. How is that, Mr. Kane?"

Kane grunted, gurgled, and then stepped toward him cautiously, stopping a few paces away when LaRue looked like he might have a case of butter fingers. "Please," he husked, rubbing his chest. "That vase is a family heirloom. My mother will come over to your house and personally kill you if you break it, but before she does that, she'll kill me first."

I couldn't help chuckling, but covered it up by sitting down on a Victorian-styled settee. "Why don't you make yourself comfortable, Mr. Kane? We don't work with Nichols and Carver. They were simply an advance team who should never have told you that you wouldn't receive another visit.''

My bogus explanation seemed to calm him, especially after LaRue obliged and placed the vase back on the mahogany sideboard. Kane sat down on the end of the couch, stalling by taking a deep breath and knuckling his eyes. ''I'm sorry. It's been difficult for me to talk about.''

''What has? Bernard Horn's death?''

Kane frowned. ''No. What's this about Bernard Horn?''

I leaned forward and LaRue walked over to join us. ''Didn't the other agents want to know your affiliation with the opera singer?''

''No, they didn't. They wanted me to talk about my experience.''

''With what?''

He swallowed and his Granny Smith bobbled. ''Extraterrestrials.''

When I get my next paycheck, I'm going to have a T-shirt printed up that says ONE OF THE FEW WHO HAS NOT BEEN ABDUCTED. This particular phenomenon has gone on unabated for a hundred years or more and underground religions have grown up around the abduction experience. It is a sad statement of our times. Life on planet Earth is too much of a trial, and the only way folks can think to relieve the pain, frustration, and boredom is to join those who claim to have been taken aboard an alien spaceship.

''What did Nichols and Carver want to know?'' I asked.

''They wanted me to tell them about the Zeladrite,'' he answered.

''What is Zeladrite?''

''Not what, who. They came to our world eons ago and made their home in the hollow earth.''

''Mr. Kane, I hate to be the one to break it to you, but our planet has a molten core.''

''Yes, but our planet also has a deep mantle riddled with fissures and caverns. They don't need to live in the center of the earth—they just need a place from which to operate. Ten or twelve miles below the surface. That's all.''

LaRue warmed to the subject and stomped into the interview. ''What are the Zeladrite doing here?''

"They're at war with the Barishi-Roo of the planet Carna," Kane answered softly. "Carna is a huge world located in the Pleiades star system and its star is called Maya. Well, that's an earth term, you see. Maya was one of the Seven Sisters of Greek mythology and the Pleiades is a system with seven suns." He shrugged. "The scientists who named the stars were romantics, I guess."

"So the Zeladrite are at war with the Barishi-Roo," LaRue said. "Why?"

"The Barishi-Roo are the Knowledge Bringers, Marshal. It was this race who transmitted information to the great crystal of Atlantis. It was the Barishi-Roo who made it possible for humanity to survive. They work in our behalf to instill us with a sense of wonder and creativity." Again, he stopped, and took a hard breath before taking a seat aboard the Insane Train. "The Barishi-Roo are our benefactors. The Zeladrite want to destroy us."

"Why us?" LaRue asked. "Surely, we aren't a threat."

"But we are," Kane answered. "Thousands of humans have emigrated to other worlds. We're a growing problem."

"All right, if that is the case, why are we a growing problem?"

"Because we are the most brilliant species known in the universe to date," he answered flatly. "We threaten the other races with our abilities."

Hearing this, I knew for certain that Mr. Kane worked as the flagman on the train.

He continued after rubbing his chest. "Many of the people who left for the Seven Sisters have become representatives of our planet. They have become business people, administrators, and VIPs in the government of the Barishi-Roo. They have managed to set up business deals with the other worlds located there."

"What kind of business deals?"

"They've been selling Earth's natural resources as well as resources claimed from dead or dying planets."

"Earth has the right stuff for long-term exploitation," LaRue said.

Kane nodded. "Yes, that's it in a nutshell. The Zeladrite

are a warlike race who have had more downs than ups in the last few centuries. They accuse the Barishi-Roo of forming an alliance against them."

"Did they?"

"Apparently there is some sort of military blockade," he answered. "Getting information at this level is difficult."

"Why haven't the Zeladrite blown us to space dust?" I asked sarcastically. "Why all the sneaking around?"

"If they openly attacked us, they would wipe out the only source for free graviton particles in this end of the galaxy," he said. Clearing his throat, he added: "The Barishi-Roo are technologically superior. They would see it as a direct assault against an allied world and they would wipe out the Zeladrite." Kane paused again. Then: "At least, that's what I understand."

"What do they use free graviton particles for?" LaRue asked.

"It's necessary for their weaponry."

"Are the Zeladrite the reason behind the abductions?"

"Yes."

"Did the Zeladrite abduct you?"

He nodded and when he did, his slight frame shook with his head.

"Why?" I asked. "Because you threatened to make them pay environmental taxes?"

Kane turned to stare at me. "You don't believe. That's what makes this so hard. I've almost lost my job over this."

"Why didn't you?"

"I don't know," he whispered.

LaRue pushed by my thoughts to entertain the fantasy. "Why, Mr. Kane? What good are you to the aliens?"

He sneered. "Believe me, Marshal. I'm nothing special. The Zeladrite can't mine the uranium ore necessary to collect the free graviton particles. It makes them sick."

"I got news for you, buddy, it makes humans sick, too," I said.

"I know. Since becoming an experiencer, I've developed several strange blisters that have turned out to be melanoma."

It sounded like he'd developed a strange melanoma in his

brain. "Did the agents ask you about the PHO Rejuvenation Facility?"

"No," he said. "I don't know anything about that."

"I can't believe they took time to listen to your story about the Zeladrites," I growled.

"They wanted to know about our efforts to stop the illegal abduction of citizens."

His sentence stopped my belligerence and abruptly ended LaRue's visions of spacesuited maidens from Venusia.

"What efforts?" he asked.

"The experiencers, of course. We have banded together under the leadership of an avatar who is determined to grant us our freedom from this intergalactic abuse."

"Who's the avatar?"

"We know him only as Turquoise."

"What does he have you do?"

"We have gatherings," he answered. "Unsanctioned meetings, and he sends the participants. The government refuses to recognize the threat, so we've had to move in secrecy for the time being. Still, the word of our dealings has gotten out."

"Are you suggesting you spread seditious material?" I asked.

He started to shake his head and kept it going as he answered. "Absolutely not! These are parties, complete with food and music where we actively trade ideas and sorrows."

It sounded like a bunch of freaked-out housewives who were bartering over bent plastic bowls while scarfing down toast points heaped with cat food. "But what do you talk about?"

"That's up to the individual. Mostly, we report about our lives since the abduction experiences. I always lead a meditation and a prayer for those who have been abused."

"Are you paid for this service?"

He glanced down at the threadbare carpet. "A pittance, Marshal. Nothing more."

"Do you take donations from the experiencers?"

"No," he answered. Sitting back, Kane took another deep breath, and then spoke on the exhale. "I have no chance of ever becoming a rich man because of my extraterrestrial abduction. Would you deny me a few extra credits?''

I'd deny any of the wolves at the ETA, but I wisely didn't reply to his question. Instead, I said: ''Are you an active member of the Spark of Creation Movement?''

''No. Honestly, we're just trying to help experiencers. Especially the children.''

''Why the children?''

''Because in the end, they are the ones who are abducted and never returned.''

TWENTY-SIX

LaRue hammered Kane some more until the guy got too esoteric even for my partner. By this time I smelled a government scam that ran as deep as the Black River and stank just as bad. Finally, it was my turn to nail the bureaucrat's weenie to the wall, and with malice and impatience in my heart, I used the biggest rivet I could find.

I reached over and grabbed Kane by the shirt collar, dragging him in my direction. I misjudged my lycanthropic strength and felt the material rip beneath my hand, but I bunched it around my fist to keep him in my control. Nose to nose, I got my point across. ''There are no people from the center of the earth and no alien abductions,'' I snarled. ''What we have here is a Class-A stall. Now, Mr. Tax Man, I would suggest you talk to us without the bullshit, because if you don't, I won't have any trouble relieving this world of another buggering parasite. Do we have an understanding?''

The fruit bowl in his neck moved when he nodded. I released him, rose, and took a turn around the room just to give me a second to vent some steam. For a low man on the bureaucratic totem pole, I noticed that Kane had some nice things. The fact that he was doing well for himself grated me more now that my own wealth had disappeared and my roommate had been beaten to a bloody pulp.

Spinning on my heel, I lanced him with my most lethal look. "Tell us about Bernard Horn."

Kane's head snapped back like I'd hit him. "I don't know anything about him. I only met him once."

"When he came to perform for your dog-and-pony show," I said.

"My gathering," Kane corrected.

"Did he speak to you or your audience about the Spark of Creation Movement?"

"No. We may be abductees but we're not disloyal to the government. We're just different. We're trying to find ways of fitting into society better. Believe me, we would conform if we could."

"Did you get the impression that Horn believed this?" I demanded.

"I didn't get any impression at all. Mr. Horn was very open and up-front with his loyalties."

"What about Turquoise? Is he loyal to the current government?"

"Well, yes, of course. It's said he's a bureaucratic stickler."

"Did Horn admit knowing Turquoise?"

Kane thought a moment like he couldn't quite remember. "As a matter of fact, I believe he did, but the gathering was in full swing and I had to attend to guests following the meditation. I never got around to asking him."

I sat back down, taking a moment to stretch before asking my next question. "Did anyone come with him when he performed?"

"No. He showed up at my door alone. Someone must have driven him, though."

"Why?"

"Because he was a cripple. I don't think he could have taken public transportation. When he arrived here, he used two canes."

"I hope your building's elevator was in service then."

He nodded. "He couldn't have made it up the stairs. I assume he had arthritis. Whatever it was, I could tell he was in a lot of pain. His singing was affected by it, but the people in the room were so appreciative of the concert that they paid him a great deal of attention.''

''What about the people who attend your parties?'' I asked. ''Where do you think Turquoise finds them to send to you?''

Kane sighed, but then tossed out the answer. ''They come from the tax rolls.''

I glanced at LaRue, who wore a lovely frown. Turning back to Kane, I demanded a reckoning. ''What tax rolls?''

''Those issued on people who have had some financial problems in their lives, such as tax evasion, underpayments, and bankruptcy.''

''Why are these people selected?''

''Because they are all abductees,'' he said. ''Two out of three people granted permission by the government to file for bankruptcy have had some prior experience with extraterrestrials.''

''What a crock,'' I mumbled.

''It's true. Statistics don't lie. Take a walk through your district database and have a look. There are several reports that are open to Class-A investigators at the ETA. It is the reason that's given in many cases.''

''Who puts together the guest lists for Turquoise?''

He stood and went to a small secretary. Pulling a drawer open gently, he removed a business card. ''I'm not really sure who does the legwork or how big Turquoise's operation is, but this is my contact.''

Kane handed me the card, and when I read the name there, I almost dropped the brass plating off my attitude. It was Myra Fontaine, my former psychiatrist.

TWENTY-SEVEN

Dr. Myra Fontaine was a physician without a correct sense of ethics. She'd compromised our relationship by double-dealing me in the worst way, and for that, I would always remain angry. Yes, I know, I hold grudges, but sometimes you just have to. Now, when it really counted, I could use my rage to make the squeaky-voiced bitch toe the line, even if it were only for an hour. Vindictiveness was almost as good as revenge.

Instead of going over to Fontaine's comfortable office, we invited her to our greasy pigsty, and found her there upon our return—fuming, fussing, and singing the same old funeral hymn. She sat at the smudgy table in our interrogation room, her irate outburst delivered on a squeal. It immediately made my eyes water, but I ignored her, long enough to mount a chair pony-style and wait for my partner to slide into his own saddle. We both stared at Fontaine until she finally stopped chattering about the indignity of being hauled out of a patient session by two smelly ward cops. After she shut up, I spoke.

"You are here concerning the murder of Bernard Horn. If you refuse to cooperate, then the law grants us permission to enter your name as an accessory before or after the fact. And you know me, Myra. I'll pull your panty hose up over your ears and tie them in a knot behind your head.'' I paused, leaned on my pony, and asked the question that was on my mind. ''We want to know who Turquoise is.''

She stared at me, but couldn't hide the surprised look on her face before I saw it. ''Is that all? You brought me down here for that?''

''Who is Turquoise?'' I repeated.

Fontaine sighed. ''He's no one. I made him up.''

''Why?''

''Because I'm trying to earn a living. You scrabble for your money, don't you? Well, I have to do the same.''

I reached across the table with the speed and alacrity my lycanthropic disposition gives me, stopping just short of my finger to her nose. It was enough to scare the poop out of her and she backed up, almost knocking herself and her chair to our filthy, sticky floor. ''Explain from the beginning,'' I ordered. ''Leave anything out and I'll throw you in the drunk tank with a few street folks. I'm sure they'd like to have a psychiatric evaluation while they're sobering up.''

She snorted. ''God, how did I ever get mixed up with you?''

''Talk, Myra. My patience hasn't gotten any better.''

Fontaine stalled a moment more and then reluctantly gave up the goods. ''After the fiasco between you, me, and Gibson, I was left without an additional avenue of income. We all have to eat.''

''So, you couldn't sell the medical information on me any longer. What did you do?''

''I have noticed over the last several months the increasing number of people who come to see me regarding UFO abduction experiences,'' she squeaked. ''I started studying these individuals and noticed pattern changes in their thought processes. This led me to believe they'd experienced some sort of alteration in brain chemistry. I wanted to find out what was going on.''

''So, your idea was to commit a fraudulent act and study people without their permission.''

''You make it sound like I'm poking around in their brains with an ice pick.'' She leaned forward and then pulled back hastily when the sleeve of her gray, silk blouse wound up in something gooey on the table. Fontaine made a sucking noise and dove for her purse, rifling through it for a clean snot rag. Finding one, she dabbed at the tissue with her tongue and tried to remove the dark brown spot from her cuff while she explained her idea. ''All these people claim enhanced creativity as a by-product of the abduction experience. Those who couldn't draw before suddenly become artists, those who couldn't write turn out beautiful prose.''

''You hooked them up to machines to see what physical changes occurred in their brains,'' LaRue said.

Fontaine nodded. ''Shortly after a reported experience, these patients would have observable changes in chemistry as well as an increase in brain weight and synaptic junctures. They showed heightened activity in the temporal lobes and certain areas of the cerebral cortex. I know it sounds crazy, but whatever is happening is changing their brains for the better.''

''Could some sort of unknown brain dysfunction be responsible?'' LaRue asked.

''Good question,'' she said. ''That was the very one I asked and which prompted me to set up my own testing arena. These patients are highly creative, but they shouldn't be, because they each suffer a variety of neuroses that should be the lock on the door, so to speak.''

''I thought highly creative people were neurotic,'' LaRue said.

''Creative people don't fit that definition by a long shot.'' She sighed impatiently. Then: ''Let me see if I can explain this so you can both understand. Our brains are what we call a dissipative system.''

I interrupted her. ''We know what a dissipative system is, Myra. We know that the brain needs to make new connections prompted by incoming stimuli.''

''You've been talking to Lane, have you?''

I knocked her question away. ''You're saying that these folks had a closed system because of their neuroses and shouldn't have handled the incoming stimuli in creative ways.''

Fontaine clapped and tossed me a smirk. ''We know it doesn't take much to change our brains' physiological setup.

For instance, a neurotic patient suffering from generalized anxiety disorder has troubles getting past his worries long enough to be creative. Certain biochemicals in the brain can actually become addictive to the organism. A person with this disorder needs the enzymes that produce the worries as much as a man who is addicted to cigarettes needs that first puff in the morning.''

''How can that be?'' LaRue said.

She shrugged. ''Who knows? There are many mysteries about the brain. We'll probably never find out for sure. At least in our lifetimes.'' Shaking her head, she went on. ''It doesn't matter. The reason I invented Turquoise was because it was the only way I could collectively control this group without them realizing what I was doing.''

I sat back to stare at her. ''Kane kept referring to Turquoise as an avatar.''

''That's right. He's one who leads, who they can pattern themselves after. You see, Merrick, this blind study is growing. More and more people are coming forward with abduction stories and creative talent to boggle the imagination. The more times they claim abductions, the more intense their creativity becomes. With these people's backgrounds, it shouldn't be happening.''

''And you don't think the Office of Intelligence is behind this?'' I said.

''No, I don't. I think something is changing in our brains and the patients relate the event to UFOs. The phenomenon doesn't necessarily have to be extraterrestrial contact. It could have just as easily been near-death experiences. I believe the UFO connection is primarily the influence of technology and the growing anxiety about the stability of our planet.'' She paused to dab at tiny beads of perspiration threatening to mess up her makeup.

''You don't think it's a mass hallucination?'' LaRue asked.

''No. That has always been the cop-out excuse for this phenomenon and as far as I can tell that theory just isn't possible. We're evolving as a species and those people who claim abduction experiences are the ones who are on the cutting edge of this growth explosion. It's fortunate it's happening within predictable boundaries as far as experiencers. We can gauge how a person should act according to his psychological makeup and history and then make assumptions. It's empirical data right now, but I hope to change that soon."

"Turquoise is the glue that keeps the team functioning without obvious interference from you," LaRue said, sliding to a stand.

"Yes. It's a perfectly legitimate psychoanalytical technique."

"Perfectly legitimate? Dr. Fontaine, it's downright dishonest."

"That, too, is a matter of perspective," she answered, turning to stare a hole through me.

"What's that supposed to mean?" I said.

"We all use our patients to some degree to further our careers. Take your precious Dr. Gibson. He's screwing you, isn't he? Look at the truth that's right there. He's just jumping into the sack with you so he can keep you around for more tests and more money. You can't deny it, Merrick. That reality won't go away like the wolf does after a full moon."

A thousand things crossed my mind when she said that, and then I realized she knew exactly which of my emotional buttons to push. I took a minute to stuff my rage down into a lonely pocket in my mind before asking the one question that really concerned me. "Was Bernard Horn one of your patients?"

Fontaine smiled sadly. "Yes, he was. Bernard suffered from a variety of neuroses. That's why he never made a splash in the music world. He had the talent, but couldn't cough up the full measure of it because he suffered from a somatoform disorder." When we just looked at her, she knew she had to explain that last concept. "Somatoform disorders are anxiety-based neurotic patterns. The person complains of physical problems, but none can be found."

"Hypochondria," I said.

"That's right. Bernard was highly self-critical and it gave him pseudo-arthritis."

I glanced at LaRue. At least we had a reason why he was in the mine in the first place. Swinging my gaze around, I studied Fontaine for a moment. "Tell me, Myra. Did Horn claim to be an abductee, too?"

"Not until a few months ago. The moment the change came about, Bernard started utilizing all of his musical gifts." She paused, then added: "The sad thing about his death? People were finally starting to notice his new talent and singing style."

TWENTY-EIGHT

Fontaine knew the law better than we did, and in the end, we had to release her without getting much more information. The moment she walked out, we had another interviewee waiting, and luckily, we got to this new person before Nichols and Carver. Her name was Louise Tanya Reseda, and she was the sister of Betty Victoria, Horn's fiancée.

Reseda was a petite woman with long, auburn hair and thick lips that were painted a luscious shade of pomegranate. LaRue just loves those pouty-mouthed broads, so I scanned her file while I let him ask her the questions.

He sat next to her in the interrogation room and warned her not to drag her sleeve through the goo on the table. She thanked him with some sweet murmur and lowered her hands to her lap.

"What can I do to help, Marshal?" she cooed.

"You can begin by telling us about your sister," he said sweetly.

"Oh, she was devastated by Bernard's death," she answered.

"We understand she's in another district performing with the District Opera Company."

Reseda nodded. "Yes. Betty has been committed to these engagements for several months."

"We understand the transport left the day after Mr. Horn was found dead."

"That's right. The next morning. It was all she could do to step on the bus. If she can sing, it will be a miracle."

"Why didn't she stay home?"

Reseda pulled on a dejected expression. "Oh, the poor dear. She would have lost her position with the company if she'd refused to go. And now with Bernard gone, she'll need her job."

"Were they pooling their resources?"

"Yes, I think so. Bernard had money."

"He did?" LaRue asked. "Was he investing in backdoor projects?"

She shook her head. "I don't know. Betty didn't talk about it and I didn't ask. It's not polite."

It was my turn to boing this lady. "Did Horn ever mention a woman named Myra Fontaine?"

"No. The name's not familiar."

"Did Horn ever mention any involvement with a man named Turquoise?"

She thought a moment, closing her eyes as though this might extract the required info from her brain. Finally, she squinted at me. "He was a friend of Bernard's."

LaRue grunted, glanced at me, and back to Reseda. "Did you ever meet him?"

"No, but Betty did. She said he was a very courteous gentlemen."

"Did she say where he lived?"

"No. She didn't say much, Marshals. I'm sorry. I do know that Bernard and Turquoise worked together."

"For the Spark of Creation Movement?" I asked.

She gasped. "Oh, my no. That's the most ridiculous thing I've ever heard. Have such vicious rumors started so soon after his death?"

"Was he that upstanding an individual?"

"Bernard was extremely loyal to the government. Just check his service records. He was a humanitarian who devoted most of his time to helping orphans and disadvantaged children."

"Really?" I said. "How did he help them?"

"He taught music at the orphanages and gave free concerts for people who have Class-D designations and below."

"What about your sister?" LaRue asked. "Did she help Horn in his efforts?"

"No. My sister prefers to be left alone. She doesn't go out of the house much and doesn't get involved in these sorts of activities."

"Wise woman," I muttered.

"Did you ever hear Horn say that he'd been abducted by space aliens?" LaRue said.

Reseda smiled sadly. "Yes, of course."

"What did he say?"

"Nothing," she answered. "He didn't need to say anything. I understood his experience without hearing his words."

"You accepted his story?"

"Yes."

"Why?" I barked.

She studied me calmly before pushing the icing off the cake. "I've been abducted myself."

LaRue and I both leaned toward her. "What about your sister?" I asked. "Has she been abducted?"

"Marshal Merrick," she said, "my whole family unit has been abducted. All twenty-nine of us. Thirty—if you count my cousin Trina, who was pregnant with her last child when the aliens grabbed her."

"You're going to have to explain this, Ms. Reseda," I ordered. "What has happened?"

"Every member of my family unit is an unwilling slave for the Zeladrite," she said. "We do what we're told."

"When was the last time you were abducted?"

"Late last year. I didn't have to do any work in the mines, though. I haven't been doing that for about ten years."

"What have you been doing?"

"I've been serving as a breeding vessel. My job is to mix my DNA with the Zeladrite DNA."

"In other words, they make you pregnant."

"No. It's not pregnancy like you understand it. It's more a stewardship of alien life. The cells need merely bond and then the Zeladrite scientists take over."

I wanted to laugh my ass off at this asylum case, but bit my tongue instead. LaRue abruptly moved his chair, clearing additional space between him and the nut bar.

"Why do they want to mix with the human DNA?" he asked.

She placed the palm of her hand lightly on the table. "Simply because it angers the High Council of the Barishi-Roo. They are tainting the gene pool, you see."

"How many times have you been used this way?"

"I'd say I'm close to five hundred visits, now."

"Can't you do anything to stop these abductions?"

"No. When they want you, they just find you by the diaphanous insert."

"And that would be?"

"A special device that they stick up your nose and lodge into your brain. It's alien technology and can't be found until the person is dead and someone has opened up his skull. I think it may have some sort of force field to protect it, but I'm not into the mechanics of it."

"So this diaphanous insert is a locator beacon," I said.

"That, and more. The Zeladrite want to know humanity's secret. They want to know about our emotions and what it's like to have imagination."

"Don't they have emotions or imaginations?" LaRue asked.

"No, they don't," she answered proudly. "They are as dead as the fish in the Black River. The Zeladrite link right on up to the human slaves and experience these things when we experience them. They simply love the creative process."

"Have you found yourself more creative after your abduction experience?"

"Yes," she whispered. Pausing, she gathered a deep breath and then spoke forcefully. "I've displayed a marvelous ability for writing. My problem is my natural rebellious nature. I know I'm being manipulated and I don't like it and I'm not going to give the Zeladrite any more of a chance to use me than they already do."

"How do you fight them?"

"I fight them by fighting my creative urges. I refuse to write anything, not even a letter or thank-you note. The other members of my family unit flaunt their new talents, though." She paused and shook her head disgustedly. "It seems that the people I know who've been abducted want to show off their creativity, like it's some sort of compensation for being abused by aliens. I keep my life as bland and as boring as I possibly can because it's the only form of protest I have."

"Can't the Zeladrite force you into complying?" I asked.

She shook her head and smiled. "Fortunately, they don't seem to have any way of making me perform. I don't know why that is. They've changed my insert several times and still I managed to defy them."

TWENTY-NINE

It sounded like what Louise Tanya Reseda had was not an abduction experience. It was more an experience of apathy, self-loathing, and sadness. I understood how the trials of daily life could foster such denial, and after we let her go home, I found myself wondering if my lycanthropy was a scream for attention that was just as loud as those claiming to be abducted.

It was a lousy thing to think about, but thankfully, I got lucky and could put my considerations on hold. We had just sat down in our cubicle to go over the case list when I received a call from a snitch who had a line on my stolen stuff. According to my source, everything showed up at the apartment/showroom of a backdoor fence called Pigeon. The food was already gone, but the blankets, books, and vids were still in stock. Hearing this pissed me off so bad, I charged away with LaRue at my heels, desperately trying to calm me down.

"Ty, take it easy," he pleaded. "If you go in there like this, you'll kill the bastard before he can tell you who brought the goods in."

I stopped walking to stare at him, suddenly open to what he was saying. Turning away, I nodded. He was right. I had bloody eyeballs from seeing red, and for the first time in my life I realized the difference between being outraged and being enraged. The anger I held was so deep that it had transformed me into a roaring tiger, but the animal was trapped within, straining at its chains.

"It's the audacity, Andy," I whispered. "How dare these thieves hit me?"

My partner, ever the one to be metaphysically pragmatic, leaned an arm casually across my shoulder. "What goes around comes around."

"I assume you're referring to my own illegal forays?" I said frostily.

"You can find ways of fooling yourself, but you will never get one by the universe."

I rolled my eyes. "Like you've paid so big yourself."

He dropped his arm and stuffed his hands into his pockets as we strolled down the street to the car. "I suffered at the hands of thieves right in our own squad room a few months back. And in my opinion, I lost big."

I ground to a halt to face him. "You never mentioned getting ripped off."

"I know. You would have laughed."

Was I that skeptical that my friends saw me as uncompassionate? I started walking again just to hide my expression. "What happened?"

"My mom gave me a large, brown bag full of charm sacks," he answered. "She asked me to deliver them to her customers before I came home from work. It was a warm day and some of the sacks had raw garlic in them and I didn't want them to spoil, so I brought the bag inside and put it under my desk. We went out to interview someone, and when I came back, the bag was gone. No one ever confessed to swiping it." He kicked at a rock in the cracked sidewalk and sighed. "I suppose it was someone who thinks I'm a metaphysical fruitcake."

"That would be everyone, including me," I said, with a smile.

He grinned, but then his expression retreated into a frown. "It cost me two months pay to replace those items. Anyway, I got over it. I've swiped enough stuff from crime scenes to expect to pay my dues once in a while. You should, too.''

Well, I didn't. ''If you expect the universe to throw you the dried fruit in that cake, then dried fruit is what you're going to get,'' I said. ''Personally, I would have taken big chunks out of someone's ass.'' With that, I marched off to do just that.

We arrived at Pigeon's dilapidated hidey-hole and burrowed our way down to the basement entrance amid trash and cardboard boxes. LaRue muttered something about calling the fire marshals in, but in the next moment he had found the door and kicked his way inside. Pigeon, the little varmint, was sitting in a sea of stolen property, eating a bowl of noodles with a pair of chopsticks.

Before he knew what was happening, I snatched away the bowl and flung it across the room before grabbing his eating utensils and his shirt collar. Getting into his face, I aimed the pointy pins toward his eyes. ''It's going to be really hard to gauge the condition of items if you can't see them.''

He smelled like soy sauce and I thought about jabbing him just because he stank, but I managed marginal control when he immediately started whimpering. ''Take whatever you want, Marshal. If I got some of your stuff, I'm sorry. I would have given it back to you if I'd known. Can't fault a man for earning a living.''

''Yes, but most of us have to pay taxes on what we earn,'' I snarled.

He blubbered some more while LaRue took a turn around this closet filled with used stereos, TVs, dilapidated computers, irons, pots and pans, and the entire stock of Baba's trash blankets.

''You knew the shit was mine,'' I growled. ''My name was carved in most of the stuff. I ought to drive these stakes clear into your brain and put you out of your spineless misery.''

''What?'' he wailed. ''What do you want?''

''I want to know who ripped me off.''

''I don't know who did it. I only know who brought me the stuff.''

''Who?'' I barked, inching perilously close to the mark with the chopsticks.

''It was those lousy hoods in Ward 13,'' he panted. ''You know. They call themselves the Scorpios. I don't think they did the stealing, though.''

Goddamned street punks. These hoodlums never did the dirty work; instead, they usually rolled the thief to get their goods. All of which meant: there was not a hope or prayer that would let me find out the identity of the bastards who'd whacked Baba, and the only ammo I had was in the form of an empty threat, but I delivered it anyway. ''You tell those assholes that if I see any of them on the street, I'll take out my service revolver and start shooting them where they stand.''

THIRTY

We loaded up the Trabi with my stuff, and while we were at it, we took a nice TV and vid machine to replace the ones that were swiped. LaRue's old car was riding on the bottom of the springs and so we went back to my flat to drop off the goodies before continuing on with our day. When we arrived, Baba was in the bedroom snoring, her friend Craia was nowhere to be seen, and the phone was ringing.

It turned out to be Gibson calling to bust my chops about showing up for a medical appointment. I tried to avoid the conversation by signaling to LaRue to take a message, but this time my slide wouldn't work and my partner looked serious as he beckoned me to take the receiver.

"What now, Gibson?" I asked irritably.

"Merrick, I want you and Andy to come down to my clinic," he said. "I need to do a specific test on you both."

My aggravation leaped into concern. "Why?"

"Just come," he answered. "I'll explain when you get here. And Merrick?"

"Yeah?"

"Don't go into the mine before you come here. I mean it."

With that, he hung up and I was left with the residue of Gibson's salty intensity. It gave me a moment's pause, because the good doctor, though excitable, doesn't play games. I waved to LaRue and off we went, trepidation improving our speed.

Upon arriving, we found Gibson talking with an old man named Robert Bennet, who contentedly stroked his yellowed goatee throughout our introductions.

"Why did you call us over in such a rush?" I asked, sliding onto the ratty couch beside LaRue.

Gibson was doing a damned good job of keeping his fire under control, and so spoke in a low voice to maintain the status quo. "Robert is a xenobiologist."

Bennet propped up this statement by nodding and murmuring: "Yes, yes. One of the last of my kind."

"Pardon my directness," I said, "but should we be impressed by this?"

Gibson sucked in a chuckle. "I swear, Merrick, you are such a pain in the ass sometimes. A xenobiologist studies extraterrestrial organisms."

Now I understood why he was the last of his kind. "Bet your career has been one jolly after another. Met any aliens lately?"

"Actually, Marshal, I have," he answered forcefully.

I glanced at Gibson, but he ignored me by making a to-do about sitting down behind his desk.

"What kind of aliens?" LaRue whispered.

"Well, I haven't met any little green men, but I have studied a variety of extraterrestrial bacteria." Bennet paused to readjust his position in the chair before crossing his legs and patting down the wrinkles in his threadbare wool slacks. Giving his beard one more snatch, he explained. "You would be amazed at the diversity of extraterrestrial life existing upon this planet."

"How does it get here?"

"Well, it comes in on meteors mostly. Perhaps you could say these chunks of rock are the ships of celestial messengers."

"Poetic," I said. "But what does this have to do with us?" Settling my gaze on Gibson, I demanded an answer. "You sounded like there was something wrong."

''There is something different,'' he said. ''Let Robert finish.''

Properly chastised, I sighed and sat back, letting the old man continue his lecture.

''There is such a diversity of alien life that we've catalogued much of it and divided this bacteria into a variety of strains, collectively known as dirium. The one we're concerned about here is a rather rare strain which we call, radio-dirium. What makes this particular bacteria different is its ability to withstand large amounts of radiation.''

When he mentioned radiation, my heart fluttered. I tried not to give away the sudden feeling in my face, and so instead of clasping my chest, I masked my mouth while Gibson stared at me with an unwavering ferocity. Damn him for his curiosity. He saw me as a lab rat and I wanted to smack him for his smugness, but LaRue's next question dragged me past any possibility. ''Are you saying we've got radio-dirium on us?''

''No,'' Gibson answered. ''It's in you. At least, it's in Merrick. In her lungs. We normally carry a certain amount of radio-dirium, but her levels are higher than they should be.''

His reply made me lose all my control and I started coughing. LaRue patted me on the back until I found my composure and raspy voice. ''Do you think I breathed it in while down in the mine?''

''That's why Robert is here.'' Gibson turned to study LaRue. ''Andy, I'm going to have you breathe in a tube. It won't hurt a bit.''

LaRue nodded and demanded another answer. ''How can anything be resistant to radiation?''

''Radio-dirium actually consumes the energy and converts it to heat,'' Bennet said.

''What's it doing to me?'' I asked.

''Well, from the levels indicated by your medical scan, you should be ill.''

''With radiation poisoning?''

''Yes, Marshal.''

I flapped a hand toward my partner. ''But Andy looks okay.''

''That's why I want to check him out,'' Gibson answered.

"Is my lycanthropy preventing me from getting sick?"

"Yes. Your metabolism is chewing up the waste material given off by the radio-dirium." He stopped to change expressions, selecting a gentler, more compassionate look. "Do you understand what this means?"

"No."

"Over the last several years there's been an increase in planetary radiation. Right now the rumor mill has it that a few segregated localities have reported a rise in radio-dirium levels, and with this escalation, there has been a corresponding increase in radiation sickness."

"And I might be some kind of walking cure," I said. "You could sell that for big bucks, couldn't you, Gibson?"

He glanced down at the desk, but didn't answer. There was no reason to and no response that would change the truth.

THIRTY-ONE

My lycanthropy makes it possible for me to heal from injuries quickly, and on top of that, I can defend against diseases that would cripple or kill a normal person. Still, I feel like a walking petri dish, sometimes.

It seems that our world is collapsing not just by beams and posts, but it's going down at the microbic level as well. There are demon plagues that are so far confined; yet fencing in a virus for any length of time proves impossible. The pollution left from three centuries of environmental mismanagement has settled the score for the earth. Humanity has become a ticking target for avengers so small, a whole colony can fit on the head of a pin.

Gibson returned from the clinic's examination room to retrieve some instrument of medical torture. He glanced at me when he walked in. For once, I didn't make him drag my concerns out of me.

"I've had a fluttering in my chest," I murmured. "Do you think it's the radio-dirium affecting my heart?"

He frowned. "Why didn't you tell me this before?"

"I didn't think it was important," I lied.

He paused, slid onto the couch, and scratched his forehead. "It may be the bacteria. That worries me, because it could be putting a strain on your heart. When Bennet is done with Andy, I'll find my stethoscope and have a listen.'' Gibson stopped speaking to pinch the bridge of his nose. Then: ''I'm sorry to sound so callous about this, Merrick, but we may need the credits your tests can produce.''

I shook my head. ''Exactly where would we spend it?''

''What's that supposed to mean?''

''Are you blind? We're heading for civil war. When that happens, money isn't going to be any good. We'll have to live by killing and stealing.''

''I can't believe the government has lost that much control.''

''You are blind. Of course, it has. This Spark of Creation Movement is the driving force behind the takeover. I've got a feeling these bastards are wedged in the bureaucrats' back pocket so tight, it would take a bucket of lard to loosen them up.'' I pushed to a stand, and then walked over to his desk to the telephone. ''Tell me, Gibson. Have you talked to Myra Fontaine recently?''

''No. What does she have to do with anything?''

''I think she might be a player in the SoC,'' I answered. ''Myra may have sold out her common decency along with her professionalism.''

''She helped you, Merrick.''

''Did she? As far as I can tell, she used me. You used me. In case you don't realize it, my brain is not fuzzy over past events. It wasn't me who got konked on the head.'' I forgot the telephone and the person I was going to call. ''She's taking advantage of these poor, neurotic lunatics by feeding on their delusions about being abducted by space aliens.''

Gibson took a deep breath. Upon hearing it, I knew I'd wandered into a sensitive area. His gaze zoomed off in the middle distance as he floundered in private thoughts. Instead of picking up the phone, I returned to the couch.

''What's the matter?'' I asked.

''You should have a more open mind,'' he said softly.

''About Myra?''

''No. About experiencers.''

''Why?''

His answer came driving in. ''Because according to words from your very own mouth, you're one of the poor, neurotic lunatics who has been abducted.''

THIRTY-TWO

The lycanthropic stretch that brings me into the full moon and total submission to the wolf is also the one that leaves my brain crippled. From what Gibson tells me, my gray matter swells, the synapses strain, and before I know it, the whole dissipative system overloads. Some lunar peaks leave me with a partial mind wipe, while other times I find that my supernatural disease has totally evaporated my memory cells. So, when Gibson told me I'd admitted to being abducted by aliens, I stood on the rubber mat of my stubbornness and called him a liar.

"I don't believe you," I said.

"I have transcripts," he answered.

"You taped me?"

"You let me."

I sat back and stared at him, suddenly overwhelmed with sorrow. It never changed between us. We both were afraid to show the measure of our emotions and one always hid something from the other. Gibson abused our relationship by using me for his financial gain as well as to test his confessions before he actually had to make them. He's admitted his love for me while I was in no position to remember and then withheld this fact until a dangerous situation pressed him into revealing his feelings. Now this. What else did he hide?

Gibson stood and walked to his desk. ''Maybe you should hear the tapes.''

I panicked for a moment, not sure I wanted confirmation of insane ramblings prompted by my lycanthropy, but in the end I had to know if the good doctor had doctored the records. The only way to find out was to hear for myself. Sliding from the sofa, I followed him to his desk, and without a word, I took the tape, turned, and walked out of the clinic.

Carnival was suddenly in the air. I hadn't noticed it when we'd first arrived, but the drab buildings were spiffed up with banners and wreaths. Someone had spray-painted a bright mural on the wall of a gray, tattered tenement. Beyond that, I saw a makeshift market where merchants did a brisk backdoor business by openly flaunting their goods—feathers, plastic, and tin—all the materials one might need to put together a costume for the parade. Before all the changes in the government, this kind of gathering would hinge on public disobedience and people would have been arrested, but now the ward cops added to the celebration by shopping along with the citizens.

I tried not to consider the implications of this new freedom and hurried on toward the Trabi. Halfway there, LaRue caught up with me.

''Do you have the little radios, too?'' I asked.

He shook his head as he fished his car keys from his pocket. ''No, I'm clean.'' Heading toward the Trabi, he called over his shoulder. ''Gibson said to tell you he would be over tonight.''

I climbed into the car before answering. ''Andy, tell me something. Have I ever mentioned having an encounter with space aliens during any of my full-moon stretches?''

''Aliens?'' He choked the Trabi's engine while he thought about it. ''You talk about a lot of things during the full moon. Mostly, you're off in your past lives, though.''

I smiled to myself. My lunar seizures are laced with dandy hallucinations and feelings of displacement. LaRue swears I touch past lives, but if you ask me, I end up between lives.

Flapping the tape at him, I explained. "Gibson caught me candidly."

"Doesn't he think it's just some manifestation of your mind?"

"I'm sure he does."

LaRue swung his gaze my way and I saw a swath of distrust in his expression. "Do you think Myra has used your fuel for her fire?"

"I didn't want to ask, Andy. I just don't want to know."

He started the car. "I can see how you wouldn't." Then, as though he knew I needed to change the subject, he steered us toward our next interview.

We decided to see a lady named Margarite Mallow, a back-door market oracle and bookie. Margarite would skin a customer using her special brand of psychic bullshit before enticing him to place a bet on some unlikely supernatural occurrence. The last time we talked, Mallow was giving odds on when there would be proof of life after death as well as humanity's first alien contact. Everything she did defied the laws on gambling, but she was so popular that she had never been raided by the district.

Mallow kept shop in a dilapidated trailer wedged between two crumbling brownstones in Ward 43. This neighborhood smelled like a sewer, but the carnival decorations kept drawing my attention away from the gutters bubbling with filth and disease.

We knocked on her door and waited only a second before she pulled it wide. Mallow was a hefty woman, one that LaRue always referred to as healthy. She had curly blond hair, big earlobes, and too many chins. Seeing who it was, she invited us in with a flourish, showing us to a couple of overstuffed chairs before coaxing cups of tea from an ancient samovar.

"Where have you two been the last few years?" Mallow asked. "I've expected to see you when some of the really big bets started coming down. You could have made some nice coinage had you come to see ol' Margarite."

I accepted the steaming, black tea before answering. "What kind of big bets are you talking about?"

"Payoffs have been in the hundreds of credits. Once, I got

into triple zeros. Did you know someone hit the spread when the government announced that they'd breached the barrier between this dimension and the next?''

I couldn't help glancing at LaRue. My partner's hand shook as he tried to sip from his cup. ''How did the scientists do that?''

She shrugged. ''Don't know, Andy Dandy. All I require is documentation. Government seals, vids, tapes, scientific confirmation. I received all that and so had to satisfy the wager to the tune of five thousand credits. I was saving that money for my heart surgery. Now it looks like I'll have to put off getting that new aorta for a few more months. Sure hope I can last that long.'' Mallow stopped talking, took a sip, and then did exactly what I expected—she opened a parlay. ''I should never have taken that bet. It means there's a possibility that interdimensional travel will be a reality before the end of my lifetime, and look at me, would you? Again, I'm caught holding the bag.''

I glanced around. Her surroundings weren't rich, but the trailer was clean and comfortable. ''You don't look like you've done so bad, Margarite. Most folks don't have a roof over their heads, much less one that doesn't leak.''

She nodded, conceding the fact. ''It's true; I won't deny it. I've got some wagers that have stood for years, quietly earning interest. But if the scientists should ever find a way to actually travel between dimensions, I'll be broke for good. Because of that, you just have to understand, my friends. I can't give out confidential information for free.''

I thought about threatening her with impeding an investigation, but I simply didn't have the energy. Digging through my pockets, I scrounged up a broken, gold-plated necklace, a box of raisins, and a chipped quartz crystal. LaRue copied me, producing a rusty switchblade and a couple of cinnamon-scented charm sacks. We placed our items on the heavy, wooden coffee table.

''That's all we've got, Margarite,'' I said. Poor-mouthing, I continued on. ''I was robbed this week and the thieves got everything. This is about all I have left.''

She stared at the meager objects and then, sighing, she nodded. "I'll take the switchblade. You can keep the rest."

We scooped up our goodies with a thank you and then LaRue opened the interview. "We've heard rumors about the Spark of Creation Movement. We want to know if there's been any local action."

Margarite snatched the knife from the table, studied it, and then gave us the answer. "The Spark of Creation Movement has been the subject of a lot of hot betting. I'm running low odds, too. Ten to one in favor of the Sparkers."

"Who's been in to place bets?"

"Locals. If you're going to ask me if they're members of the SoC, then I can't answer. I don't know. It's none of my business."

"What about Bernard Horn?" LaRue said.

"The opera singer?"

"That's the one. Has he stopped in to place any bets?"

At that point I think Mallow was sorry she'd fallen for my hard-luck story and taken the whole cache when she'd had the chance. She swallowed like an elephant, a sound I could hear from where I sat, and finally sighing loudly, she replied. "Yes, he was here."

"When?"

"About three months ago."

"What did he take a bet on?"

"He didn't take the bet for himself. It was for his fiancée."

LaRue jabbed me with a look before he repeated his question. "What did Ms. Reseda want to bet on?"

"On Mr. Horn's health," she answered.

"In other words, she took out a life insurance policy," I said.

"Apparently so." Mallow sipped her tea and then explained. "I gave her low odds because he didn't look so good."

"Have you paid off?"

"Why, yes. Betty Reseda stopped by the morning after Mr. Horn's death was announced."

THIRTY-THREE

According to Margarite Mallow, folks had been placing bets on new laws, new propaganda, and new people taking over various governmental offices. The disheartening news was that wagers had been placed on a coming civil war, and from what Mallow indicated, people thought this event would happen sooner instead of later. So, rather than calling it a day on this particularly unsettling note, we decided to visit Horn's residence in hopes of finding a hidden trail.

He lived in a dingy walk-up on the south side of the district, and when we finally convinced the landlady, Mrs. Johnny Domini, to open the door, we were in for a big surprise. The suite had been turned into a sound studio. Someone had pasted up hundreds of cardboard egg cartons on the walls and ceiling in an effort to muffle the noise to others. Several layers of rugs covered the concrete floor and the one, large window facing the street was swathed in heavy, black velvet curtains. The center of the room was a clutter of dilapidated computers, recording equipment, and banged-up microphones. Mrs. Domini explained the reason for all this.

"You know, Marshals, my Johnny was a big opera fan. He worked for years as a gardener over at the concert hall, ya see. Every night that they'd have a performance, he would go there and stand in the service entrance to hear the music and singing.'' She paused, patted her bangs, and took a step inside the apartment. ''We got this building at an auction. The district was going to tear it down, but we came up with the credits to buy it. Ya see, it was Johnny's dream to give struggling artists a place to live while they worked on their crafts. My Johnny—he was such a humanitarian. Saint Ophelia, bless his soul.''

We moved into the flat with her. As LaRue stepped off toward the next room I cornered Mrs. Domini. ''How long had Bernard Horn lived here?''

''Oh, at least ten years.''

''Do you know what he was doing with this recording equipment?''

''Why, of course,'' she chirped. ''He was recording his voice for posterity.''

''Did you think he had a good voice?''

She nodded. ''Bernard grew into his talent, Marshal. At first, he was a tentative singer, and because of it, he lacked the acoustical range for serious participation in the opera world. Ya see?''

Not really, but I went along with the lecture. ''How did he grow into his talent?''

''Well, there now is the one subject that Johnny and I differed on. He thought it was all the practice Bernard had been putting in; and yes, there was a considerable amount of that. Morning until night, five days a week.''

''But you think differently?''

''Yes, yes, I do. Practice hones the talent that is already there. It doesn't elevate it. As far as I'm concerned, the amount of talent you have comes with the package. Ya see?''

''So, you believe Bernard had some sort of shift in his initial talent for singing.''

She nodded fiercely. ''His talent changed. It grew. It expanded. It held new meaning.''

''What do you think caused this?''

''A mystical experience.''

''Such as?''

''I don't know. It happens sometimes and it's always a miracle when it does. Ya see, it takes cosmic intervention to change the talent one is born with. I've seen it happen one other time. It was a soprano. She had a near-death experience, and when she came back from the light, her voice had deepened and enriched. What a singer she could have become."

"Why didn't she?"

"Unfortunately, she had a second death experience. One she didn't return from."

I turned my attention to study the room. "Horn didn't have a high labor designation. How did he acquire so much equipment? Did you and your husband help him?"

Mrs. Domini stepped toward the door, frowning slightly.

"Ma'am?" I said.

She took a hard breath and spilled the news. "No, we didn't help him. One day, he just had it and we indulged him."

It was time for the hundred-dollar question. "Did you know of Mr. Horn's affiliation with a group called the Spark of Creation Movement?"

"I don't know anything about that organization," she answered, with a huff. "I doubt Bernard did either."

"Why do you say that?"

"Because he was the most loyal citizen I've ever known." That said, she frowned again, and left the apartment.

LaRue returned from the other room carrying a handful of music discs. He walked over to a recorder and placed one in the player. "Horn has a storage bin full of these things. They're all unmarked." Hitting the play button, he started the machine.

Much to my surprise, the first notes I heard were the very same tones I'd been hearing inside my head.

THIRTY-FOUR

We took a sampling of discs from Horn's apartment and then LaRue dropped me by my flat. I went inside with my part of the music collection to find Gibson standing by the propane stove, cooking a chicken. His glance my way was quick, but mine was quicker.

"I thought you could use some provisions," he said.

"Thanks," I answered. "How's Baba?"

"Baba has been at her loom today, from what your neighbor tells me. She's asleep right now. That old woman is as bad as you. She never cuts herself any slack."

"You know the old saying: strive without end." I unsnapped my utility belt and threw it on the couch before turning to my shoulder holster. "What's the real reason you're here?"

This time he sent me a volley of intensity. "It's not to make money on you if that's what you think."

"I do. It's always the same, Gibson. I'm crazy for being crazy for you."

He smiled. "I need a place to crash until the paperwork comes across on my new apartment."

The good doctor's high-rise had been condemned by the district after the hurricane and he'd been bunking at the clinic while getting permission to relocate. "Are you even sure you'll get the paperwork now?"

His smile flashed into a dejected expression and he tried to look away before I saw it. "I doubt it. Don't worry. I won't get in your hair. A couple of days is all I should need."

"Stay as long as you like," I said. Turning, I flopped into my ratty recliner. "But tell the whole truth. You're here to be with me when I listen to your tapes of my abduction confession."

"That, too."

"You know I talk bullshit during the full moon."

He stepped to our rickety kitchen table and proceeded to open a can of peas. "Have you ever wondered why your seizure is so much more violent at the lunar peak?"

"I just figured it had to do with the pull of the moon."

"Keep believing that and you'll keep fooling yourself."

"Why?"

"Because it doesn't affect us with that much force. What you've heard about the magnetic pull of the moon is crap."

"We've been around and around on this subject."

"Yes, we have, but I still want to know why you suffer in various ways at the peak of your lunar cycle. The clues we need to control your lycanthropy are wrapped up in this event somehow."

"Well, if they don't put you in a labor camp for fraud, we might be able to find out one of these days."

Gibson scowled, pulled the lid off the can, and dumped the peas into the pot. "I don't think it will go that far."

I snorted. "You'll be walking to the gallows cursing yourself for being wrong. The SoC is taking over—like it or not." I rose and placed one of Horn's discs into the new player we'd liberated from Pigeon, turned it on, and was stopped immediately by the haunting sound. The recording was nothing but a conglomeration of instruments and voices continually repeating the same tones. Listening to it suddenly gave me a headache. I flipped the machine off before rifling his medical bag for a packet of aspirin. When I found what I needed, I chewed two of the tablets, letting the bitter pills coat my throat.

Gibson joined me at his case of torture instruments, removed a stethoscope, and pointed to the couch. I reluctantly slunk back to it, sticking out my chest for the examination. Just as he pushed the plungers into his ears, I screwed up his analysis by talking.

"I keep hearing that sound," I said.

He removed the stems to stare at me. "The sound on the disc?"

"That's right. Only, it's inside of me. A by-product of the lycanthropy, I think. I noticed it shortly after my last stretch."

"Our brains have a way of catching a tune and holding on to it," he explained. "It's what neurologists have come to think of as a mirroring effect. The sounds are trapped within a certain set of neurons and unable to move down filtering pathways in our gray matter. It's like the pattern bounces off the cell system, causing an echo."

"You make it sound like it's nothing."

He shrugged. "Trust me. It has nothing to do with your lycanthropy. I'm sure of it."

"Now, why would you say that?"

His response was matter-of-fact as he readjusted his stethoscope. "Because I've been humming those same notes for a week."

THIRTY-FIVE

According to Gibson, my heart sounded good and strong with a nice slow beat. He should have checked it after I started listening to the tape.

I usually feel disconnected from the full moon once the monthly experience is over. It's as though the wolf awakens to total maturity and power. My efforts to prove my freewill are futile and there is nothing I can do but obey the dictates of my lycanthropy, and hearing myself seemed to heighten this feeling of distance. For that, I was grateful, but the words I spoke had such an ominous ring to them that they made me cringe.

My monologue began during an incident when I was four years old. The experience took place in my home district before the earthquake wiped out most of the population, including my family. It was early evening and I walked alone on a dusty road toward a distant village. Near the horizon, I noticed a glowing light. As I approached the town, the light began to come toward me until it stopped in my path. I heard loose gravel roll away; felt the heat; and smelled a tart, vinegary scent on the wind. The light was so bright, it nearly blinded me and I went down upon my knees, screaming as only a small child can.

I must have passed out, because the next thing I recalled was waking up in a strange, metal room. Glancing around, I saw a young man with black hair and black robes. This man began speaking in low tones, explaining to me that I was aboard a spacecraft hovering gently in Earth's upper atmosphere. He also told me that I was infinitely old and wise, and because of the special properties of the ship, I could shed the restrictions of a four-year-old mind and clearly understand my manifest destiny.

This being apologized for abducting me, but said it was necessary so that the emulators could restore my memory and allow me to access the otherworldly talents I possessed. His discourse rambled, but I followed it straight to a story about me being a cosmic traveler, one who had left her home world to bring truth and light to those planets where the people still lurked in the Stone Age. My extraterrestrial mentor explained that I would one day command my true source of self and do grand and powerful things.

Sitting there next to Gibson, facing down an intolerable situation of poverty and insecurity, I sincerely wished this last fact were true. I was no better than anyone else when it came to fooling myself by pretending I was worth more than the collection of chemicals making up my body.

After I heard my lecture on fractured particle waves in faster-than-light commuting, I flipped the tape machine off. I sighed and glanced out of the window at the revelers celebrating the start of carnival by gathering on the street corner with a keg of home-brewed beer. Hooch out in the open. I never thought I would see it.

Gibson must have sensed my disorientation because he threw a medical theory at my feet. "There is something called cryptonesia or false memory syndrome. It is where a person thinks he remembers an incident, but in reality, he is remembering unconsciously collected facts."

I turned back to him. "So, it's entirely possible I saw a vid about an alien abduction and applied it to my own case. Is that what you think this is?"

He licked his lips, and seeing it, I knew he was about to tell me something I didn't want to hear. "Your story is identical to many of the patients that Myra has studied. The similarities in the abduction scenario are remarkable, and if it were simply a case of cryptonesia, then there would be disparaging things. The brain regurgitates the facts, but will get some of them wrong. It's as though the information crosses the wrong circuits and gets jumbled. I can't tell which ones are false, but I can tell you that you never vary from your claim."

"Just how many times have you had me repeat this story?" I said.

Gibson pulled on a sheepish expression. "Five or six times. It's always the same, right down to the color of your underwear."

"What are you saying? That I've lost my mind?"

"No," he answered immediately. "But you did mention an underground group called the Society of Intergalactic Travelers?"

I shook my head. "Is it a real organization or did I make it up?"

"They're a real group who believe that they are cosmic travelers, here visiting from other worlds. When I listened to the tape this morning, I wondered about that and did some checking." Pausing, he swallowed and then leveled his wild-eyed gaze at me. "Your name appears on their membership list."

THIRTY-SIX

From what Gibson told me, my membership with the Traveler's Aid for Galactic Wackos began shortly after I came down with lycanthropy. He explained that I was in good standing with these folks, though the man he'd talked to said I never showed up for any of the meetings.

Psychiatrists say that crazy people don't know they're crazy. That's pure horse hocky—especially when you have someone like Gibson to tell you otherwise. After this conversation about my lycanthropic activities, I excused myself, climbed into bed, and pulled the covers over my head. There I lay until dawn, when I changed my uniform and snuck by the good doctor as he snoozed soundly on the couch.

When I arrived at the office, my partner was already there, busily slopping the innards of an egg-and-ketchup sandwich down the front of his uniform. He pointed to a bag sitting on his desk, causing me to hastily dive inside for a container of fried onions flavored with cinnamon. LaRue brought me up-to-date while I stuffed food down my gullet.

"Did you know that the presence of radio-dirium in cattle has actually boosted their immune system responses?" he said.

"That's nice," I mumbled, licking my fork.

He smiled at my obvious pleasure in the food and then

continued. "Frank pulled a P.M. shift last night. I asked him to stop by the mine and test a few folks at random just to see if they displayed high levels of radio-dirium. He also checked the bodies when he got back. Out of the sample, you're the only one whose readings are off the scale."

"Isn't that always the way it is?"

He smiled gently. "You may have gotten it when you wiggled your way into that hole."

I nodded as I slurped a soggy onion, and then talked while I chewed. "How do you figure the bacteria got way down there in the mine?"

LaRue sat back, took a bite, and shook his head. "I asked Mr. Bennet about that when I was taking my test. His theory is that it's been embedded in the rock for millions of years, lying in a dormant state."

"How can that be? Wouldn't it fossilize or something?"

"According to Bennet, this bacteria travels through space for untold millions of years just to get here."

"Sounds like something out of an old sci-fi vid."

He nodded, taking a large bite. Part of his sandwich escaped and flew at me like a yellow missile. Before we were done provisioning ourselves, I wore most of my partner's meal.

Finally fortified, LaRue turned the conversation in a new direction. "Did you listen to those discs we picked up from Horn's apartment?"

"Yeah."

"Did you recognize the intro music?"

"The set of musical notes," I answered. "I can't get the noise out of my head. I thought I was making the music up until Gibson told me he's heard the combination before, too."

"I'm sure he has. I played the discs for my family and everyone recalled hearing the music. It backdrops everything—television, radio, social and sports events. We turned on the TV to watch the evening news and there it was again."

I sat back in the chair and dabbed at the food stain on the breast pocket of my uniform. "What part did Horn play by recording the music?"

"You know, Ty, I think it's nothing deep, dark, or mysterious."

"You think it's more likely that Horn was turning over some major, tax-free profit."

"We all do it to some extent. He comes across like a real humanitarian zealot, but come on. How many of those still exist?"

He had a point there. I glanced at him and then beyond the short walls of our cubicle to see Nichols and Carver in deep conversation. "Bilking the ETA might well be the reason the goose steppers have led on this investigation." I paused, shook my head, and burped onion at the same time as I set my indignation loose. "It grates me having to pass them reports."

LaRue grunted. "The queen witch over there made me explain several paragraphs in our sheet this morning."

"What was her problem?"

"She wanted to know what good it did to see Margarite Mallow."

"What did you tell her?"

"I told her that we'd stopped in to get a feel for the mood of the citizens and to place a bet."

"A bet for what?"

He grinned. "I bet that Nichols and Carver would find themselves sucking wind at the end of this investigation."

I laughed. "Andy, you're going to get us fired and then executed."

"Naw. The most they'll do is raise our taxes." LaRue leaned close, changing the subject and speaking in a whisper. "Horn may have been the spearhead for the movement, Ty. He might have been a propaganda official's dream come true."

That idea brought up all kinds of possibilities. If Horn were the King of Creativity, then he certainly had lots of enemies. It made a convenient motive and placed our distrust on both sides of the coin. Did the ETA knock him off and then try to cover their asses by sending in the agents to deflect suspicion, or did the SoC, tired of his outspoken attitudes toward them, decide it was time to shut him up? At this point no one wanted to admit being linked to the Sparkers and they gave me more cause to wonder. Who the hell were they besides some anarchist group hiding behind metaphysical ideology?

"Andy, have you ever heard of the Society for Intergalactic Travelers?" I asked.

He blinked and stared at me. "No."

"Well, apparently, I joined years ago during one of my full-moon fits. I've also been paying my dues, though I don't remember doing any of it." I rose woodenly and patted down my cammies. "There might be a connection to the Sparkers, and thanks to Gibson, I just happen to have the address of the society's chief executive officer."

THIRTY-SEVEN

Roscoe Turner was the spiritual head of the Society of Intergalactic Travelers, but he fancied himself a cosmic travel agent more than the leader of a cult invested with the secret knowledge of the spheres. I have to tell you that I felt ridiculous at having Turner recognize me by my name. From the way he acted, you would have thought I was the high priestess of the abduction set, but once inside his posh flat, I realized it was my continued support that he focused his attention upon.

If my dues had bought him this luxury, I decided right then and there to kill myself. How could I have been ignorant of the dealings of the wolf? Had I shared this dual personality from the start, never knowing what my supernatural half was up to during the full moon?

The flat was filled with style—thick-pile carpeting, fine furniture, a wall of books, brand-new electronic equipment, as well as paintings and sculptures of old masters that had been lost to the bootlicking families that had followed Duvalier. The alien business must have been good.

Still, I have a hard time with wealth, especially when I'm the one without it, so I spoke frostily in an effort to remain neutral. ''Mr. Turner, I smell a scam.''

Turner was a flesh-and-blood double for Orson G. Welles

and his reaction to my announcement was as classic. He swelled his chest by filling his lungs with the breath of indignation. When he finally spoke, I was sure he was going to tell me that Martians living in glass houses shouldn't throw stones.

"Please, Marshal Merrick, let's get to the truth of the matter. You came to collect on your money."

"I want every penny, including interest."

"Well, the document you signed is legal and binding and was filed as a personal loan agreement between us. You agreed to the terms. I'm merely the custodian of the funds."

"Loan agreement?"

"That's the way we were able to file it. You agreed to this, so you don't have any other recourse."

I wanted to scream something about having the recourse of shooting him in the head, but the radio-dirium must have been affecting my energy level, because I couldn't muster enough passion to tell him off.

LaRue took a slow turn around the apartment and his inspection deflated Turner's hostility, replacing it with apprehension. I couldn't help a small smile as I watched my partner get greasy fingerprints on porcelain figurines and polished brass mirrors. Turner followed his every move, concerned, I'm sure, that some of those pieces would end up in LaRue's uniform pocket. I sat down heavily in a wing-backed chair and used the moment of defeated concentration to hammer Turner with questions.

"Let's talk about what your group does," I said.

He nodded and answered, but his eyes never left LaRue. "Our organization maintains the galactic jump-point depot here on earth."

"Jump-point depot? What's that?"

"It's a wayfaring station for intergalactic travelers. When they visit our planet, they often come to us for assistance until they can make the next time-space jump. Earth is on the galaxy's arm and there aren't that many portals in this region of space. Those that are operational cost their weight in gold to maintain and are always overloaded with transport ships. On top of that, there's a big problem in Sector 92 in the Pleiades

Star System. Everything happens there because it's a commerce hub."

"You're referring to the trouble with the Zeladrite?"

He nodded. "They are nothing more than parasites. In fact, they look like bugs." He paused and pointed at LaRue when my partner picked up a fancy heirloom. "Please, don't touch that. It came from Perseus Minor."

"Greece?" LaRue asked, turning it over. "It doesn't look Greek."

"Perseus Minor is a planet in the Pleiades."

We both stared at him until this fat man took a heavy sigh and flopped down in a chair to explain. "The worlds residing in the Pleiades are a union who function like a galactic trading center. Travelers, merchants, politicians, and thieves from every race in the Milky Way converge there to lie, steal, cheat, and gamble. An agent of mine just happened to be there when that piece came up for auction."

LaRue slid right past the insane story. "What is it?"

"It's a lip cup," he answered. "The Wujina Tribe place them between their lips and front incisors to eat."

"Why?" I asked.

Turner shifted a cold eye onto me. "Because they have holes in their chins."

Goes to show you what I know about aliens. I stared at the man, trying to figure out if this scam came from the heart or the pocket, but truth to tell, I just didn't know. "What kind of service do you personally perform for your members, Mr. Turner?"

"We're a diversified operation, Marshal Merrick. We assist in the routing and transportation of intergalactic guests. When visitors come here for an extended stay, we make sure we help them find employment and housing."

"Oh, I get it," I said. "You falsify district documents. That's against the law, Mr. Turner."

"I never said I did anything of the sort," he answered belligerently.

LaRue placed the lip cup on the table with a clatter and Turner focused on him once more. "Please, have a seat, sir."

My partner ignored him to pick up another object, while I

asked a new question. "Why would travelers want to come here? Earth is a garbage dump."

"Earth has great potential and is the center of the universe right now," he said. "We are on the Aquarian Cusp; that is to say, we are a race who will either blossom or wither on the vine. Our decisions about the stewardship of our planet cannot be based on political aims, greed, or coercion." He stopped, shook his head at LaRue, and then settled his attention onto me. "The travelers who come here have lofty aspirations. Their duty—your duty—is to put this world back on track so we can flourish and become an active, vital part of the intergalactic community."

"I understand the Zeladrite want to keep this from happening," LaRue said.

"Not just the Zeladrite—many races."

"Are you a traveler, Mr. Turner?" I demanded.

"No. I was born of Earth. I'm a cocreator."

"What's that?"

"A person who has been abducted and fitted with a diaphanous insert."

That particular confession drew LaRue from this tour. "We've heard about these diaphanous inserts. Please tell us what you know about them."

"They're bioelectronic packets of information placed into the brain by the Pleiadian Teachers. They help stimulate the creative process. The Teachers are from a very old race who have come in spaceships to monitor our progress."

"It sounds like they're impeding our progress."

Turner bounced back a quick reply. "Not in the least. Inserts were invented by the Pure Caste on Zenon III. When a lower technology attempts to scan for the packets, the insert emits a negative ion field that prevents it from being identified by a probe. Hence, the name—diaphanous. The Teachers see how functionally illiterate we are. We have these enormous brains and yet our evolution is termed backward by the more advanced races. It's a genetic defect that we all suffer from. Well, there are a few who overcame this limitation. Albert Einstein for one; Vivian Duvalier, for another."

I snorted. "Duvalier got us into this mess."

"Duvalier was a humanitarian. His ideas were worthy of the great experiment. Unfortunately, the Zeladrite got in the way before the society was fully formed."

"So, what did they do to put a kink into the humanitarian process?" LaRue asked.

"They started abducting people for their own uses, mostly as slave labor. They would remove the diaphanous inserts so the Teachers couldn't relay the necessary information. Slowly, we became indentured to them. The Teachers are fighting a war for our souls and our freedom, and the Society of Intergalactic Travelers helps to maintain the status quo by doing everything we can to assist in our resurrection."

"Your beliefs make me wonder if you would align yourself with the Spark of Creation Movement."

Turner stared at me. "You forget, Marshal, you're a member of the SIT. Your beliefs are supposed to be like my beliefs."

I ignored his insinuation. "What about Bernard Horn?"

Turner blinked slowly. "What about him?"

"Was he a member in good standing?"

"I don't know. Many of our members prefer to use secret names or code numbers."

Great. Not only was I throwing money away, I was openly throwing it away. I leaned forward. "Mr. Turner, you still haven't told us what your position with the Intergalactic Travelers entails."

"I invest membership dues on the galactic market," he said. "Your share right now is over twenty-five thousand credits. That came from shrewd investing in mining operations on the Juno asteroid. You see, the thing was loaded with anatelsic alloy. Our affiliate companies sold a million tons of rock to the refineries on Jessat-elt and we pulled out a bundle."

The mention of the asteroid reminded me of the radiodirium and my mind leaped ahead to strange, incomprehensible possibilities. Instead of going into them, I focused on the subject that really bothered me. "I want my twenty-five thousand credits right now."

Turner shook his head. "Can't. You understood the terms of investment when you applied for membership."

"Refresh my memory."

"Your investment was not without risk," he said. "You would double your present earnings and receive payoff after twenty years and not before." He leaned back and crossed his hands over his barrel chest. "I'm sorry, but there's nothing I can do."

THIRTY-EIGHT

It seemed that idiocy had been my birthright. As much as I wanted to get medieval on this character, Roscoe Turner held all the legitimate cards. Any other time, I might have roughed him up if nothing else, but now, with the bulldogs sniffing our shorts, I didn't dare. It would tip my hand, even though I had no idea what I was holding.

The anger I felt over my stupidity threatened to erupt, and so to contain this volcano, I let LaRue finish the interview with Turner. My partner saw me sitting there red-faced, and so to get me out of there before I did any damage, he demanded a copy of the society's computer records. Turner begrudgingly gave up the goods and we quickly left this strange man to his galactic confusion.

When we stepped onto the crowded street, I found that I could not speak, effectively silenced by my turmoil. It was all right, though, because my partner talked enough for the both of us.

"I think Mr. Turner has one too many sets of diaphanous inserts in his brain," he said. "Maybe there is something to that mass hallucination theory."

I shrugged, unconcerned about the possibilities right now, because my mind played with the potential of what I had unwittingly done. Worse than that was my irritating ability to see the darkest side of every scenario. At some point in this mysterious game, I'd come to believe the abduction experience at a subconscious level or I wouldn't have told Gibson of it. My tale of aliens and intergalactic travel was not so bad in and of itself. The problem surfaced in the lack of context, because suddenly I'd discovered that I was not the master of my thoughts and actions.

We climbed into the Trabi and LaRue started the engine the same time he started down a new avenue of reasoning for my current, unfathomable dilemma. His ideas roved across light-years and extended into theories on how the retrograde motion of the planets could cause selective amnesia. I registered his words, but could barely get past the screaming in my head. Had I given away my hard-earned money to this insanity and not even known? Just how brain-dead was I?

When we arrived back at the office, my aggravation was further complicated by being forced to deliver an oral report to Nichols and Carver. LaRue and I joined them in the interrogation room, where we could talk without the world overhearing the conversation.

We all sat down at the table, choosing sides like we were drawing the line for a Mexican standoff. I couldn't help staring at Nichols and my scrutiny made her uncomfortable.

"Do you have something you want to say?" she snapped.

"Yeah, I have a lot I want to say," I answered. "For one thing, I want to know what you and Carver are up to."

"I don't know what you're talking about."

"Oh, come on, honey, of course you do. You two are up to your thyroids in this Bernard Horn mess."

"That's enough," Carver ordered. "We're law-abiding citizens. You're making accusations that you can't back up. Now give us a report on your activities before I file a memo of record about your lack of professionalism."

I was about to crawl across the table and rip his tongue out through his asshole, but LaRue stopped me by placing his hand gently on my arm. "We have reason to believe that Bernard Horn's murder was motivated by money."

Nichols and Carver took their turns staring at us. "Not revenge?" Carver asked.

"Revenge?" LaRue said. "Why revenge? What do you know that we don't?"

Carver sputtered as Nichols tossed him a scowl. "I just assumed that he was murdered because he was a threat to somebody."

"To whom?"

"That's what you're supposed to find out."

"Then help us. Tell us what you know."

They turned to glare at each other and I could practically see the blame kicking up sparks between them. Finally, Carver spoke. "Bernard Horn had some trouble. Someone had submitted a petition to sue him."

"Who was it?" I asked.

"We don't know."

"Why don't you?"

"Because the records have been destroyed."

"Oh, of course, they were."

"Why was he being sued?" LaRue asked.

Carver shook his head. "It was a paternity case."

"Why would this make someone want to kill him?"

"Don't you see?" Nichols said. "The suit was denied because he was a humanitarian designate. He couldn't be involved in any kind of litigation."

I rocked my chair onto its back feet and balanced it against the wall before swinging my feet onto the table. "So, what you're telling us is this: Bernard Horn was a womanizer who couldn't be caught in his misdeeds."

Nichols wrinkled her nose at seeing my dirty running shoes close up. "Yes. We suspect there were a variety of women and half-grown children who wanted to see Horn dead."

THIRTY-NINE

If there is one thing that I certainly understand, it's the concept of futility. It colors everything we do in our society and it touches us at levels we don't often consider. My life as a district marshal has further jaded my viewpoint, because more than anything else, I can see the futility in telling the truth. There was just no knowing for sure if Nichols and Carver were being honest, and suddenly it didn't matter. I was floating in falsehoods, particularly those I had told myself. So, before I did something I would regret, I walked away, leaving LaRue to deal with the goose steppers.

A stinky breeze blew in off the Black River to flutter the banners decorating the street. Carnival was fast approaching, and as I walked down the street toward my flat, I wondered if I would survive the changes that might come. I was a freak among freaks, an outcast whose life was an open book to the current government. Did I have a chance to come out on top or was I merely lugging along a knapsack of hopelessness? I was able to see clearly how corruption overturned corruption, but like everybody else aboard this sinking ship, I could also see that I was too insignificant to pump the bilge by myself.

When I reached my apartment, I found both Gibson and Baba home. My roommate defied the better judgment of the good doctor, and sporting a bandage across her noggin, she worked at her loom, threading in a bobbin filled with surgical gauze. Gibson lounged on my sofa and they both listened to a disc I'd brought home from Bernard Horn's musical cache.

"We've been listening to the opera," Baba said. "That fellow had a beautiful voice. Just full of vibrato. Crying shame he was murdered."

I wired my gaze to Gibson's and then lied just for the hell of it. "I was just told that the music is laced with a subliminal message about committing civil unrest. You shouldn't be listening to it."

Gibson rose, switched off the player, but then batted the ball back to me. "There has never been any conclusive proof that subliminal messaging works. After years of studies, there are no signs of significant changes in the brain. Now, if it's supported by regular hypnotic applications, then there might be something to it."

I nodded, but didn't reply, because frankly, I didn't care. Instead, I glanced at the trash blanket Baba weaved. "Are you selling that one?"

"Yes, my dear. Lane has been kind enough to give me a box of bandages. It makes a nice, airy effect, don't you think? A summer blanket. I could probably get a hundred credits if I pitch it right." She paused to work a knot and then cursed softly.

"What's the matter, Baba?" I asked.

She looked up with a valiant expression. "Oh, nothing, my dear. I just have the tremors. I suppose that comes from being konked on the head."

I looked at Gibson, who nodded. "I think it's a temporary thing. Let's hope so anyway."

I grunted, relieved, but unable to admit it. Instead I decided to confront Baba about my supposed abduction experience. Sitting down on the couch, I brought the subject abruptly to a head. "Has anyone from the Society of Intergalactic Travelers ever tried to get in touch with me?"

Upon hearing my question, she fumbled the shuttle and a minute went by in which I could tell my roommate was debating her answer. Finally, she decided to stall. ''Why do you ask?''

I sighed again, the feeling of weariness tracing through my whole body. ''Please, Baba. Tell me the truth. Has someone tried to contact me?''

She stared at me, but her expression was soft. After adjusting the placement of the bandages around her head, she answered. ''Yes, but it hasn't been for a long while now.''

Upon hearing this confession, my stomach came loose from its moorings and sank down into my feet. ''Did you talk to their representative?''

''Yes.''

''Why?''

''He was setting up a plan for paying your membership dues.''

I closed my eyes to ask the next question, as though the darkness behind my lids could somehow hide my emerging shadow self. ''When did I supposedly join this organization?''

''Oh, quite a few years ago. I know you don't remember doing it.''

I opened my eyes, but then buried my face in my hands. Baba continued gently, but relentlessly.

''You came home one day and announced you'd joined,'' she explained. ''You told me this story about being abducted as a child and how important it was to keep in touch with other folks who'd had experience with flying saucer aliens. I do understand your needs, my dear. You were an orphan—no family unit, no long lost relatives. Your early years were erased after that earthquake brought down half the continent. The way I see it, being part of some group, any group, is important to you.''

I lifted my head to flash her an incredulous expression. ''How can you say that? I'm a loner.''

''On the outside you are, but on the inside, you want a place in the chicken coop along with the rest of us. How long are you going to lie to yourself, Ty?''

Maybe forever, if it was easier. ''Why didn't you tell me I joined this group and they were chiseling money out of my bank account?''

"Because they weren't chiseling your bank account," she said quietly. "I was giving them my money in your name. You see, they wouldn't deduct the funds from my account, so I had them take it from yours and then transferred the amount back in when I got my pension check."

"Did I give you the number of my bank account?"

"Yes, dear, you did."

I sat back, feeling more the loner than either of them could ever suspect. "Why did you go to all this trouble over the years?"

"Because deep down inside, I know you believe your own story, and I guess I do, too. I started asking around about the group and found out that lots of people right here in our neighborhood had joined. I don't know if any of them are intergalactic travelers, but I could see the sense of membership, and so I thought I'd invest some of my money for you. You know, an inheritance of sorts. It's safe to say that I'm not going to give my money to any of my goddamned, ungrateful kids." She paused to pick up the shuttle. "I wanted to do something nice for you, Ty. And I wanted it to be a surprise for when I'm gone."

My overreaction had led me astray into fields of betrayal and disloyalty, but here, the liberated truth spoke of love and understanding. These elements, which had seemed so rare in my life, had always been there, quietly lurking on the periphery of my perception. If I had indeed been abducted by more advanced extraterrestrials, why hadn't they found a way to relieve me of my own stupidity and shortsightedness?

Still, as touched and comforted as I was by Baba's admission, I was still not straight on the whole thing. "Thank you, Baba. I had no idea, not even a clue." Leaning forward, I asked the question that was starting to give me a rash. "What kind of investment did this group allow you to make?"

"A savings plan," she answered. "Tax-free."

Oh, sweet lord of the Sterling Credit. The ETA had my name and was going to take me down for tax dodging.

FORTY

How could I possibly tell Baba that all her money had gone to buy strange trinkets like lip cups? Worse than that—how could I tell her that I was helpless to prevent it and that I was going to take the biggest hit of my life and go from the District Marshals Office to tax evasion prison? Sadder still was the lie I told myself. On the outside I was all bravado, but on the inside I'd actually spent a moment wondering what kind of food they served in the joint. It sustained me until my guilt traveled in on roller skates.

Baba's innocence, trust, and love had led her to throw away thousands of credits over a full-moon blunder on my part. It was all my fault, as was the obligation to explain how she had been duped by a man who openly flaunted his thievery. In the end I couldn't do it, and so again, I left the flat, but this time I couldn't get away from Gibson.

"Where are you going?" he asked, when we stepped onto the front stoop.

"To see a backdoor oracle by the name of Lizzie Borden."

He snorted. "Lizzie of the Twenty Whacks?"

"That's the one."

"Why? You don't believe in her invisible magic shtick. Do you?"

"No, but a lot of people do. She's the most famous light worker around. Everyone knows her name."

"You're wondering if Bernard Horn visited her?"

"I'm wondering how many of the folks she ministers to could be Sparkers."

"Again, I ask why?"

"Because I want some feel for the numbers." Actually, I wanted to know more than that, but I really didn't feel like trying to explain it to Gibson.

We walked the rest of the way in silence and soon arrived at the tent town that ran along the Black River past the coking plant. Even here, amid the squalor and filth of life on the street, there were signs of the carnival—prayer flags, mystical symbols, and open containers of homemade liquor. I sensed a gay atmosphere despite the dismal poverty, and the moment that we hopped a stream of raw sewage running down the muddy street, we actually heard a couple of drunks singing a ditty about flying to the moon. Following their noise, we soon found ourselves entering Lizzie Borden's cardboard box.

Lizzie of the Twenty Whacks had nothing to do with the old story about the daughter hacking up her parents with an axe. Years before I was born, she'd been attacked by a ward cop whose brain had turned to goo from excessive use of the drug quantum. He used his nightstick to crack Lizzie around the head, face, and shoulders before concerned members of the citizenry came to her assistance and killed the crazed officer with his own gun. The woman almost died, and did, in fact, claim a near-death experience. When it was all said and done, she also asserted that the twenty whacks had changed her from a normal human being into a master of supernatural light spinning.

What Lizzie really had was a nice backdoor scam going and a reputation to back it up. Whether of her own design or the gullibility of her clients, people sought her out to take a look at the amount of light contained in their bodies.

Lizzie's shack was like a sweat lodge, from the smoking fire and the hot rocks of her sidewalk hearth. She greeted us from her dirty floor pillow, a seat that, in my estimation, was situated too close to the blaze for normal comfort. The woman wore a simple black cloak, and even though she was by herself, she had the hood pulled forward so no one would see her demolished face. Pasting her hands together, she bowed her head until her fingers touched her lips. "Ty Merrick," she said in a low, gravelly voice. "I make respects. Welcome to my home."

Making respects was a common practice among many people, especially those living in street shanties. It signified obedience and honor to authority. It also meant that the honored one had to fork over a gift. The Marshals Office gives a monthly allowance to gather up trade goods that are necessary when working the street, so I pulled out a wormy apple and offered it to her. She bowed again, took the fruit, and stuffed it into the voluminous folds of her filthy robe.

"Who is he?" she asked.

"This is Dr. Lane Gibson," I said, settling down on a cinder block. "He's a friend of mine."

Lizzie nodded under her hood and directed the good doctor toward a scruffy section of rug. After he made himself comfortable, she pointedly asked the purpose of our visit and I pointedly answered.

"I need information from the streets, Lizzie. I need you to tell me everything you can about the Spark of Creation Movement."

"I'm an old witch, Marshal. I work with the light. I don't minister much to the Sparkers. They're an odd lot, they are."

"Why are they odd?"

"Because they don't believe in the old ways," she crowed.

"What old ways?"

"They don't accept nothing on face value, these people. They don't like the government, but then I say: who can blame them on that? I'd spit on the members of the District Council if I got half the chance to." She snorted. "It's not so much their attitudes on the humanitarian lifestyle; it's their disregard for the way the magic has always been. They want to change the laws by which it works, you know."

I shook my head. "But, Lizzie, the magic doesn't work."

"So you say. It's only because you haven't been touched by it like I have. Like everybody else has. You act as though it ain't there, but it is, and denying it won't make it go away.''

I didn't feel like arguing about the supernatural. ''How do they want to change the laws of magic?''

''They think that all magic except kundalini magic is bogus and they want to drive the beliefs from the people. That ain't right. There's merit to things like charm sacks and voodoo dolls. It don't make sense to accept one kind of power and not the other.''

''Your shtick revolves around kundalini magic. That should make you happy.''

''Not really,'' she said. ''Their form of kundalini doesn't match mine.''

''What do they believe?''

''They believe in a bastardized form of the kundalini,'' she answered. ''It ain't the right form, mind you.''

I leaned forward and my lycanthropic sense of smell told me she needed a bath in the worst way. ''What form of kundalini do they worship?'' I growled.

''Worship?'' Lizzie started cackling beneath her hood. After a moment spent in some hilarious, private joke, she sobered enough to say: ''You can't worship the kundalini.''

''Why not?''

''The kundalini is the light force in the universe. You use the light to find the diamond mind. This is the thing the Sparkers just don't understand.''

Why did I ever come to this old woman? She always talked in riddles. ''Diamond mind?''

''Yes, Ty Merrick, the diamond mind. That is the point of complete clarity, when all that can be known is known.'' She paused, cleared her throat, and began one of those incomprehensible metaphysical lectures that only LaRue understood. ''The Sparkers concern themselves with drawing out energy from the lower chakra centers, those that give us the source of our creativity. This ain't bad, if you ain't consumed with expressing the diamond mind. For that, you have to engage all the chakra centers. There's nine of them, you know. It takes a right long time for a person to ease the power out, and they can't do it until they are lit from the inside.'' It was her turn to lean forward. ''Lit like you, Miss Marshal.''

Gibson swerved the conversation the same way LaRue took sharp, right turns in the Trabi. "Exactly what do you do, Ms. Borden?"

I could tell the old crone was smiling behind her hood and it was only a moment before she happily explained. "What I do can be done by anyone who has been hit in the head at least twenty times. I have the ability to see the number of tachyon particles present in the body's cell structure."

"Tachyon particles are only theoretical possibilities," Gibson said. "Researchers have been trying to prove their existence for years, but nothing has ever come out of it."

"Science ain't caught up to reality, sir. Tachs are there, existing in the cell's nucleus."

"But tachs are supposed to move faster than the speed of light. Why would they be present within the very heart of the cell?"

"Because humans have the ability to transmute light." She paused to cluck at him. "Don't you understand, sir? We are light. After water and the odd chemical, that is all that we are, and that's the thing that the Sparkers don't accept. They think the power comes from outside of us, from another dimension of reality. They say we channel it through the chakras. That, of course, is the wrong way."

Her answer made Gibson frown. "How does a person transmute light?"

Lizzie sat back on her pillow and paused to fold the frayed cuffs on her robe. As bad as she smelled, I was surprised to notice how clean her hands were and how neatly her fingernails were trimmed. "We're straying dangerously close to a consultation," she announced.

A grin got me and I flashed it Gibson's way. Pay up or shut up.

He did just that by dropping a five-credit note on the rug. When he spoke, his voice was dark with intensity. "Tell me, now."

Lizzie scooped up the fiver and obliged him. "The cell is a reservoir of light, Dr. Gibson, and buried deep in the DNA are tachyons. When the body has reached a certain level of evolution, the light particles are turned on. This burst of light transmutes the cell and fills it with energy. When that happens the kundalini starts to rise. We call this energy, the serpent. In Atlantis, oh, maybe ten thousand years ago or so, this building energy was likened to the serpent god, Yezratez. Yezratez represented the diamond mind to those folks. He knew all that could be known.''

She began to hover over a metaphysical cloud, but Gibson pulled her back to science. ''What turns on the light and signals the transformation of the cells?''

Lizzie pointed toward her head. ''The brain. Inside, you find something called the pineal gland. It is the vestigial remains of a third eye that so many early people had. Those in Atlantis had three eyes, but our evolution has been on such a lower order that we never did use the thing right, so time buried it for us until we were smart enough and compassionate enough to see with it properlike. But it's still connected in a pathway to the optic nerve, and when stimulated, it starts the light transmutation.''

''How do you know this?'' Gibson asked. ''Were you some sort of doctor?''

''Ain't you been listening to me?'' she snapped. ''I can't work with the light if I don't have the kundalini myself. I know this stuff, because the serpent rose in me. Knowledge comes with the light.''

''Obviously, Gibson's diamond mind needs polishing,'' I said.

He pummeled me with a pissed-off expression, but then went right back to jumping on my interview. ''The pineal gland controls our circadian rhythms,'' he said.

Lizzie continued to explain without letting on to Gibson that she had long ago been a midwife over at the PHO hospital. ''Yes, our sleep/wake cycle. Light and darkness affect the amount of the hormone melatonin. When the pineal gland awakens structurally, it goes to feeding a similar chemical into the person's body. It's this chemical that stimulates the tachyon particles.''

''What happens after the stimulation begins?''

''Nothing, for a while. The person has to wake up to the fact that his body is now sensitive to light. He's got to understand that he functions at a different level. The only way a person can do that is to balance the chakras.''

''And that's what you do?''

''Oh, yes. Have for years.''

''So, the person who has his chakras aligned is rewarded with the diamond mind.''

She nodded. ''Yes, yes. A state of great clarity. To know all that is knowable. What higher order can there be in the universe?''

''But the SoC doesn't see the need to reach beyond the lower chakras,'' I said. ''Why?''

''Why? Look at the truth, Miss Marshal. It's hanging there in front of your nose. The Sparkers want to control the world like old Duvalier did, but they ain't giving us nothing new, nothing that ain't ours by right of birth. They want to control our natural vision and vitality. They want us to believe we are creators *with* the universe, but they don't want us to know that we are actually the creators *of* the universe.'' Lizzie left her discourse with a shrug and moved the inquiry into a parlay. ''Baba was in to see me the other day. She thinks you need an etheric enema.''

I grunted. ''I'm trying to find a killer, Lizzie.''

''Yes, well, that's your job, isn't it? Maybe you would think better if I balanced your tachs.''

''Only if you tell me more about the Sparkers.''

''I suppose that's a fair deal.'' She turned to a small cardboard box sitting beside her pillow and pulled out a handful of pine needles. Tossing them into the fire, she sweetened the cardboard shack with a delicate scent while she sweetened the bargaining pot. ''Once you have a good cleansing, you'll be able to understand things better, Miss Marshal. You've been lit for years, but in bad need of an energy leveraging. How many times have I told you this?''

''Every time I check out the tent village during my public service days.''

''Since you've got the gift of brightness, why don't you start using it? It might be this brilliance that will save you in the end.''

''What's that supposed to mean?'' I asked.

"I mean that if the Sparkers take over, they'll either grab folks like you for their talents or they'll kill you out of fear. You're going to need the clarity of the diamond mind if you're going to figure out how to stay alive. And Miss Marshal, you can be sure the SoC already has you in its sights."

FORTY-ONE

"How much to get Merrick glowing?" Gibson suddenly asked.

I glared at him, wondering why he was playing the part that LaRue usually took.

"Another five will cover a general removal of tachyon toxicity. For ten more credits, I'll realign her chakra centers." Lizzie studied me under her hood. "She needs that more than anything, and since it ain't been done before, it might take a while."

Gibson peeled off the precise amount, but I stopped him from giving the money to her by touching his hand while I addressed this misplaced metaphysician. "No deal, unless you answer my questions, too."

"As you wish." With that, she scraped up the money, burying it in the greasy folds of her getup. She pointed to a frayed mat lying next to the flimsy wall. "Make yourself comfortable, please."

I felt like an idiot, but I did as she requested. I decided not to give her a chance to hem and haw about answering me, so started asking questions immediately. "Have you heard of any other people the Sparkers know about?"

"Here and there. No names stand out. You got to understand that these people have been around a long time."

"I'd never heard of them until this past year."

She laughed. "That goes to show you what you don't know, Miss Marshal. I've heard them called by other names—the Light Raiders; the Sun Chasers; the Dawn Traders. Now they're the Sparkers."

"Have you ever been visited by a man named Bernard Horn?"

"I don't recall him, but then, it ain't necessary for me to find out a person's identity to do light spinning."

Lizzie touched the top of my head, and then pressed gently with her hands. I started to say something, but she hushed me and started explaining my condition. "You're a light bearer, Ty Merrick," she reported quietly. "You are definitely lit, but your chakra centers are so out of tune that you only receive the grace of diamond mind at certain times. It is as though your energy balances of its own accord, with no conscious help from you."

There was no great news there. Everyone in my ward knew I had lycanthropy and most knew how it affected me.

"You got a right good blockage in your throat chakra," she announced. "Just relax."

I tried, and for a moment I felt the comforting heat from her hand on my neck, but Gibson got as mouthy as LaRue and broke my concentration.

"Have you ever heard of radiation being applied to enhance the latent properties of the brain's pineal gland?"

Lizzie was silent for a minute. She began to massage my head and I suddenly felt myself drifting. "You would be referring to the tachyon-infusion bridge."

"How do you know about that?" he demanded.

"Diamond mind," she answered simply.

"What is this bridge thing?" I mumbled.

"Quiet," Lizzie ordered. Her hands moved down my shoulders. "It was an experiment a long time ago—way back before Duvalier's time. Some university tried to find out if radiation would flip on the lights for a person."

Gibson took up the explanation. "Studies showed that exposure to radiation stimulated the pineal gland. The focus was not to flip on the lights so much as it was to see what kind of chemicals the gland would secrete under certain conditions. They found out that it produced a hormone that they called Anna-19, named after the test subject. When this hormone came on-line, Anna's intelligence level shot up dramatically. Before activation, she was an average thirteen-year old. Afterward, she had brainpower that nearly rivaled that of Albert Einstein."

"That's nice," I murmured. As bad as I didn't want to admit it, Lizzie had magic in her hands, for whatever she did lulled me with a sense of calm. She moved her fingers gently across my chest until she centered them above my heart. The strange fluttering came back, but this time it was like a hundred butterflies flitted through my breast.

I enjoyed this interlude of quiet until Gibson threw the kundalini switch by saying what was on his mind. "A person might get enough radiation exposure to stimulate the pineal gland after spending only a few hours in a radon mine. Merrick, with your condition, you might have brainpower like never before."

FORTY-TWO

I grasped Gibson's meaning the second my heart burst and I was thrown into a lycanthropic stretch. The pain was so intense that I howled, and yanking away from Lizzie, I tried to control the expanding supernova of agony by curling into a fetal position, but the explosion was no longer contained in my solar plexus, so it did nothing to relieve the crackling in my chest.

Gibson crawled toward me, grabbed my hands, and placed his knee against my right thigh to keep me from thrashing and rolling into the fire. He spoke to me, but his words made no sense, because this rising power pushed all the air from my lungs and I was more concerned with the struggle against this release of my life force. Gibson saw I was having difficulty and did what he could by rolling me onto my back and massaging my torso hard enough to break a couple of ribs.

Suddenly the pain was gone; and then, so was I. In fact, I floated overhead, adrift like my thoughts. I watched Gibson from behind and saw his frantic efforts at getting me to suck in air. I saw Lizzie of the Twenty Whacks acting with calm self-assurance, as though her procedure had been responsible for my soul's freedom.

Spinning gently, I took a quick peek around the cardboard

cabin, and then traveled straight through the soggy roof without getting any goo on myself. I floated skyward, glancing back when I cleared the tallest building in District One. My home was there—dark, dirty, despicable, but instead of feeling the usual shame at humanity's excesses, I felt full of understanding and compassion. I comprehended the marvels of the universe with stark clarity. I knew the knowable. Somehow, I had arrived at diamond mind.

As abruptly as it had started, my journey ended. The stretch was over and I was tugged earthward again. I was not concerned that I would be turned into potted meat when I hit the material plane, but I should have been, because landing in my body was like smacking into a brick wall. I took a hard suck of pine-scented smoke and coughed until I was sure that pieces of my lungs had been flung out with my spit.

The minute I slid into recovery, I realized that there had been a dramatic shift in my awareness along with the physical changes. It was as if my mind had expanded with this stretch and had failed to zing back into place after the dust had settled. Still, the malleability of my thoughts during my out-of-body experience had been lost in the return and the only thing I remembered about diamond mind was how the clarity felt.

I found myself staring at Gibson while I tried to get an emotional handle on what had just happened. I'd stepped into virgin wilderness and it scared and pissed me off all at the same time.

"Ty," he husked. "Are you all right?"

He used my first name. I had him worried, so I let his concern build by taking a minute to catalog my lycanthropic changes. My vision picked up the glitter of sunlight filtering through the open doorway; my nose smelled the sharp scents from nearby campsites; and my hearing was once more decorated with sterling, crystal tones, but this time the exquisite sounds were accompanied by a far-off weeping voice, quivering with vibrato. I frowned, trying my damnedest to hear this beautiful noise past Gibson's insistent questions.

"What's wrong, Merrick? Can you sit up? Do you have pain?"

Lizzie saved me from answering by gently touching Gibson's arm. "She's fine, young doctor. Just confused. It happens after the initial flight."

"What are you talking about?" Gibson barked.

"I had just released the energy from her heart chakra," she answered matter-of-factly. "When all of the power was forced from the center, it was like the universe drew a breath for her. She was swept from her body by the cosmic tide. This is the energy contained in the rising power, and if you ain't prepared for it, the experience is joyous and terrifying all at the same time."

Gibson helped me to sit up before pronouncing his medical opinion on this mystical interlude. "I think the radio-dirium is affecting you, Merrick."

No doubt there, Doc. I stared at him, seeing beyond his concerned expression to his need to grasp this latest event by applying the safe parameters of scientific logic. Unfortunately, there was no answer I could give him. Gibson, himself, was fond of saying that the hallucination is real to the person who experiences it.

FORTY-THREE

I won't concede the fact that Lizzie charged my DNA with magic, but I will admit to having one of the best night's sleep I'd had in years. The next morning I woke up to Baba's bitching as she complained about the electricity not having come back on the grid when scheduled. I also awoke to the wonderful smell of eggs frying. Gibson flipped those greasy babies pretty fast and we all sat down to a cozy, domestic morning. By the time I walked in to work, I was feeling full and satisfied—something else I'd not experienced in a hell of a long time.

I met LaRue, who was on his way out. When he saw me, he noticed my good mood but couldn't identify what was different about me. "Are you wearing makeup?" he asked.

I laughed. "Maybe it's the light you see. I had a session with Lizzie Borden last night."

He stopped walking to face me in the middle of the busy hallway. "You went to see Lizzie of the Twenty Whacks?"

"I went to see her for the investigation, Andy. Gibson came along to pay for the session."

"What happened?"

I turned toward the entrance and stepped out onto the street before answering. "I had an out-of-body experience."

My partner stared at me, trying, I'm sure, to figure out if I'd been in the garlic vodka that morning. He abruptly decided I was sober. "What was it like?"

"It was amazing. I flew. At least, that's what it felt like. I know it was some manifestation of my mind, but it was so real."

LaRue's stare turned into a squint. "Did it come on the tail end of a stretch?"

"Yes, it did. That's never happened before."

"I'm so jealous," he said.

The only thing I could do was chuckle and slap him on the back, assuring him that with his metaphysical bent, he would probably eventually find the key that turns on the flight of fancy in the brain. It was all I needed to say before he jumped into the conversation and started telling me that most alien abduction victims report occurrences of OBEs. He talked about it until we arrived at the District Theater to have a conversation with Gina Nailor, diva, twenty-year employee of the government's Art Commission, and a self-proclaimed visionary who produced shows for the District Opera Company.

The theater seated over five thousand people and looked like a Russian had designed it—heavy velvets, gilt edgings, and lots of maroon. It was a huge hall filled with comfy seats and a stage big enough to drive in a herd of cattle.

Upon making our wishes known to some opera lackey, we were immediately taken down the main aisle and introduced to Nailor, who stood center stage, reading silently from a sheaf of papers. She was a small, pear-shaped woman with short, mousy-brown hair and a bulbous nose. To tell you the truth, I didn't think she was capable of belting out an operatic tune without a mike, but when she spoke, I realized she was a bellowing elephant dressed in chiffon.

"Marshals?" she boomed. "This is about Bernard Horn, isn't it? Damn him! Wasn't he enough trouble to me when he was alive? And now, look! Even after he's gone, he's found a way to annoy me."

Nailor's assistant chimed in to speak sweetly. "Gina, you poor darling. We all knew how Bernard could be."

We sat down in the front row and I took a moment to marvel at the comfort of the chairs, but my fascination was short-lived when LaRue opened the interview. "Please tell us how Bernard could be."

Nailor slapped the papers against her hip and marched to the edge of the stage. "Infuriating! Worrisome! Unreliable! Indignant! And too goddamned full of his own trumped-up self-worth."

"Well, we're each all those things at one time or the other. What in particular bothered you?"

"For one thing, he had an annoying habit of arriving late for rehearsal," she snapped. "How can you expect to get the lead in an opera if you don't show up on time for work?"

"He wanted the lead, but couldn't live up to the pressure."

"That's right. He cost the government money because of his need for recognition." She paused and sat down on the stage to study us for a minute. By the time she spoke again, her voice had shifted down a few octaves. "You must think I hated Bernard. I didn't. A long time ago I learned to work with the talent I'm sent. Make do. Improvise. Just don't cost the government any more money than you have to. Less if you can afford it."

"Why was he always late for rehearsal?" I asked.

"Because he had too much going on. He was so involved with his collateral activities that he started ducking rehearsals altogether."

"What kind of collateral activities did he have?"

Nailor glanced around for her assistant and then for confirmation. "Wasn't he doing something with kids?"

The assistant nodded. "It was something that had to do with public welfare. Bernard didn't talk about it much. If you want to know more, you should ask Betty. She could tell you."

"You're speaking about Betty Victoria Reseda, Horn's fiancée?"

"Yes. Oh, she was terribly broken up about his death. She just couldn't believe it."

"Did Horn have any fans who might have been considered bothersome?" LaRue asked.

"Stalkers?" Nailor hooted. "You must be kidding. He didn't have enough fans for that."

"He had recognition," he said. "What about his humanitarian award?"

The assistant twittered and we all turned to size up her timing.

"What is it?" I asked.

She clasped her hand over her mouth and shook her head while she mumbled. "I'm sorry."

"Why did you find it amusing?"

The girl glanced at Nailor, who nodded. Dropping her hand, she explained. "Bernard was designated a humanitarian treasure because he was considered disabled due to his arthritic condition."

"It was a government regulation designed for fair and equal treatment under the law," Nailor said.

"So, in his mind, he didn't earn it?"

"No. Perhaps later he started to believe he'd earned it." She waxed metaphysical and it was all I could do not to snort my opinion. "Some people have a difficult time dealing with the concept of cosmic receiving. The universe gives them a gift, but unless they've earned it in their thoughts, it's nothing more than a burden."

"What about his amazing comeback?" LaRue asked. "He claimed he was abducted by aliens and his voice became much better."

"Aliens. That's a bit much. Even for Bernard."

"You don't believe he had an abduction experience."

"The only abduction experience he ever had came at the end of a bottle of homemade hooch."

"You're saying he imagined it all?"

"What do you think?"

LaRue shrugged and I jumped into the conversation, afraid that my partner just might answer her question. "Do you think he was insane?"

"No," she said, stretching. "He had his neuroses like everyone else. If you ask me, he should never have been going to see a psychiatrist."

"You're talking about Dr. Myra Fontaine?" LaRue asked.

"Yes. That was her. She would come down sometimes to listen to Bernard sing during rehearsals." She paused. "The few rehearsals he managed to make, that is. She was the one who filled his head with this nonsense, and then she convinced him to start filling other people's heads with it, too. No, Marshal. There was no change in his voice. It was good publicity and a great line. Divine talent delivered through alien intervention. It should be an opera.''

I forced a smile down, but it got through anyway. ''It was all in his mind, then?''

''Well, isn't everything? Our strengths are found there, as well as our weaknesses.''

''Believing in yourself is important.''

''Yes, it is. But duping the public is something else again.''

I let a chuckle fly. ''Everyone's a critic.''

Nailor smiled, but didn't get into the humor. ''Society demands certain standards from its artists. That's the way it's always been. Conform to the status quo; don't trot out your creativity and flap it in people's faces. We're all told what to do by the government. There's no room for outlandish ideas.''

Did she realize how ridiculous it all sounded? Wasn't creativity an essential part in the process for the critic to judge? Society didn't demand standards. It demanded censorship. ''Was Horn full of bright ideas?''

''Bernard wished he was. I think in the end, he deluded himself more than he fooled anyone else.''

''Was Horn open about his affiliation with the SoC?'' LaRue asked.

''The Spark of Creation Movement?'' she sang, adding a lilting warble to her response. ''Bernard, a Sparker. Now, that is funny. If anyone was involved with that group, it would have had to been that good-for-nothing-no-talent mentor of his.''

''Silvio Valinari?''

''That's the one.'' She stood in a fluid motion, despite the weight she carried in her behind. ''He could have been a Sparker because he always harped about Bernard singing for the masses. Bernard was in this world for success and money. Anyone who would hire him, he would sing for. He didn't care about appealing to a bunch of no-brained people.''

''Was Bernard wealthy?'' I asked.

Nailor shrugged. ''Personally, I think he had gold-plated gonads.''

FORTY-FOUR

Gina Nailor told us that Betty Victoria Reseda had returned to the district with the rest of the opera company and could be found at her quaint, little house on the outskirts of the district. We immediately stopped by to find a woman who, in this tiny hut she called a home, filled out a room. Literally. Reseda must have weighed four hundred pounds and stood as tall as Gibson.

She seemed pleasant enough, and despite her size, she maneuvered through the tight maze of furniture in the parlor without knocking anything on the floor. After pointing us to a U-shaped settee, Reseda took a moment to squeeze into a purple armchair. She fluffed the bottom of her large paisley caftan and finally spoke on the hind end of a heavy sigh.

"You're here about Bernard. You want to know if I had anything to do with his death. Well, for the second time, I'm telling you no."

"We weren't here before," LaRue said.

"The others were. Agents Nichols and Carver."

"Did they accuse you of anything?"

"They told me they thought I killed Bernard for his money."

I used my own performing abilities to play along. "His money? Was Mr. Horn a wealthy man?"

She inched forward, which, upon review, involved only a slight movement of her neck. "Bernard didn't have any money. At least, none he ever told me about. I don't know where you people get your information."

"Is that why you took out an insurance policy with Margarite Mallow?"

Reseda leveled me with an even look. "That was not my idea. Bernard did it on a whim."

"A whim? The man took a bet about his own death."

"He was feeling good about his life," she answered quickly. "He thought he might be able to get his arthritis under control. It was a whim."

"It sounds like he was worried about dying to me. Maybe someone had been threatening him."

"No," she snapped. "I told you. He was feeling confident that his health would return after he took rehabilitation at the mine." She paused to work up an operatic wail. "I loved him so! I didn't care if he was broke."

LaRue stomped back into the conversation. "Did he have financial difficulties?"

"Yes. It happened years ago. He got a woman pregnant and she made him pay through the nose."

"What was this woman's name?"

"I don't know. Bernard refused to tell me. Whatever happened, it ended him up in bankruptcy court and I guess he considered himself grateful that he was given permission to claim the loss. I asked him about it several times, but he said he didn't want to discuss the past, his or mine." She snorted. "Like I have any."

"Why do you say that?"

"I've spent my life right here, honing my singing skills. I have talent, just like Bernard did, but we were both trapped singing chorus and bit parts. My weight is my problem, Marshals. Even in the opera world, I'm too fat. The costumes have to be specially made for me and it costs too much money. It's easier to wrap a bedsheet around me and stick me by the curtain." Reseda stopped her bitter explanation to return to the subject of her fiancé. "At least, Bernard began to break out of the mold. He was being noticed."

"Yes, but by whom?" I asked.

She turned a squint onto me. "What is that supposed to mean?"

I burned a minute studying her before lying. "We understand that Bernard Horn was involved with the SoC."

"Bernard?" she trilled. "That's insane. Utterly ridiculous."

"Why?"

"Because the government had given him his life from infancy until his death. Would you throw a kink into the machine by joining the Sparkers?"

"What about Silvio Valinari? Did he have such leanings?"

"Not that I know of. Silvio wanted Bernard to sing for the masses, but those were the words spoken by a frustrated artist."

"Why was he frustrated?"

"Because he has no real talent for the opera. How does that old saying go? Those who can't—teach."

"What about Purceval Walker?"

She was taking a breath to reply when I asked the question, and now she held it tight in her chest. When she finally exhaled, the breeze fluttered my hair. "Purcy," she whispered. Then, louder: "What can I say about Purcy? I didn't like him."

"Why?"

"Because he had the heart of a two-bit hoodlum. I didn't trust him and I thought Bernard was blind to this boy's deceit. I think he was a liar." Reseda paused, took another explosive breath, and then just as I thought she was going to get to some meat, I found out it was her prejudice that was talking full tilt. "I suppose you can't expect much more," she said. "He's an orphan after all. Bernard rose above it all and managed to escape the mediocrity of this doomed class of people, but most are like Purcy. They hide behind civility and yet they're nothing more than thieves, rapists, and petty criminals."

I clenched my teeth and tried to speak without growling. LaRue saw my building anger and took over the questions immediately.

"Why did Agents Nichols and Carver think Horn had money?" he asked.

Reseda shook her head sadly. "I'm not sure. Maybe there was some problem with his quarterly payments. I really don't know."

"Did Bernard charge for work done under the table during his singing gigs?"

Reseda turned on an incredulous expression. "Dodge taxes?" she asked. "Why, of course. Doesn't everyone?"

It was time to spell out the last point. "We understand that you were abducted by extraterrestrial aliens."

She chuckled. "You've been talking to my sister."

"That's right."

"Well, the fact of the matter is this: you can't believe anything Louise says because she's crazy."

FORTY-FIVE

Betty Reseda sent us to visit one of Horn's under-the-table students, a young musician by the name of Alita Bavol. I expected another woman with a glandular condition, but was pleasantly surprised to find out that she was a wisp of a person—tiny, dark-haired, and flighty.

Her apartment was her orchestra pit and she told us immediately that the junk, ranging from glass bottles to soup cans to rocks, was her musical instrument. To demonstrate, she picked up a pair of drumsticks and started tapping a beat on the end of an oatmeal container. We smiled indulgently until she finished her solo before we began to ask her questions.

"Ms. Bavol, you are a member of the District Symphony," I said. "Is that correct?"

"Well, sort of. I'm an employee of the Agency for the Arts and Humanities. I'm a clerk. I process applications."

I plopped on a scowl. "As talented as we were told you are, I'm surprised. We just assumed you were a musician."

"I am," she said. "Unfortunately, the district government doesn't see it that way. I only have a Class-C designation. The musicians carry A-plus or more." She sighed. "I suppose it's the luck of the draw. Not everyone can get the job they want."

"How long did you work with Bernard Horn?" I asked.

She tossed me a frowny face as she answered. "Oh, Bernard. I just loved him. I'm so sad that he's gone. Of all the people in this world, Bernard understood my music. He understood my need to be creative. It drives everything I do. Without him, I'm lost—simply lost."

Her theatrics were a bit overdone, but I let it slide by. "How long did you work with Bernard Horn?" I repeated.

"Six years. Six wonderful years." She stood and began to adjust a glass bottle being held aloft by a length of copper tubing connected to a metal post. When done, she moved to play with the tinkle of several nails hanging from this contraption by strings of braided yarn. Sucking in a deep breath, she explained. "We met through an encounter group."

"What kind of encounter group?" I asked, taking a stroll around her flat.

"Well, I'd rather not say. It's personal."

I started to jump mean on her about withholding evidence, but LaRue spoke first. "Ms. Bavol, we understand that it's not easy to talk about things that are painful or that we wish to keep a secret, but Mr. Horn is dead. He was murdered in a horrible way. Would you like to see his death go unavenged?"

She gave him a wet, doe-eyed look and then shook her head, whispering: "Of course not."

"Then please tell us about how you met him."

Bavol took a moment to adjust her seat on the plastic crate and gently began to thrum some metal wires. "I was in therapy because I am an experiencer."

"You've been abducted by aliens?"

"Yes. We prefer to call them extraterrestrials, though."

"What happened?"

"I was a child and they took me from my home."

"What did they do to you?" he demanded.

Bavol swallowed hard and then replied, "They placed a diaphanous insert into my brain by way of my nose."

It was all I could do to keep this bullshit from leaking out into my expression, so I pretended to admire a photo of Bavol and Horn taken during a concert while LaRue hit her with another question. "What exactly does this diaphanous insert do?"

"I don't know exactly, but I think it has increased my creativity. Yes. That's what it feels like."

"Creativity has a feeling?" I asked.

"Yes. Haven't you ever experienced the euphoric rush that comes with creating?"

"Apparently not."

"It expands your awareness at all levels. It's a communion of sorts."

"You met Horn at a gathering of folks who each received a diaphanous insert?"

"I can't say they all had DIs, but most."

"Did Horn?"

"Yes."

"Was this therapy session instigated at the suggestion of a person named Turquoise?"

"Yes. The workshop was run by his assistant, Dr. Myra Fontaine."

"Did Dr. Fontaine talk about these diaphanous inserts?"

"A little. She told us that we needed to exploit them."

"How? By joining the SoC?"

"No, by joining the network of groups who take our claims seriously."

"Has either of you been involved in a group called the Society for Intergalactic Travelers?"

"No, but I've heard of them. You have to understand that there are a lot of these organizations, maybe four or five hundred small groups in this district alone. Our numbers are growing worldwide from what I hear, but you have to be careful you don't run into a scam."

"Did you ever meet Turquoise face-to-face?"

"No, but I talked to him on the phone."

"Did he call here?" I asked, trying to hold my hope in check.

"Yes. He sounded like a young man. He had a beautiful, baritone voice."

"What did he want?"

"To talk to Bernard. I left the room to give him some privacy, so I don't know what their conversation was about. I assumed he was passing on a new message for Bernard to deliver.''

''What kind of message?''

''A message of peace. Turquoise wants us to love one another and allow each other the space to demonstrate his or her highest creativity, for this creativity is the First Law of the Universe. It is the only reason we exist and society shouldn't restrict this basic right of the immortal soul.''

God, that sounded grand, but it was such idealistic twaddle that I thought I'd puke. ''To your knowledge was Horn involved in the Spirit of Creation Movement?''

Bavol swallowed past a lump in her throat again. ''No, not Bernard. He was a loyal humanitarian.''

''This message of Turquoise sounds like its perfectly wrapped for the SoC.''

She hesitated before maintaining her stance. ''No, Bernard wasn't a Sparker. I'm sure of it.''

FORTY-SIX

Gibson had talked a colleague into giving me a brain scan, and so when we left Bavol's apartment, LaRue swung by the hospital to drop me off. The good doctor threatened to strap me to the table so I wouldn't run off before he was done, but the moment the machine beeped its completion I hauled ass back to the office. I was in no mood to find out how big my brain was, because in the end all it did was press on the inside of my skull and give me a headache.

I found LaRue huddling in our cubicle as he sifted through the files that Roscoe Turner and Elbert Derry had forked over.

"What's going on, Andy?" I asked quietly, sliding into my chair.

He glanced at me and then settled his attention back onto the monitor while he answered. "The brass just called Julie upstairs. She was heated, Ty. I could see it in her eyes."

"Well, the steam is rising, isn't it?" I answered. "Do you really think Julie hasn't been playing both ends against the middle? If she isn't, then she's pretty damned stupid." I flapped a finger at him. "Personally, my whole existence has been a walk down skinny stairs, and I'm tired of trying to hold my balance, too."

He flipped me a look. "The wheel of life eventually turns."

"Yeah, and with it goes our innocence." I pointed to his computer "Got anything besides coded names in there?"

"Not much. I'm sifting through the notes old Roscoe made on everyone. He had some strange ideas and opinions. He also has two sets of accounting books, but I'm still looking for something we can use."

"What about Elbert Derry's PHO scam? I'm sure he had one."

"According to the records, Derry was new to the facility. His PHO service files give him outstanding marks all along the way. There is one interesting thing, though."

"And that would be?"

"Derry is in deep guano with the ETA."

"Why?"

"He claimed bankruptcy and hasn't paid a lick of quarterly taxes in two years."

"How the hell did he get to claim bankruptcy?" I asked.

"It's who you know, Ty. He probably paid someone over at Treasury to issue the permission slip."

"Well, if he got to go free on his bills, why didn't he keep it low profile and pay his taxes?"

"Excellent question." LaRue studied me, but I could tell his brain fiddled with a faraway idea.

"What are you thinking about, Andy?"

"I did a little digging on Roscoe Turner," he answered. "He claimed bankruptcy, too."

"What about his quarterly tax payments?"

He shook his head. "I can't get a secure pipe into his tax account. Someone shut that information valve off."

I nodded and shot my gaze beyond him to take in the back of Nichols's head. "What about yon goose steppers?"

"Well, just for the hell of it, I happened to see where they stood with their little tax bills," LaRue said. "They're on the money. Paid in full." With that, my usually talkative partner shut up and went back to his sorting job.

I spent the next half hour trying to look busy by doodling on a sheet of paper while I listened to the aria in my head. Since my out-of-body experience, the music had gained a whole new integrity and was loud enough to distract me. It continually caught my attention, holding it like Gibson's hypnosis tricks. Several times I tried to ignore the enchanting sounds but surrendered to the beauty instead. Thankfully, my labored musings were interrupted by Frank Wilson. He stood over my desk staring down at the picture I'd drawn.

"Damn, Merrick," he said. "When did you learn to sketch like that?"

His interest alerted LaRue, who leaned over to see my pencil painting. He let his gaze track across the paper only a moment before fixing it upon me. "That is really good, Ty."

"What are you guys talking about?" I asked. "It's just scribbling."

Wilson shook his head. "No, it isn't."

I followed his line of sight and studied my own handiwork. Much to my surprise, he was right. I'd drawn an odd landscape composed of shadow and light, laced with delicate forms. My picture had perspective as well as feeling—and all this from an untrained eye and hand.

When I realized it was a new lycanthropic display, I clenched my hand, and not gauging my strength, I broke the pencil in half before pushing the paper under a file folder. "It's nothing," I muttered. Then, louder, I said: "Do you have something for us?"

Wilson plopped down in the available chair. "We lifted a clear set of fingerprints from the back of Jenna York's hand. You are not going to believe who they fit."

"Who, Frank?" I asked, trying to hide my sudden impatience.

"Elbert Derry's missing six-year-old son, Hewitt."

FORTY-SEVEN

We immediately had Dr. Derry and his wife, Noreen, dragged in for a conversation. They came quietly, and as they sat down at the table in the interrogation room, I noticed that Derry's rude manner was gone. Instead, he shared Noreen's nervousness. Clearly, they did not know who to trust and that was the only detail that made me feel compassion for them.

Noreen had way too much eyeliner on, and from one look at her, I could tell she'd been weeping. There were dark splotches dirtying her lids. "We haven't done anything wrong," she wailed.

I adjusted my chair while LaRue did a little pacing. "You're not under arrest, Mrs. Derry," I said. "We want to ask you questions concerning the Bernard Horn case."

She looked at her husband with a surprised expression. "I don't understand what this is all about. Elbert?"

Derry's lips started flapping in the breeze, but no words passed between them. I leaned forward and cocked an ear in his direction. "You were saying, Doctor?"

After a few more fluttering attempts, he managed to speak. "I—I don't bring my work home, Marshal. Noreen doesn't know anything."

"Isn't this about Hewitt?" Noreen asked.

"Hewitt Derry," I said. "That would be your eldest child. Is that correct?"

Noreen abruptly collapsed into hysterical sobbing and LaRue was forced to fetch her a cup of gritty water while she fumbled through her purse looking for a bottle of nerve pills. Thirty minutes later she was able to control her emotions and, in fact, was slurring her words.

Derry patted his wife's hand gently and explained. "My wife has not been the same since Hew was kidnapped."

"What happened?"

He shrugged. "One day, he didn't come home from school."

"He was a bright, little boy," Noreen blubbered. "So smart. So friendly. I guess that's what went wrong. He was too friendly and too trusting."

"When did this act occur?" LaRue fired.

"Two months ago," Noreen said. "The Marshals Office has put out bulletins for his safe return, but nothing has come of it."

As sad as her tune was, it was nevertheless time to stir the soup. "It must have been a bad year for your family unit. Hewitt's kidnapping happened on the heels of a legal financial restructuring."

She nodded. "A horrible year. We lost everything—our house, our possessions, our child."

"How did you get into such a financial mess?"

Noreen turned to her husband. "I can't go through this again, Elbert."

He glanced at me. "Would you allow my wife to sit outside? This conversation is extremely painful to her. She needs time to heal."

LaRue showed instant compassion by leading Mrs. Derry to an empty chair in the homicide pen. He returned quickly to sit down at the table, and using a dark, menacing tone, he got down to business. "You better tell it straight, Doc. We want to know everything. If not, we'll bring your lovely wife back in here."

Derry inserted a pause into the conversation by rubbing his eyes and grunting. Then: "I got us into the financial mess."

"How?"

"By trying to make money under the table. I had my own scam going, Marshals. Only problem was, the ETA had been the ones to set me up in the first place."

"What happened?" LaRue demanded.

"What didn't happen?" he answered. "I was making house calls, seeing folks on the side, and I didn't report any of the income." He snorted. "Income—that's a laugh. Most people want to pay you in potatoes. I had one old lady who wanted to give me a charm sack that was supposed to magically confirm my diagnoses."

I thought of Gibson. The good doctor was always making house calls and always being paid in chicken feet and dried squid. "So, the ETA sent in a phony patient."

"Yes. Several, actually. They obviously had it in for me from the start. Well, someone did, at any rate."

"Any idea who?" LaRue asked.

"No, not really. You know how it is. You make your share of enemies if you live long enough."

"Were you involved with the Spark of Creation Movement at this time?"

He shook his head emphatically. "No. If I was, I didn't know it. I treated a lot of people. I suppose any one of them could have been Sparkers. I just never talked about it."

LaRue hammered him with an astute observation. "You were engaged in a criminal activity, Dr. Derry. Why would they allow you to claim bankruptcy? That's a privilege reserved for very few."

Derry gathered a head of steam and leaned forward. "Let me tell you the truth, Marshal. Claiming bankruptcy is not a choice and it's not a privilege. It's a punishment. A legal punishment. Once you've been added to the list, you lose your class designation and so do the members of your family unit. It costs big money to buy it back. And you and I know that unless you have that piece of paper, your life is worth less than a load of manure. Period. If I hadn't gotten it back, we would have been shipped off to labor camps. As it is, I still don't have the money to purchase Noreen's class designation.

She was a social worker for the PHO. Now she sits at home and cries.''

''So, how did you buy back your class designation?'' I asked.

Derry sighed, taking a moment to study us before answering. ''Will you promise not to tell my wife what I did?''

''It doesn't matter to us,'' LaRue said. ''Provided you're going to fork over the truth.''

''The ETA signed it back over to me, but in payment, they wanted my son, Hewitt.'' He paused to point toward Nichols and Carter. ''Those two came and took him away.''

FORTY-EIGHT

The minute I heard Derry's confession, I knew that Nichols and Carver had been sent in to bumfuzzle us. They wanted to keep a lid on certain information and that tranked me up tight. "Why would they want your child?" I demanded.

"Because he was bright," he answered. "Beautiful and bright."

"I take it they wanted to make him into a tax adjuster?"

Derry scowled. "This is not a laughing matter, Marshal."

He was right, but my sympathy meter wasn't running. "Do you know any other family units who have had their children taken from them?"

"No. I swear."

"Was Nurse Jenna York aware of your secret?"

"Not that I know of." Then, like a drowning man, he grasped for the life preserver. "She had tax problems, herself."

"You're suggesting the ETA put the tap on her? How? Did she have children?"

He shook his head. "They made her work in the facility, of course. Listen, in case you missed it, the District Council has granted the ETA the privilege to assign public service in lieu of money owed on quarterly payments, and a few years back they got the right to begin taxation on offspring beginning at the third year of the child's life. Most people don't have that kind of money and get into trouble. Gone are the days when the government actually gave you money to have a kid. Now they want the money, the labor, or your firstborn."

"Was Nurse York close to anyone on the staff?"

"She kept to herself. She never socialized. In fact, she acted as if her service at the facility was beneath her."

"What about Horn? Did she get along with him?"

"He didn't complain about her, so I suppose everything was all right."

"Did you check out Mr. Horn's claims of arthritis?"

"I looked at his records."

"Did he have arthritis?"

"Yes."

I leaned across the table. "Are you sure, Dr. Derry?"

He wet his lips and studied me. "I had charts. X rays. Whoever the negatives belonged to had arthritis. One never knows if the picture is authentic or not, but the bone structure looked like it could have fit Horn, so I went with it."

"Who referred Bernard Horn to the facility?" I asked.

Derry thought a moment. "It was a governmental request. Bernard Horn had just had a change in his tax status due to his disability and qualified to receive health maintenance services."

After I was tied to Gibson's medical umbilical cord, the district had changed my tax rates to fall into a similar bracket. If I kept playing the game with the good doctor, my taxes rang in only at 15 percent.

"It was a little odd, though," he murmured.

"What?"

"I had a conversation with Horn one day and he mentioned his psychiatrist thought it was a good idea for him to take the therapy."

"Psychiatrists are medical doctors, too," LaRue said.

"Of course. That's not the point. Jenna York's day job is the point."

"And?"

"Jenna worked for his psychiatrist, but when she was introduced to him during his admission, she acted like she'd never met him before."

FORTY-NINE

After our conversation with Dr. Derry, we zipped over to Myra Fontaine's office and found her suite vacated. It did not look good as we hurried to her house to discover it empty, too. Obviously, the shrink knew when to shrink into the woodwork.

"Damn!" I barked, stomping on the back porch of her house like a petulant kid. "To think I let that bitch tinker around inside of my head."

LaRue tried the door again, but it was still locked. He paused to peer once more through the chink in the curtains before satisfying himself that nothing had changed during the course of my sentence. "She must have known it would only be a couple of days until we caught up with her double-dealing. I don't see a stick of furniture."

"If it's all gone then she knew were were closing in on her trail."

He glanced at me and spoke in a low voice. "Do you think she was the reason Horn was where he should have been for this hit?"

"Who knows?" I answered. Sitting down on the top step, I took a moment to study Fontaine's backyard. There was a lot of dead stuff—weeds, dying roses on a rickety arbor, and a pine tree that looked like it had already had an out-of-plant experience. "It's a good bet Myra thinks Jenna York stuck Bernard Horn. Whether she gave the word or was a willing accessory is anybody's guess."

LaRue didn't answer. Instead, he clomped down the stairs and started around the side of the brownstone walk-up. I followed, thinking he had thoughts about breaking and entering, but found that he headed for the Trabi instead. Without asking, I knew it was time to get along to our next interview at the district orphanage.

The facility was housed in a crumbling, seven-story building situated in the center of the locality and surrounded by poverty, filth, and hopelessness. Inside, it wasn't much better.

The kids were dirty and thin and their spirits were as threadbare as their cotton uniforms. Silence invaded these dismal hallways, sharing the space with the sharp scent of urine and the smell of cabbage cooking in the cafeteria. I took a quick glance into the bunk rooms, but found no surprises. The cots were marked according to number, and by number, the children responded.

Try as I might, I couldn't help sympathizing with Purceval Walker and his early exploits against authority. Living like a chained animal did nothing for the child except to turn him toward violence. If the evolving brain were ever to transform enough to save humanity, then it would have to move away from rage to peace. Staring at the sad, angry eyes of these orphans, I couldn't see how our species had a chance.

We were introduced to the facility's current director, Kingsley Turlow, who greeted us in the associate's lounge. This room, though dressed with sturdy furniture, suffered from peeling wall paint, broken windows, and decaying ceiling panels. The electricity had been rotated off the grid for this ward, and when we entered this suite, we heard Turlow curse the wind for blowing out a crooked candelabra of candles. The director apologized upon realizing we were there and stalled to study us by brushing his hand through his long, gray hair.

"The day is dark, don't you think?" he asked, pointing to a couple of plush chairs. "And this room is darker than the punishment pen."

Punishment pen: a cell designed with uncontrollable children in mind, where they may find the necessary solitude to consider their wrongful actions. How many times had I done a tour of duty in the PP? At least twenty times between ten and twelve years of age.

Though he didn't glance my way, LaRue obviously sensed my discomfort and took charge of the interview. "Mr. Turlow, we need to discuss two individuals who grew up here—Purceval Walker and Bernard Horn."

Turlow nodded, but instead of answering, he walked to the window. Once there, he busied himself by taping newspaper over the missing windowpane before answering. "It was a shame about Bernard Horn. We shall miss him."

"Did Mr. Horn support the orphanage?"

"Oh, yes. Well, what he could. He found ways to offer his time to the children and the facility. Many a day, you could hear him leading them in song. The kids loved him." He stopped his work to look dead at me. "Bernard always carried a pocketful of sweets and they knew it. They also knew he was an orphan. Children can sense these things without ever being told. It never fails."

I could do nothing but agree with him, but didn't utter a confirmation. "Did he ever give money to the orphanage?"

"No. He was never a rich man as far as I understand."

"How long did you know Mr. Horn?" LaRue asked.

"He was already an adult by the time I took the position. I suppose I've known Bernard almost fifteen years."

"Did he ever come by for a visit and bring a woman named Myra Fontaine?"

Turlow frowned. "Not that I recall."

"Did Mr. Horn ever have conversations with you regarding his belief that he was abducted by extraterrestrials?"

Turlow chuckled. "No, I'm afraid not."

"What about his involvement with the Spark of Creation Movement?"

LaRue's question was enough to draw the administrator's attention from his repair job. He stared at my partner for a good thirty seconds before answering. "We never had a discussion about the subject."

"Are you sure?" I asked.

"Yes. In my opinion, Bernard was devoted to the humanitarian principles of this society. He worked within the system and was honored for it. Why would the government make him a treasure if he was tied to the Sparkers?"

"Why, indeed?" I murmured.

"What do you know about a man named Silvio Valinari?" LaRue demanded.

"Silvio is a volunteer social worker. He occasionally trains some of our more talented children in music arts. Silvio isn't that interested in the kids, though. His efforts stem from an old tax penalty he's trying to repay with public service instead of money."

I glanced at LaRue and back to Turlow. "How old is the tax penalty?"

"Silvio has been trying to work off the tax owed for as long as I've been here. Apparently, he worked at it several years before that." Turlow coaxed a piece of tape from the roll and then tried to apply it to the paper without wrinkling it. "I don't think he'll ever see the end of that bill. How could he? He works for five credits an hour, but interest alone heaps up at a hefty twenty percent per month."

"Perhaps he doesn't intend to pay it off," I said. "Maybe he's investing his real money somewhere else."

"Tax dodging? Silvio? Now, that I'd believe. He makes no bones about not liking the government."

"What doesn't he like?"

"Everything. He thinks the humanitarian values are pointless and the bureaucrats keep people from pursuing their own destinies."

"He sounds like a good candidate to be a Sparker."

Turlow finished plastering the hole shut and then returned to his candles to fight with the matches, cursing softly until he finally had fire. "I never heard him admit to allegiance to the SoC."

"What about Purceval Walker?" LaRue said.

"Purcy? Part of the Sparkers? Nonsense. Purceval is going to be a doctor. The government is giving him a chance to excel and serve humanity. Why would he throw that opportunity away?"

"When was the last time you saw Walker?"

"It's been several months. He's been going to the university and living on campus."

"Did Walker know Horn?"

"Yes, he did. They were quite good friends, too. Purceval respected Bernard a great deal."

"What was Walker like as a child?"

"Quiet. He was bright, though. I could tell that from the start."

"If he was so bright, why did he end up in a public training program picking pumpkins out of the fields?"

Turlow finally managed to light the candle, and when it flared to life, he shifted his gaze to me. "He was selected for duty. I can't change the labor designations."

"Well, then, explain how Walker went from digging 'taters to studying medicine."

"After his last, great escape from the training program, Bernard intervened," Turlow answered. "He petitioned the District Council to give Purceval the opportunity to change his labor designation. The Council acquiesced, but would only consider the change if he passed a battery of psychological and intelligence tests. They discovered that he was not only bright, but brilliant, a resource they couldn't justify squandering."

"Who administered the tests?"

"A friend of Bernard's. A psychiatrist with a license to have a private practice. I don't know the name of the doctor, because the documentation was never sent to the orphanage for our records." He sighed after lighting all his candles. "It should be easier to save more of our children in the future."

"What's that supposed to mean?" I asked.

"Ah, well, it's the statistics," he said. "There are less and less children on the public dole. The district is literally running out of orphans. There's talk about shutting down the facility."

FIFTY

We left the orphanage and did some quick checking through a friend of Gibson's who worked in the university's student records department. We found out that Walker was neither bright nor brilliant. He was below par in all his studies and the dean had recommended his expulsion if he didn't straighten out, and according to the good doctor's buddy, Walker hadn't.

We decided to take a break from all the aggravation and stopped at a greasy spoon called Smelly's Deli, where we fortified our bellies with garlic sausages wrapped in cheese, onions, and pita bread before returning to the office. As we ate, LaRue entertained me with his theories on spatial dynamics in the supernatural world. I appreciated his chatter, because it helped me let go of the ghosts that cling to a person when he walks into an orphanage. My mind was off doing something else when my partner's words cut into me.

"Do you recall many runaways during your time spent at the orphanage?" he asked.

I glanced at him. "Not many. I suppose in all those years only a couple of us tried the great escape."

"A few of us? Does that include you?"

I nodded. "I was about eight or nine and I simply walked

out the front door. We had a truant officer working for the facility. I guess she knew all the places a kid would think of going, because she flushed me out after two hours on the lam. She brought me back to face Mrs. Cagney and the lesson book.''

``What was the lesson book?'' he asked, before biting into his hoagie. Processed cheese oozed out of the wrapper to plop onto his uniform.

I handed him a dirty towel while I explained. ``We were forced to learn the tenets of Saint Ophelia—all fifty-nine of them. She would then quiz us on the rules like a game-show host. Miss an answer and she got to whop you with a wooden paddle.''

LaRue winced as he chewed. ``How many hits did you take?''

``Out of fifty-nine, I got one right. The most important tenet.''

``Which was?''

``It is the task of the people to suffer.''

LaRue swallowed, shook his head knowingly, and then shoved the sandwich into his mouth.

``You know,'' I said, ``it doesn't seem possible that so many orphans are running away. They condition you from the first day to bow to authority and to not think for yourself. The facilities want control. Free-spiritedness is not condoned.'' I paused to nibble at an onion. ``Orphanages turn out the obedient drone. That's their primary function.''

LaRue smiled. ``What happened to you? You don't have one obedient drone bone in your body.''

I returned his smile. ``The ones that do are easily molded.''

``I see what you mean. What's say we have another visit with Ralph Kane?''

I agreed and we finished our lunch, polishing off our meal with strong, black coffee, so by the time we walked into the ETA building, we smelled of various strong odors. There we found Mr. Kane working alone in a cubicle that fit his desk like a cocoon. This small space didn't stop LaRue from being intimidating, because he leaned over the desk, grabbed Kane by the tie, yanked him forward, and blew his stinky breath into the slug's face.

"We think you've been holding out on us," he said.

The smell of garlic sausage must have started melting Kane's skin. His eyes watered as he desperately tried to disengage from LaRue's grip. It was nothing doing until the puke remembered his own tenet of Saint Ophelia—bow before authority. "I—I can't help you if I can't breathe," he complained.

LaRue let him go and I realized that my partner had used his strength to pull the guy out of his seat. Kane's ass hit the chair with a thump.

"Why did you have to come here?" he whispered while he adjusted his tie.

"Would you have rather been escorted out of here by a couple of hard-nosed ward cops?" LaRue demanded.

"No," he answered. "No, of course not. I don't know what you're talking about, though. I didn't hold out on you."

"We had someone do a quick database search on your name," he said. "You didn't tell us you were an orphan."

Kane frowned. "So? That's not illegal, is it?"

I almost smiled, but fought the urge, satisfied with our abilities at deduction as well as our abilities to lie.

"You were assigned to the District One facility?" LaRue said.

"Yes."

"When did you leave there?"

"What does that have to do with anything?"

"Just answer the question."

"I left when I turned eighteen."

"Why weren't you placed in the public work program?"

"Because I had a talent for math. The proprietor used me to keep the accounting books for the orphanage. When it was time to be chosen for labor in the fields, he helped me out by submitting my name as an exceptional case. It's how I managed to go to tax school. I'm telling you the truth. You can verify it if you want."

LaRue pushed his explanation away with a barking question. ‘‘When was the last time you saw Bernard Horn at the orphanage?’’

Kane frowned, but didn’t reply.

‘‘I don’t think he heard you,’’ I said.

‘‘Obviously not,’’ LaRue answered. Then, at the top his lungs, he repeated his question.

The employees swiveled in his direction and Kane cowered, hiding his face in his hands. ‘‘Please,’’ he murmured.

It was all I could do to look at this groveling excuse for a man, not because I felt shame for him, but because I felt elation that I’d managed to guard my freewill during my childhood.

‘‘Bernard Horn was around the whole time I was growing up,’’ he whispered. ‘‘The last time I saw him at the orphanage was about a month before I left for the ETA Training Academy.’’

‘‘Did Horn help you get the bump up on your labor designation?’’ I asked.

Kane raised his attention to me like he was raising a flag. ‘‘Yes, he did. He worked with the proprietor on submitting the forms to the District Council. How did you know?’’

Instead of answering his question, I strained the juice out of another possibility, hoping for a hit. ‘‘Horn also helped Purceval Walker find service suitable to his intelligence.’’

‘‘He and Purcy were close.’’

‘‘How many children did Horn help?’’

Kane shrugged. ‘‘I don’t know. Several dozen, at least.’’

‘‘When did you have your first abduction experience, Mr. Kane?’’ LaRue asked.

‘‘I was six.’’

‘‘Did you share this experience with Walker?’’

‘‘No.’’

‘‘But you told Horn about it.’’

‘‘Yes.’’

‘‘What did he say?’’

‘‘He said I was special. One of the chosen ones who will bring the new day.’’

‘‘So, he supported you in this.’’

‘‘Yes.’’

"Did you ever meet Horn's mentor, a man named Silvio Valinari?" I asked.

"No. I've heard he was a friend of Bernard's but I never met him."

"Did Horn link you to Turquoise and Dr. Fontaine?"

Kane nodded. "He told me they could help me. I was suffering from these experiences. I needed to talk to someone, to know I wasn't alone. But, honestly. I never met Turquoise. You've got to believe me."

"Do you believe your exceptional mathematical ability is a result of your abduction experience?"

"I didn't think it was. At first."

"But Horn convinced you otherwise?"

"No. Dr. Fontaine made me believe in myself. She made me explore my innermost feelings about the abduction. When she did that, I discovered I had a variety of other talents that had remained hidden."

"Such as?"

"Art, literature, and music." He pointed to a nice, if uninspired oil painting hanging on the wall behind his desk. "I did that. I also compose songs and have three-quarters of a novel finished."

My mind flitted back to Gina Nailor and her assertions about critics and the status quo of society. Kane might have talent, but more likely he had energy, desire, and drive. I stared at the painting, unable to see the creativity associated with it while LaRue hammered him with a final question.

"Did you meet Dr. Fontaine's assistant, Jenna York?"

Kane glanced at his desk. "Yes. We're acquaintances. She's an abduction victim, too."

"I got news for you, Ralph," I said. "She's a dead abduction victim now."

FIFTY-ONE

That evening we met with Julie in a back alley in Ward 2. Night had swung in on us without much notice, and when we arrived we found our watch commander sharing a bum's barrel with two homeless men. They huddled over the fire burning in the steel drum, trying to avoid the flying sparks and still stay warm. Julie greeted us with a weather report.

''There's a stiff wind from the north,'' she said. ''The carnival is going to kick off just in time. A couple more weeks and it will probably snow.''

The bums agreed with her, as did LaRue. ''It's an El Niño year,'' he said.

Julie nodded and pulled the hood up on her flimsy jacket. She then stared directly at me. ''I'm sorry I haven't been totally up-front with you. I'm trying to walk on both sides of the bridge.''

I grunted. ''Aren't we all?'' I squeezed into a space around the barrel so I could see her face by the firelight. ''I suppose we should be grateful.''

It was her turn to grunt. ''I don't expect gratitude. I'm doing what I'm doing for me, Merrick. If you and LaRue are strong enough swimmers, then you should be able to follow me no matter what way the current is running.''

"What way is the current running, Julie?"

"As far as I can tell, it's still flowing in favor of the present government. Luckily, I have friends on the trapeze who are keeping me informed. Rosebud is up to his ears on this."

The intergalactic travelers weren't the only ones who had code names. Rosebud was Graham Kanata, the sixth man of the twelve-man District Council. Kanata's purview included public funds and the overseeing of the ETA. Occasionally, he would supply the Marshals Office with information about criminals by searching closed tax records.

"Which way is Rosebud swinging?" LaRue said.

"It looks like the Sparkers are going to announce their majority presence in the government, and tell us all how entrenched they are throughout the Treasury Department. It's damned dicey. We don't know for sure how many people are in place within the bureaucratic ranks because of SoC influence, and how many were already at their jobs before being coaxed over to the power grabbers."

"What about Nichols and Carver?" I asked.

"Rosebud sent them over," she answered. "He thinks they are as crooked as the ETA calculating machines, but doesn't know exactly why. You understand how it is—one hand doesn't know what the other is doing."

"Why the bullshit?" I said. "Why do we have to report to these people?"

"Because Rosebud is hoping they might tip their hand." She sighed. "I was ordered not to give you two the heads-up. I'm violating a direct line command right now. The bigwigs think the less you know the better."

"Why are you telling us now?"

"Because I don't trust the goose steppers. I never have."

"Why are we it?" LaRue asked. "Why didn't the brass string those two onto someone else?"

"Your mental-health-test results. It was a matter of convenience. Killing two birds with one stone. If you two leap over the edge, then they have the opportunity to get rid of the deadweight."

I took a couple steps away from Julie and then turned back

to speak once my expression was hidden in the shadows. "Whose side are you on? Really?"

"On the side that signs my paycheck," she answered. "Right now I don't care who that is."

"Are they expecting a reshuffle to take place at the top of the heap?" LaRue asked.

She shrugged. "I don't see why not. The District Council is so corrupt it crackles. Maybe in the long run, it's not so bad a thing. That is if they don't take away the government's promise of a retirement pension."

FIFTY-TWO

Julie didn't have many answers for us and she left before our questions became more persistent, so LaRue dropped me off at my flat before swinging by his girlfriend's place. To my delight, I discovered Baba was spending the night with Craia and Gibson had left a note about trying to break into his clinic or something. I had the apartment all to myself.

I came in and threw my gun belt on the kitchen table. Groping by the light of the rising moon, I found a box of matches and lit a few candles, each stubby chunk of wax having been donated by Gibson. The moment I had light on the subject, I stopped my worrying for a few moments to concentrate on heating up a dented saucepan of chicken noodle soup.

Filling a mug, I strolled to the window. People clamored in the street, celebrating their newfound freedom and desire to express their creativity. Firecrackers, gunshot blasts, laughter, decadence; and everywhere you looked, you saw masks. Not a face could be seen clearly; no identities could be detected. This then was a scene from Sodom and Gomorrah, where not even God knew the names of those who partied. No one trusted this new thought. No one had any reason to.

Why should we? My situation was a case in point. The only thing I had to trust was my faith in brotherhood. I'd known

Julie a long time and she'd always gone by the book, but now? Survival in a changing world often meant chewing on someone else's liver while masking your feelings with a smile.

I had a feeling Bernard Horn had been doing exactly that.

Bazooki music filtered up from the street to charge my thoughts and make me think of Gibson again. He had the audacity to slurp soup from two spoons as well. Maybe that's why I was so attracted to him. In the midst of all the lies we tell ourselves about our supposed self-worth, we end up judging love and honor on how well that person dupes us with half-truths and kisses.

I had just set my soup mug on the table when one of my many lies hit me squarely in the face. On the outside I maintain a scientific rationale about my lycanthropy, but during those times of solitude when my supernatural interloper attacks, I find that I must silence this objectivity in favor of the theory that the wolf is a predator who uses me to gain access to the material plane.

The stretch came on so fast that I hit the floor without realizing I was falling until my chin contacted cracked linoleum. I wriggled and moaned against the growing burn, fought off a howling scream with everything I had. Again, the energy blossomed in my chest and surged through me like a dragon. I tried to take a deep breath to help me recover from the agony, but my lungs refused to work. I lay there, gasping, coughing, and praying for the end. It was then that my awareness split from my body and I escaped the torture I was enduring.

I've listened to LaRue expound on subjects such as out-of-body experiences and yogic energy, but the real thing does wonders for your understanding. I floated above me, and while still attached at some synaptic juncture in my brain, I was, nevertheless, whole, free, and able to maneuver. There was something else, too, some unseen force that seemed to buoy me up. My diaphanous self glanced around, hoping for a face-to-face meeting with the wolf, but wherever it was, it remained hidden to me except for the knowledge of its presence. So, rather than stick around to watch me writhe on the floor, I decided to take a stroll through the ceiling and out of the building.

The sensation was glorious! I'm not often impressed by these metaphysical claims, but this was the best feeling I'd ever had. I was actually having a stretch without feeling the pain.

Swimming through the atmosphere, I ascended the buildings until I floated over the district, and all the while I could feel my invisible friend accompanying me. The locality was in a shambles, but my new perspective intensified the glitter in my lycanthropic eyesight and the place actually shimmered.

It was at the next moment that I entered diamond mind. I was scraped clean by clarity and depth of vision. My understanding had a pristine quality to it, one I never wanted to give up. I literally knew the knowable, and managed to enjoy a whole ten seconds' worth of infinite wisdom before I was abruptly sucked back into my apartment and my body.

The stretch was over, and lying there panting, I sensed that I'd grown in bone and sinew. My hair felt thicker and wilder, and my hearing had a crystalline quality that reverberated against the back of my eyeballs. I had inside-out fur, a condition whereby my nerves lit up like Lizzie Borden lighting the DNA in cells. It produced an odd sensation of wearing a pelt just below my skin. Stranger than that was a new feeling overtaking me, one that I can only describe as mirth, because upon settling fully into my body, I started giggling. I heard myself doing it, and then before I knew it, I launched into full-blown laughter. It had a maniacal edge to it, but for the first time in my life the moments spent in diamond mind had made it possible for me to dip into the well of profound joy. It had also given me an idea about Bernard Horn.

FIFTY-THREE

My metabolism was supercharged from all this lycanthropic stimulation, and after soaking half a loaf of brown bread in the leftover soup, I sat on the floor to stuff the meal down my gullet. Fortified, I changed into a longer set of cammies, loaded up some firepower, and hit the street, wearing Bernard Horn's mask.

The party goers barely noticed me moving through the crowd, so intent were they on dropping coins to watch snake charmers coax cobras, psychics read crystal balls, and frustrated stage magicians claiming to be powerful sorcerers with the answers to life. I did stop a couple of times—the first, to chase along Twiddle Thumbs Harden, an infamous pickpocket who was known to be the clumsiest thief around. The second time I was waylaid was my own fault. I walked into the middle of a community polka and ended up taking a turn around the intersection with some old guy who danced better than I did.

I know, it doesn't make a damned bit of sense, this gaiety I felt, but what was the use of overanalyzing a state of lightness?

Once untangled and safely through a conclave of boozers, I reached my destination, the high-rise where Moody Mike Jackson lived. Of course, the electricity had been rotated and

I was forced to haul my ass up six flights of stairs. I found Jackson at home, his flat ablaze with candlelight and smelling wonderfully of roasting meat and pumpkin pie. Jackson took a step back when he saw me standing there in the mask, but after whipping it off to reveal my true identity, he paused to scream at his kids before inviting me to join him and his wife, Helga, for a dish of dessert.

The three of us sat in the alcove that served as the dining room. Jackson complained nonstop about all the noise coming up from the street and how people should be ashamed of themselves for their loud, obtrusive behavior. This muttering and bellyaching was the reason he'd been nicknamed Moody Mike. The fact of the matter was, he loved all the frivolity or he wouldn't have volunteered every year to organize the annual Autumn Carnival parade.

"I heard you got robbed the other day," Helga said quietly. "My condolences. How's Baba?"

"She's fine," I answered. "Thankfully, she's so hardheaded that a jackhammer couldn't split that skull of hers." I dipped into the pie and luxuriated a moment in the smell of spice before popping the bite into my mouth. Then, back to business, I glanced at Jackson. "I need your help to find a killer."

"Working during carnival, are you?" he said.

"I have no choice. If I catch this guy, I may be able to keep my job."

He nodded and ran a hand through his long snarl of blond hair. "A lot of that going around. Helga, here, got laid off at the canning factory."

"Tough break," I said. "Sorry to hear it."

"It's okay," she murmured. Helga sat back, rubbed her eyes with the heel of her hands, and then crossed her arms over her chest. "Mike thinks I'm talking treason, but, Ty, I hope to God the Sparkers get into power."

Jackson beat her with his lips. "Helga, hush. You're talking to a government employee."

"Not a problem," I said. "I'd like to see the world get a little better, too." I grabbed a quick bite and then told them the reason for my visit. "My tail is bleeding from being rubbed across a gravel road by a couple of ETA agents. LaRue and I have to score on this investigation by going around these goose steppers, and that's why I'm here. Conventional means aren't working."

Jackson grinned. I could tell by the wicked expression he wore that he was all for sticking it to the tax collectors so long as no one spoke the truth out loud.

"I checked out the carnival schedule and I see that the District One Opera Company is going to be performing and they are also going to be in the parade."

Jackson dove into his piece of pie and answered, spewing grains of crust as he did. "Goddamned opera singers! Like a bunch of whales with stubby legs. You know the district likes to haul out their vintage autos and show them off during the parade. Do you know how hard it is to fit one of those elephants in the front seat of Duvalier Classic? Them bastards can't squeeze their knees in. I told the District Council it was a bad idea, but they were heavy into promoting the arts this year."

"So, if they're such a problem, what did you do?"

"He bitched about it," Helga said. "That's all he ever does."

Jackson didn't contradict her, but instead, pulled on a sheepish look. "I made do. Seems that a lot of the singers aren't all that big."

"Have you met any of them?"

"Yeah. We had to fit them for costumes before we fit them into the seat of a Volkswagen Beetle."

"Did you work with a fellow named Bernard Horn?"

Jackson took another mouthful of pie and nodded. "He was going to be grand marshal of the parade. Damned shame about him getting murdered like that. I suppose you're looking for his killer."

"That's right."

"I didn't notice nothing odd going on."

"You wouldn't," Helga said. "You get so wrapped up in counting roses for the floats that you don't know what's going on around you." She picked at her pie and then paused to scream at one of the kids.

Jackson continued. "I remember he was a real nice guy. Polite and all. We did some sound checks and stuff, because he was also going to sing at the carnival's opening ceremonies."

"What piece of music was he going to use?"

Jackson shrugged. "It was something he wrote, so he said. I've heard it a lot lately. Someone up the line must have taken a fancy to him, because the tune is played in all the district stores. I heard it being played over at Dino's the other day. And you know him. If it ain't a person with real Italian olive oil running in his blood, then Dino swears he can't sing opera."

"It is a catchy tune," I answered.

"Horn said it was a clarion call for folks who wanted to change the world."

The moment he said it, I pulled a piece of the puzzle from the pile. "Clarion call? Do you mean that when people heard him sing this song, they were supposed to join into a cohesive group?"

Jackson shrugged. "He never did say, but I figured it was like the trumpet of Archangel Michael calling the legions to battle."

Horn had indeed forged the iron on both ends. While playing up to the ETA with talk of loyalty, he had gone underground to promote the beginning of a social revolution through the Spark of Creation Movement. I had a feeling that his clarion call was only one of many that would be echoed throughout the world at the opening of carnival. In that, Horn had been small potatoes, but someone out there may have seen this as reason enough to murder him.

FIFTY-FOUR

Not only was Horn swinging the ax back and forth, it was a good bet that his collateral activities saw him making money by minting underground recordings. He was famous throughout the district because he'd flooded the backdoor market with his music. If this was a fact, then Silvio Valinari knew about it and probably appreciated the illegal enterprise.

When I arrived at work the next day, Valinari was already being interviewed for the second time by Nichols and Carver. The old man appeared to be putting up a good fight, and after watching the concert for forty-five minutes, LaRue decided we should join the conversation. We stalked into the interrogation room, my partner announced our intentions, and then we all stood there staring at each other until Carver finally gave us a curt nod. I glared at Nichols, and for once, the tax collector had an attack of good sense and reluctantly backed off.

We crossed the room to the table and climbed onto our chairs. I glanced at Carver before turning to Valinari. "I suggest you take a moment to listen up, since the ETA is floating its goiter in this mess."

Neither agent said a word, but instead crawled into the shadows. I paused to yank the battered light fixture down over the table and then took a moment to study the maestro. He looked like he'd been chucked in the "preacher's hole"—a tiny, concrete closet in the office lockup designed to keep unruly patrons out of sight. This lounging area wasn't big enough to lie down in and the air grew so rank from the lack of circulation most prisoners huddled at the crack under the door, hoping for a breath of fresh air. My mind flicked to my childhood, the punishment pen, and a particularly hot day. If I hadn't earned my claustrophobia, no one had.

"Is this prisoner getting proper treatment?" I barked.

Nichols shrugged. "What kind of treatment does a subversive deserve?"

"You got that from the horse's mouth, did you?"

She glanced at Valinari, moved her lips to say something, but then changed her mind. Shaking her head, she trucked off to the shadows with her sleaze partner.

I turned to LaRue. "Andy, this man could use some water. Would you be so kind as to pour him a cup?"

Valinari closed his eyes and relaxed for a few moments until LaRue returned with the glass and handed it to me. By that time I had the maestro's attention and I used it. Holding the water out to him, I charged the gift with a little electricity. "The voice is an important thing, isn't it? So important and so fragile. I mean look what the lack of liquid does to a person? It dries the throat and takes the spring out of the vocal cords. Tell us, Silvio. What part did you play in Bernard Horn's backdoor recording studio? Were you general manager, perhaps?"

His nostrils flared and he tried to swallow, but I could tell there was no saliva to help his tongue out, so I gave him the prize. He bolted the water in three gulps and then looked longingly at the empty glass.

"Answer my question," I said quietly.

Valinari nodded. "It's true, we were making money under the table. Bernard would record the tapes and I would find ways to distribute them."

I smiled, picked up the glass, and gave it back to LaRue. "Andy, would you help us out again?"

My partner left the room without a word, snagging Nichols and Carver on his way out. After a momentary tussle between the three, we had the place to ourselves. I began immediately, keeping my tone as flat and impersonal as possible. "When I first heard this music, I was attracted to the tones played before each song. The sound stuck in my head. For almost a week my partner and I have been thinking that what we have here is a SoC plot involving subliminal manipulation. We've run the road around this subject, and then last night I was told that Bernard Horn was planning to deliver the clarion call during carnival, the one song that would announce the beginning of the new order. This particular confession bothered me all evening until I figured out exactly what was happening here."

"And what would that be?" Valinari croaked.

"Well, let's see. According to a gifted neurologist I know, subliminal applications are pretty pooey. They don't work without hypnosis, and then it's iffy. And if there's one thing I know about hypnosis it's this: without regular reinforcement sessions, the hypnotic influence begins to wear off. People who are hypnotized to stop smoking often go right back to a pack a day without the help of their mesmerist." I paused, gave him a second to digest this information, and watched his expression grow hooded and dark. When it baked into the perfect scowl, I continued. "Since I understand all this, I began to think that those tones at the beginning of the songs were for something else altogether."

He shook his head, but didn't speak.

"Come on, Silvio. Give us the truth. Those tones were a code to the leaders of the SoC. Every time a song was played that had those tones preceding it, the Sparkers sat up and listened. Didn't they?"

When he didn't answer, I growled. "Didn't they?"

My forcefulness was enough to dislodge a nod from him. "Yes," he husked. "It's the way the SoC sends messages to the members. But the message wasn't the song that Bernard recorded."

"It wasn't?"

"No. The message was contained in whatever song was played previously to the tones and Bernard's musical recording."

"Who are the leaders of the SoC?"

"I don't know," he answered. "Honestly."

LaRue marched back in the room and interrupted the dialogue by cursing out the ETA agents before placing the glass on the table and sitting down. Valinari reached for the glass, but using my lycanthropic speed, I snatched it from his reach.

"Who are the leaders of the SoC?"

"I told you I don't know," he snapped. "I have always received my orders by telephone and my contact never identifies himself. I was told where to deliver the recordings and then someone would push an envelope of cash credits beneath the front door of Bernard's apartment after distribution. That's all I know, Marshal. You've got to believe me. I was in it for the money, not some ideology. I mean, what difference does it make, anyhow? I'm a nobody, like a million nobodies out there. If the SoC does gain power and there's a purge, then I'm one who they'll steamroll. I don't have my doubts about the corruption in any government, no matter how lofty the talk."

"Did you convince Horn to trust the SoC?" LaRue asked.

"Bernard didn't trust anyone," he said.

"Why not?"

"Because he was an orphan. It colored his view of the world. I didn't convince him that being a Sparker was better than being a humanitarian."

"What was he doing with the children?"

"The children? What children?"

"The ones that kept coming up missing?"

Valinari had one of those faces—heavy and wrinkled—the kind that devolved with a mere frown into a simian equivalent. "I don't know what you're talking about."

"Let me refresh your memory," LaRue said. "We think Horn was responsible for snatching a variety of kids. He may have been working with the likes of our goose steppers in the other room. Now do you recall?"

He shook his head. "I know Bernard was working for the ETA. We all are. What he did? That I can't say."

"All right, an easier question. What was Horn's relationship with Purceval Walker? The real relationship?"

"Do you think I followed Bernard around like a dog?" Valinari asked. "He did have his own life."

"Of which you were a very big part." LaRue took the glass from me and waved it under the maestro's nose. "This may be the last water you get until we're done with this investigation. If we don't get the cooperation we need, you could die of dehydration."

Valinari studied LaRue and then conceded with a sorrowful nod and a long sigh before explaining. "Purcy is a bad boy. He's an idiot, too. I don't know what Bernard ever saw in him. Maybe nothing more than a willing flunky. Whatever it was, he was a dangerous young man."

"He's been missing since Horn's murder," LaRue said, leaning in. "Admit it, Valinari. You killed them both."

The man almost lost control of his bowels. "I swear I had nothing to do with this," he sputtered.

"Shall we talk about a plausible motive?" LaRue asked.

I joined in. "For years you tried to sway Horn to the SoC, but he couldn't be swayed, except for the petty stuff that earned him money. And then one day Horn had enough of you and enough of the ETA and decided to strike out on his own, playing this deal against that one until both the humanitarians and the Sparkers alike thought he was a dangerous commodity to have around."

"I didn't kill anyone," he snarled.

I leaned toward him. "You see, Silvio, it's this way. We may not be able to bring you down with the letter of the law, but being marshals, we can go around you. We're not embarrassed about trumping up charges if it bags a warm body."

He stared at me and I saw hatred in his eyes. "I'm to be that warm body."

"Not necessarily. You talk to us and maybe we can come to some understanding and agreement."

There were several moments when I thought I'd have to jump mean on the old boy, but in the end he must have seen the wisdom in what I was saying. "I don't know what Bernard was doing, exactly," he answered. "He treated Walker like gold. In fact, he's the one who nicknamed him Turquoise."

"How did he come up with that?"

"The bunk rooms at the orphanage are given names after gemstones. Turquoise, topaz, amethyst. Walker was Turquoise One. When Bernard lived there, that had been his designation."

Valinari tested his tenuous position by motioning for the water. LaRue gave it to him and we waited until he'd slugged the contents.

"Bernard spent more time than he should have with Purcy," he reported. "He was starting to neglect his music for Walker. A shameful disregard of talent."

"Did Bernard ever tell you that Walker had an abduction experience?"

He thought a moment. "He made mention of it. I blew him off, though. That stuff is just nonsense. I don't believe Bernard had a shred more talent after his claim than before. It was that it gave him something extraordinary to apply to his life. You know, help from on high; a source outside himself that he could draw creativity from." He shrugged. "I suppose it was the best he could hope for. Orphanages make a mess out of people's egos."

"Myra Fontaine thought this change in Horn was significant."

Valinari snorted. "So? Just another shrink feeding on the woes of the less fortunate."

"She and Horn were close," I said.

He hesitated but coughed up the answer. "She and Bernard were lovers."

Fontaine hadn't seemed very broken up about Horn's death. "Are you sure?"

"Yeah. She had a child by him."

"Myra?" I said. "When?"

"About ten years ago. Little boy."

"What happened to him?"

Valinari shook his head. "One day he came up missing."

FIFTY-FIVE

I just couldn't shake the questions I had about the mine and the hidden levels, so after we squeezed Valinari, we gave him back to Nichols and Carver before returning to the PHO facility. During the trip over I made LaRue promise not to tell Gibson I'd gone back into the mine.

"Well, what if the radio-dirium affects you and you start to act funny?" he asked.

"If I start to act funny and can't handle it, I release you from your promise," I answered. "There. If I die from extraterrestrial bacteria, it won't be on your conscience."

He grinned, gunning the Trabi to narrowly miss a district transport loaded with coal. "That certainly makes me feel better. But really. If we get in the mine and you feel strange or anything, please tell me."

"I will." With that, I tried to lapse into a moody silence, but my partner was having none of it. "Do you think Myra and Bernard were tapping the till at the orphanage until it looked like things were going to run dry?"

"I think the orphans make good drones, Andy. They may have enough worker bees and need some overseers."

"The kids they're swiping from family units."

"Yeah. Derry said his brat was intelligent. They may need

to sweeten the pile.'' I paused, glanced out the window and then surprised my partner by giving him a history lesson. ''You know, Andy, the Spartans of ancient Greece used to take the sons from their family units at a very young age, anywhere from two to six years old. They would place them in a facility that was segregated from the populace, and there, they were suckled, trained, and turned into perfect citizens, people who had loyalty to the state and not to any family ties.''

''When the government feeds, clothes, and pacifies, it's hard not to show loyalty,'' he said.

''Yes. Mother and father.'' With that, I finally shut my mouth and got some thinking done.

I could see how Fontaine could have set up someone to be killed, but she wouldn't have gotten her fingers dirty by committing the act herself. The fact that her nurse had access to the facility placed the legitimate blame on Jenna York, and then the nurse was killed to be silenced. It seemed like a pat scenario, but if I knew anything, it was that I always managed to find the jagged piece of the puzzle.

Before I could continue riding my thoughts, LaRue floored me with a confession. ''I was abducted as a child, Ty.''

I turned to stare at him. He kept his eyes straight ahead, and despite his attention to the road, he still slammed into a pothole. ''What happened?''

''I was seven years old,'' he answered. ''I was in a grimy side alley near my apartment building, playing bocci ball with the neighborhood kids. I'd won the game and stayed behind to pick up the coins we used. Even though I knew better, I'd lingered too long and I was alone when a man wearing a black coat and hat came down the alley. He told me he had a job for me and that I would be paid if I came along with him. I asked him what kind of work he wanted me to do. He told me he wanted me to take a nap and that was all.'' He stopped to wet his lips. Then: ''The bastard chloroformed me, Ty. The next thing I remember is waking up three days later in another alley six miles from my home.''

''Do you remember anything about the three days?''

LaRue swallowed. ''I remember taking a loyalty oath.''

''A what?''

"You heard me. For some reason, I have a fuzzy recollection about swearing to uphold the values of Duvalier's humanitarian society. You know the speech. We took it when we became marshals."

"Were you hurt?"

"No, not that I could ever tell. When I came to, I checked my pants pocket and I found a fifty credit note."

"So, they really did pay you?"

He frowned. "Yeah, but what did I do to earn it?"

I shook my head. "Maybe you got a diaphanous insert and became more creative."

LaRue glanced at me and frowned. Seeing it, I realized he was laying his heart bare and I had made a callous joke.

I sat back, scrunching down into the hole that my butt had made in the cheap seat over the years. "So, tell me, did your mom beat the crap out of you for making them worry?"

"Are you kidding?" he asked. "I told her I had the opportunity to fill in on a public training project and made the decision to do it on the spot. Since I was picking strawberries and sleeping under the stars a million miles from a phone, I couldn't call."

"And she bought that?"

"Not until after I showed her the money."

"I take it you had steak for dinner that night," I said.

"It was always chicken with my mother," he answered as he spun around a hairpin turn in the road. His heavy foot and marginal driving skills made the car fishtail, but he ignored the probability that we might crash to open his mouth. "I do remember the incident like it was yesterday, though. We had chicken and pear sauce. Uncle Pierre got drunk on homemade red wine; Aunt Lucia tried to kill us with escargots that she raised in washtubs of dirt in the backyard; and my father just kept staring at me with a funny expression on his face."

"Why?"

"I never found out, Ty. The next day he died in an accident on the job."

"What happened?" I asked softly.

"He worked at the district airport fixing the food transport planes. I guess he was nursing a hangover or something and wasn't being careful. He was chewed up by a jet engine."

I was almost hesitant to ask this next question, but tact is not a biggy with me, so I did. "Do you think there is a connection between your experience and his death?"

"Yes," he said. "A few years after his passing, my mother mentioned that my old man knew I hadn't gotten the credits from working in the fields, simply because it was too much money. She said he blamed himself for my problems."

"In what way?"

He shook his head. "I don't know. After hearing some of these confessions lately, I wonder if he had a tax problem. I know the revenuers came in and busted his still. That would have been enough to get him into considerable trouble." LaRue sighed as we went airborne over a dip in the street. "We French Canadians are a tight-lipped bunch of folks. If my dad had trouble, my mom would never admit it. Not to anyone."

FIFTY-SIX

This investigation was a little like pulling off your skin and shaking it out to get rid of the itches. Something was moving right below the surface, and had been, possibly for a long time. The problem was that no matter how we jiggled the junk, we kept getting invisible answers—circumstantial evidence stretched into the realm of implausibility. More than ever, I discounted all the stories about alien abductions, even my own.

When we arrived at the PHO facility, we immediately went to the reception desk. A pretty, young woman dressed in a dark blue uniform greeted us with a pleasant smile, and in the moment it took for us to saunter up to the desk, she'd settled her sights on LaRue.

"Hello, Marshal," she said, in a sultry voice.

My partner animated. "Ah, Vida, the love of my life."

"I thought Conchita the Tarot Reader was the love of your life," I whispered.

"Not now, Ty," he murmured, without removing the smile from his lips.

I shrugged and hung back to let him use the most creative part of his body—his mouth. He leaned on the desk to charm the fair maiden.

"Vida, my dear, you are always here when we come. Don't they ever let you take a day off?"

She smiled and sighed sweetly, pushing at the ends of her bleached-out tresses. "Well, we're short-handed. I do what I can."

LaRue nodded and then made sure he openly inspected the tilt of her big boobs. "And you volunteer your time, too?"

Vida's smile slipped a bit. I wondered if she had volunteered the same way Jenna York had. It would have been interesting to find out, but time was of the essence and we needed a permission slip. We couldn't wait to go through official channels or to get cozy.

LaRue rolled on. "All this time devoted to a cause of healing the ill. Now, that's what it means to be a humanitarian."

Her smile returned. "Well, look at you, Marshal. You're always on duty, too, helping to bring murder victims to their justice."

I was starting to feel the bullshit pile up around our feet. It was still another five minutes before LaRue finally stopped sucking wind and got to the point.

"I was wondering if you could help us with this investigation," he said. "We need to see the sign-in sheets for the last couple of weeks."

Vida leaned forward and spoke in a conspiratorial tone. "Do you think the murderer is on the staff?"

LaRue adjusted the space between them by caressing the top of her hand with his forefinger. "Yes," he answered. "I'd hate to see you in any danger from this maniac."

She watched his finger for a moment before she glanced at his face. "I'm not supposed to give out those records."

"Vida," LaRue cooed, "this guy has murdered two people by doing something hideous to their spines. He's got serial killer written all over him. Our job is to find out why he's doing this, and if we can, we'll bring him to justice." He paused. "Remember justice?"

"Yes, but my supervisor gave me orders," she said. "I'd like to help. Really I would. I just don't want to get into trouble. There's been enough of that lately."

"Our killer could be any number of people, Vida," LaRue

said. "It could be someone you'd never expect. As sweet as your are, you must have a lot of friends on the staff and I know you wouldn't want to see anyone else die." He stopped cooing and proved his creativity yet again by switching gears in an attempt to sway her onto a more personal basis. "Now admit it," he said gently. "You're so popular I don't have a chance to get a date with you."

"Not true," she trilled. "In fact, I'll write down my telephone number. Call me and you'll be pleasantly surprised."

"No doubt. But to tell you the truth, if we've got to go through channels to see those files, you may not be around for me to call."

That did it. The trollop hoisted over a black, spiral-bound notebook and then let us go into the deserted break room to look at it. Someone had brewed a fresh pot of coffee at the breakfast bar, and so while LaRue made himself comfortable on the leatherette sofa and thumbed through the pages, I poured a couple of eye-openers before snagging a bear claw from a box sitting on the counter.

I handed LaRue his coffee, took a big bite out of the doughnut, and passed it to him. Sitting down, I glanced over his shoulder at the book. "Anything jump out at you?"

"Yeah. There are a few people on this list whose names are computer-generated."

"Show me."

He pointed with his pinkie, but instead of speaking, he ate the rest of the bear claw.

It didn't need much explanation as it was what we'd expected. The file was set up on a grid with several columns—each space filled in with ID, access, and room numbers. Within this format, there was a designated place for the entrant to sign in, but in this case, this section had been crossed through with the word "auxiliary" stamped upon it.

"There's another way into this place," I said.

LaRue finished fighting the bear claw by taking a big swallow. "And it would appear that Nurse Addison comes in that way all the time."

FIFTY-SEVEN

We found Nurse Addison hard at work in her stone vault deep in the mine. When we peeped into her cubicle, she glanced up, hawkishly focusing on us over her Ben Franklin reading glasses.

"Yes, what is it?" she asked sharply.

"We need a moment of your time," I said. Sliding into the room, I stopped before her desk and placed the registration book in front of her.

She stared at me with a frown, but then readjusted her specs to study the ledger. "Yes, so?"

"Why don't you have to check into this facility like normal folks?" I asked.

"Because I use the auxiliary entrance," she answered. "Part of my job is to keep the keys."

"Show us the way to this entrance, please."

Addison rose stiffly, patting down the wrinkles in her linen skirt. "What's the problem?"

"We have a number of them. The first one has to do with the fact that we were told no one enters or leaves this place without signing in or out."

Her response was so chilly, it frosted her lips. "Well, that's not entirely correct, then, is it?"

"We have plans of the mine and this auxiliary entrance doesn't appear," LaRue said.

"Perhaps you have old plans," she answered. "This entrance was constructed within the last twenty years."

"Why?"

"Government regulations. We needed an emergency exit. I come in this way to make sure everything is in working order. You never know when the district fire inspector will show up."

She led us down a dark corridor, lighting our way by sections until we reached an open elevator similar to the one sliding up and down at the main entrance. "This is how you get to the surface."

"Who else uses this access?"

"Service workers, mostly. It's not for the general public unless there is a need."

"Are there service workers on duty?" LaRue said.

"No, not a regular staff. That costs too much. When the machinery needs maintenance, they call in the workmen."

"Where does this thing come out topside?" I asked.

"The elevator shaft runs vertically and horizontally. It comes up in a secluded place within the university grounds."

I punched LaRue with a look. He nodded before throwing another question at her. "Are there any sublevels on this side?"

Addison shrugged. "There are service shafts along the horizontal route the elevator takes. You can stop the car at various points along the way and access the heavy-equipment rooms. Having it along the elevator shaft makes it easier to bring in new equipment when something fails. I understand this is a problem that keeps getting worse now that the machinery is getting old." She stopped speaking to fish into her skirt pocket, and produced a set of keys. "If there's a sublevel, you can probably get to it by one of these. That is, if you want to go on some dark adventure." Pointing to the floor, she brought our attention to a red strip of tape running down the wall. "This is the trail to your treasure map, Marshals. Keep the strip on your right side and you'll eventually end up back on the corridor where I have my office. Please stop in to leave me the keys before you depart.'' With that, she turned on her squeaky nurse's shoe and marched away into the shadows.

We decided to burn the electric at the district's expense and turned on all the lights in the area. It didn't do much to chase away the gloom, but it did give us time to focus our thoughts. Entering the elevator, I spoke one of those meanderings out loud. ''I heard machinery when we were digging around after York's lost shoe. It sounded like the hum of a transformer.''

LaRue grunted, placed the key into the control panel, and started the car. ''Look for any doors or passages marked electrical room or substation.''

We rose slowly, stopping only when the elevator shifted to the horizontal plane. After traveling several feet, LaRue stopped the car, and rolling back the cage, we peeped down the dark tunnel. The beams of our service lanterns picked up the glitter of fool's gold and not much else. Satisfied that there were no entrances within this sector, we moved on.

We did this three times, coming up empty, but during the fourth try we found a single passage. My claustrophobia had kicked up, and despite my desire to stay where there was light and circulating air, I followed my partner so he wouldn't know I was busy dipping into my personal handbag of neuroses.

As we traced the corridor we used our flashlights instead of turning on the overheads. This was a precaution in case we happened to hit Lady Luck bending over far enough to show us her underwear, but LaRue started chattering about people from the center of the earth and any element of surprise we had was lost to his impromptu lecture. If we came across the killer, my partner would have to flog him with his wits, because he'd hear us coming and surely defend his territory. I finally told LaRue to hush when we came to a doorway marked EQUIPMENT ROOM B. I had no idea where the hell Equipment Room A was, but since this was the first egress we'd come across, I started trying keys. After sixteen attempts, I was ready to bust down the door. Thankfully, number seventeen was the answer we needed.

The door sprang open and the rusty latches screamed like they were having babies. LaRue aimed his beam just inside, found the light switch, and bathed the room in a green glow.

I felt my heart flutter and realized this would not be a good place to have a stretch. It was a low-ceilinged, stone vault decorated with a metal table. On the far side of this room, there was another door, and here our hike bogged down. Although I had the added advantage of my lycanthropic strength, it took us a couple minutes to batter open this entrance and to find ourselves in a corridor that traveled at a gentle, upward slope. Along the way we passed a series of transformer rooms, and glancing inside, we found the electric mammoths humming nicely.

Finally, after we'd started huffing and puffing from the uphill climb, we came to a topside exit. This door was a trifle easier to open, though we didn't have the key on the ring. LaRue was forced to pop out his handy-dandy breaking-and-entering kit, and after fumbling for a few minutes, he jimmied the lock and away we went.

Much to our surprise, the shaft opened into a dilapidated roundhouse at the District Train Yard.

FIFTY-EIGHT

We saw a tall, wiry man, naked to the waist, monkeying over an enormous diesel engine. He was bald, covered in black grease, and swinging a six-foot torque wrench like he was adjusting a watch instead of screwing down bolts the size of my fist.

We kicked the door shut and the noise grabbed his attention. He glanced our way and waved before he forgot his wrench and came to greet us.

"I wasn't expecting another shipment," he said. "The train ain't ready for another turn up the pike."

LaRue immediately fell on his creative talent and started talking. "We're brand-new on this run. We were told to come here and have you give us the info we need."

"Me?" he asked incredulously. "Who told you to do that?"

"Turquoise."

The man frowned and stared at us suspiciously. "That don't seem like him."

LaRue broke the tension by extending his hand. "I'm Andy, and this is Ty," he said.

The guy gave us the once-over but then smiled slightly and offered his own introduction. "I'm called Zack." We shook hands and he continued. "Why is Turquoise suddenly calling the shots?"

"Because Bernard Horn is dead," LaRue lied.

Zack nodded and wet his flabby lips with the tip of his tongue. "That there was a damned shame." He paused and fumbled through his shirt pocket for an illegal cigarette. Finding a half-smoked stub, he placed it in his mouth before lighting it with a brass flint nicker. Taking a puff, he used the moment to further size us up. Then: "So, you're the new baby-sitters? What happened to Nichols and Carver."

Upon hearing their names, LaRue almost lost his boondoggle, but he returned to character with alarming dexterity. "They're busy rounding up the new load of children."

The man grunted. "There can't be a waif left on the street after those two get done. I suspect they're stealing them from their parents now."

"How many times have they and Turquoise been through here?"

"Every time the big boys at the ETA tell them to. Which is a lot. We had three runs last month alone. It don't pay that well, but it's regular income."

"How many kids are we going to have to ride with?"

"Probably twenty or thirty. If they get out of hand, just pop 'em good and hard. They'll shut up." He pulled another puff and mused for a bit. "Of course, if Nichols and Carver are busy, it might be a bigger load. You can never tell. The more kids delivered, the more money. That might be the reason they wanted you for this run. I know they wanted to get it in during the full moon."

"Why?" I asked.

"Because it's a big day for the carnival. Makes for good cover, I suppose."

LaRue took a step toward the man, warming the space between them with a cozy voice. "So, tell me. They're taking them to work in the mines in District 24, right?"

The man guffawed, going beet red under his greasepaint. "Who told you that shit? Turquoise, I'll bet. Now that sounds like him. He's full of crap."

"Where do they take them?" I asked.

He studied me before answering. "They take them to a real nice government center, where they turn them into useful citizens." As though done with this conversation, he dropped the subject, finished his cigarette, and returned to his torque wrench. We followed him.

LaRue kept up the casual act by leaning on the engine. "Do you think Turquoise is old enough to be running the operation?"

The guy shook his head. "Turquoise is bad. He's mean and nasty to the children. Ain't no cause for the treatment he gives 'em." He leaned toward LaRue, but still spoke in a loud voice. "He likes the little girls."

"I thought the ETA didn't want any soiled goods?"

He blew off LaRue's question. "I guess it don't matter none. They fix 'em up."

"Fix them up?"

"Yeah, treat 'em right. Put 'em in school and stuff. Tell 'em how to think. That's what's wrong with society today. Folks don't think right. They think about how to cheat the next guy out of his money or his wife or his property."

"But the orphanages and their parents should be assuming that responsibility. Why is the government funding additional efforts?"

He shrugged. "I don't know, and if you have any good sense, you won't ask either." He picked up his wrench and then cursed softly. "I knew when I heard about Horn's death that things were going to get dicey. I hope you two can keep Turquoise in control."

"He's a real high-strung sort of guy, huh?"

"That's for a fact. Horn could control him, but just barely. I don't know why the boss brought him in on this deal."

"Mr. Horn was the boss?"

"Yes. Had been for years. Did a deal with the ETA two decades ago, at least."

LaRue snuggled into the conversation. "So, how much did the bastard get?"

Zack chuckled. "From what I hear, he bagged a cool million credits."

LaRue whistled. ‘‘Damn. We’re not getting a hundred credits apiece for this gig.’’

‘‘Me, neither, partner. Me, neither.’’

‘‘Well, then, what we hear is not true.’’

‘‘Depends on what you heard.’’

‘‘That Mr. Horn had gone over to the SoC and was going to rat publicly on the ETA.’’

Zack was silent for a moment, as though he weighed some heavy matter contained within LaRue’s statement. Finally, he spoke. ‘‘Everything would have been fine if he hadn’t started dating that fat opera singer. It was her fault. She got him involved with that trash. At least, that’s the rumor Turquoise spread around.’’

‘‘Did this upset Turquoise?’’

‘‘Did it upset him?’’ he crowed. ‘‘I’ll say it did. He hated the Sparkers and he hated Horn for flipping sides.’’

FIFTY-NINE

Imagine four hundred pounds of quivering, weeping woman. That is exactly how we found Betty Victoria Reseda when we returned to her house to get some straight answers. Her mother was with her, a tiny slip of a woman who had a small voice but a large temper. She greeted us with antagonism even as she tried to calm down her blubbering daughter.

"What do you want?" she demanded, before cooing to her overgrown baby.

"Your daughter may be an accessory to murder," LaRue said.

Upon hearing his statement, our opera singer started sobbing and her mother was caught answering our challenge. "This woman is a loyal citizen. She's a humanitarian. She would never help someone to commit such a dastardly act."

Reseda nodded furiously, but her bubbly reply wasn't what we expected. "It's all my fault," she wailed. "I was the one who started it all."

"Betty!" her mother snapped. "That is utter nonsense. You're just upset over Bernard."

"No. It's my fault." She sniffed, swallowed, and waved the woman away. After drying her eyes, she turned her attention onto me. "I'll tell you what you want to know. I thought I could keep a secret, but I can't. I can't."

I didn't leave her a moment to change her mind. "Did you know that Horn was illegally transporting children?"

"Illegally?" she warbled. "No. He did it for the ETA. He had government sanction." Dabbing her eyes with a handkerchief, she explained. "Bernard was a humanitarian. He did what he had to do. Everyone does."

"What is happening to the children?"

"I think the ETA is experimenting with them."

"How so? Are they going to set them all up as baby bookkeepers?"

"Bernard told me they turned them into productive citizens."

"How?"

"I'm not sure, but Bernard said they needed a steady flow of children. A new delivery every few months. But lately, it's been every few weeks."

"Why has it increased?"

"Purceval Walker. He said he could supply the ETA with the children they needed, and of course, the government saw a solution to their problem." She craned her neck toward us and spoke conspiratorially. "I think he was stealing some of the children out of the university research clinic."

"And Horn went along with him in this?"

"At first. He made additional money with every child he provided."

"But?"

"But I got in the way. I introduced him to the SoC Movement."

"How did this get in the way?"

"He started coming to our meetings. He started seeing how things could be. He realized he was hurting innocent, young people and that it wasn't necessary to give in to the demands of the government."

"Betty!" her mother scolded. "You don't have to tell them this."

"Yes, I do!" she bellowed.

"So, Horn became more and more involved with the Sparkers, and his friends and associates were not happy about it,'' I said. ''Especially Walker.''

She nodded and sniffed.

''Did you ever meet a psychiatrist by the name of Myra Fontaine?''

''Yes. I couldn't stand that woman. Her voice drove me crazy!''

I could agree with her there. ''Is Silvio Valinari involved in any of these activities?''

''Silvio is not interested in movements; only the potential of a person's voice.''

''Did he help Horn collect children?''

''No. He didn't want anything to do with it and he kept his nose clean.''

''Was Horn going to denounce the ETA publicly during the carnival?''

''Yes. It was supposed to be his moment of freedom. He kept saying it was the first time in his life that he'd had a choice to make the world a better place.'' She took a moment to cough before adding: ''You have to believe me—I don't know who killed him.''

I pulled out the mask that we'd found at the crime scene. ''Do you know anything at all about this mask? It was discovered in Horn's personal effects at the PHO Rejuvenation Facility.''

She stared at it, then shook her head as she gave us an answer. ''Those who are active in the SoC were each given one. We were going to wear them during the height of the carnival to show our allegiance to the effort.''

''Is that all?''

She hesitated.

''We need to know, Ms. Reseda,'' I said sharply.

''It was so we could tell each other apart,'' she answered. ''During the revolution.''

SIXTY

It was time for us to corner Nichols and Carver, so we waited in the shadows behind the Marshals Office that evening. When the goose steppers came outside, we nabbed them. LaRue grabbed Carver, and though he was a head taller than my partner, LaRue proved to have his own supernatural strength on which to draw. He threw Carver against the brick wall and disarmed him before his opponent could do more than grunt. I followed suit to energetically give Nichols the what-fors, and together we did a kung fu dance that saw me nearly knock her block off. LaRue passed me an impatient look that the dim light did nothing to hide, but I ignored it to drag the bootlicker over to her slimy companion.

Marshals and ward cops came and went, ignoring the altercation, the conversation, and the fact that we held these bastards at gunpoint.

''You've signed your own death warrant,'' Nichols spit.

''Yeah, yeah, yeah,'' I answered. ''Start talking or you'll find yourselves a couple of ghosts looking down at your bloated, white bodies floating gently in the muddy current of the Black River.''

They stared at us, defiant, until LaRue pushed the barrel of his revolver into Carver's ear. ''The wind will be blowing through your brain in about thirty seconds.'' He squirmed and LaRue moved with him, but it was Nichols who answered.

''I'm sure by now the great Merrick and LaRue have put together the story.''

''Confirm our suspicions, if you please. Why the hell are you working out of the Marshals Office?''

''Because sometimes we need to investigate the investigators,'' Carver said. ''You should know by now that the ETA has district jurisdiction. We can go anywhere.'' He wiggled a little more and then cleared his throat. ''The ETA had an arrangement with Horn and we knew that no one on our government team had killed him. We also knew Merrick, here, was involved in the Society of Intergalactic Travelers, a group we figure is close to the SoC and giving them money to fund their illegal activities.''

''The Intergalactic Travelers is a scam,'' I growled. ''Roscoe Turner isn't giving anyone money.''

''Don't be so sure. Roscoe Turner is a liar, too.''

''Speaking of scams,'' LaRue said, ''what kind of boondoggle is the ETA running? What are you doing with the kids you're nabbing?''

Carver glanced at Nichols and they exchanged some form of telepathic information that partners get so good at. LaRue noticed their transmission and pressed on the gun. ''We know you're shipping them off to a facility in the northern districts. Why?''

Nichols clenched her teeth. ''Reeducation.''

''Oh, reeducation,'' I said. ''What did you do—surgically implant electronic gear into their brains so they would do the bidding of the government?''

''Surgically implanted electronics?'' Nichols said. She chuckled darkly. ''That would cost too much.''

''Then why the abduction scenarios?''

''It's complicated.''

''We've got time.''

Carver finally got a little oomph and yanked from LaRue's grip. He turned savagely on my partner, but instead of attacking, he stood there with hands on hips.

Nichols blew a hard breath and then launched into the impossible story. "The SoC has been around for more than three decades and in all that time the government has been relying on covert activities to keep them in check."

"Reeducation being a covert activity?" I demanded.

"Yes, children who met certain criteria were taken to orientation centers maintained by the PHO and ETA. Here, they were retrained."

"The goddamned loyalty oath!" LaRue snarled. "By Saint Ophelia's frilly knickers. You bastards are ensuring the status quo by brainwashing people."

"What would you have the government do?" Nichols asked. "This whole thing escalated a few years ago. The SoC was gaining momentum and they were using a new technique of brain technology. People we'd already secured were starting to sway toward the Sparkers. We faced a civil war, and now, this week, we'll find out if what we did will save the world or transform it." She stopped to sneer. "What's the problem, Marshals? From what we can tell, your programming is still in place. You're loyal to the government, and in the end you'll defend it as hard as we will when the time comes." She laughed. "Do you see the beauty in this?"

I was beginning to. "Did the SoC spend all those years dishing out their brand of brainwashing?"

"Oh, sure. Who do you think was responsible for the explosion of magical beliefs and superstitions? For a long time the humanitarians were just staying even with the Sparkers."

"But then?"

"But then, technology changed."

"What's that supposed to mean?" LaRue asked.

"It means that if the SoC got to a kid first, they made sure they fixed him so it would be impossible to countermand the programming."

"How did they do that?"

"We don't know the particulars," Carver barked. "We do know that once a kid hit seven years old, something changed in the brain that allowed the SoC to use the process they'd developed. If we got to the kid before he turned seven, then we had a chance to apply our methods. If the Sparkers beat us to the punch, the kid would take our programming, and then die."

"What happened?" I asked. "Did the Sparkers up the ante again?"

"Yes, they did. More new technology. They could countermand our programming if they got to the child before he reached puberty."

"So, you're taking the children and hiding them away until they are safely past the age when the SoC finds it financially feasible to program people."

Nichols nodded. "It's expensive, but it's the only way the humanitarians can hold on to power."

"Once successfully converted, you then began to place these young adults into government positions," I said.

"Not all of them, mind you. The orphans—well, let's face it—you are one of the rare ones, Marshal Merrick. Our government needs cheap labor, so these children are programmed not to form lasting, sound relationships. They are usually cold and distant, and as expected, obedient. It's what makes a functional worker."

I heard her words and suddenly my brain puckered. A thousand curses and a thousand threats of revenge exploded in my thoughts, but at the end of this hullabaloo, I was not choked up by my indignation and resignation. My next question was the one that had been on my mind since I started hearing this shit. "Orphans are wards of the district. Why didn't you just keep them in the facilities? Why the whole abduction scenario?"

"A couple of reasons," Carver answered. "But for now, let's just say the enemy had infiltrated the farms. Covert maneuvers were required to ferret out the children who would have potential. There are conversion processes which require several stages of application."

I shivered, but did my best not to show it. "So, you sent in people like Silvio Valinari and Bernard Horn to find the kids who displayed promise and who were susceptible to the whole routine. I'll bet they tracked the process of children who'd already had their brains diddled with, too."

"Yes." He stopped to stare at me. "Don't be so appalled

by it, Merrick. Our government is made up, layer upon layer, with secrets, and there are bureaucrats whose job descriptions include thinking of insane ways to spend taxpayers money. Do you actually think they would work outside of the need-to-know network and tell schmucks like you and me the reason behind the orders?''

''What specifically did they do to the orphans?'' I growled.

He shook his head. ''Need-to-know, Merrick. Nichols and I aren't on the list. We only enforce the orders.''

''How does Myra Fontaine figure into all this?'' LaRue asked.

''She wasn't a willing volunteer, if that's what you think. The government uses the ETA records to provide quality children for reeducation. Orphans are fine, but they're questionable as far as motivation and intelligence.''

''People who get themselves into trouble with the ETA have to give up their kids to get a license to work,'' I said. ''Myra got in trouble, didn't she?''

''Yes. She and Horn both. They had a child out of wedlock and she tried to register him without proper papers.''

''You took her kid. Why did she work with you?''

''It was the only way she could visit her son.''

''Damn. That's mean, even for the government.''

Carver shrugged.

''Myra told us she was tracking the burst of creativity found in abduction victims,'' LaRue said.

''No, she was tracking the newbies. People like your buddy Ralph Kane, who have a six-degree conversion. We needed data, because we'd changed the programming slightly and we wanted to know that the reeducation was going to stick. So, the government established the different abduction encounter groups and Myra worked a few of them.''

Standing there, I discovered that my energy, my very zest for life had drained away with the truth. The bureaucrats had buggered us all.

LaRue, though, had decided not to feel sorry for himself. Instead, he drew the only card he had left. ''Purceval Walker killed Horn and you don't know where he is.''

''Yes, that's right,'' Nichols said. ''If you know his

whereabouts, it's your duty to hand him over to us.''

''Why?''

''Because he's a criminal, of course.''

LaRue took a step toward her. ''You don't want him because he's a murderer. You want him because you're afraid he'll rat the ETA out, just like Horn was going to do.''

Carver rushed to explain. ''Walker was afraid Horn would blow the operation. He was afraid of losing the money he was making. That makes him a loose cannon.''

''Looks like Horn set you up with a crazy one,'' LaRue said. ''And then it backfired on him. Myra probably helped him pull it all together, too, considering she's conveniently missing right now.''

''If I were Myra, I'd want to get even,'' I barked.

''Yes,'' Carver answered. ''She's not been treated well by the government, but hopefully her programming is still intact.''

''As I see it, Walker did a favor for you by killing Horn,'' I said. ''And now you want him dead.''

''That's right,'' Nichols said flatly. ''He knows too much. He could severely disrupt the status quo.''

I holstered my gun and then stared at her. ''You don't know how strong the SoC is, do you?''

She shook her head, pulling a weary sigh. ''No, we don't.''

Like it or not, it was time to wrestle the octopus. ''We can nab Walker for you,'' I told her, ''but we have a price.''

SIXTY-ONE

LaRue has a quaint metaphysical way of explaining my impatience and the results I usually get. He says it's like I'm constantly poking the universe between the shoulder blades, reminding it that I'm here and needing attention. After a while the universe decides it's taken enough of my shit and pokes back. The only problem is: the universe has a lot more oomph than I do, so I end up getting flattened.

I had to agree with him. What I proposed was a deal made with a faceless devil, and the worst part was, we weren't sure if the one we'd picked could do us any damned good after the tree finished shaking out. One thing was certain. Both LaRue and I knew we could cough up Purceval Walker. At that point Nichols and Carver were left straddling the barrel.

The parlay was short, sharp, and sweet. We would keep our jobs with tax-free bonus checks coming at regular intervals and I would have the reports erased against my name in regard to activities with Intergalactic Travelers. Gibson would get back his clinic and his funding, and we would all go on like the brainwashing of the world didn't matter.

Yes, I showed little compassion for the unknown plight of my fellowman, but to be honest, I'd apparently been there and done that, so I didn't give a damn about anybody else's shorts but my own. It was my icy attitude that fried Gibson's wires when LaRue and I stopped into his new apartment that evening.

After being tossed out of the clinic, he called in some markers and what he came up with was a big, basement room with a toilet. It was downwind from the coking plant and the smell wafting through the cracks in the tiny windows made your eyes turn to sawdust.

The good doctor was taking it easy in a plastic lounge chair listening to a tootling band of revelers playing on the nearby street corner. LaRue and I sat on an old, smelly couch and I began telling Gibson just what we needed from him after explaining the situation.

"If you want a chance at getting your old life back, then you're going to have to take a big risk and help us," I said.

"Doesn't it bother you that you're condemning future generations to this kind of abuse?" he snapped.

His attitude crapped me out and I spit back at him, "It's going to be done whether we vote for it or not. Get off your goddamned high-minded pedestal, Gibson, and come down here in the mud and manure with the rest of us."

"God, it really pisses me off," he muttered.

"Yeah, it bends most of us out of shape," I answered. "But the material world is just that—material. Get the goodies, folks, any way you can."

"It's such a high cost, Merrick."

I suddenly had an attack of weariness and found I didn't have the energy to drive this conversation. Slumping into the worn-out comfort of the sofa, I let LaRue convince him.

"Look, Doc," he said. "We've got to bring this guy in, and to do this, we'll have to set up a sting. We need your help."

"Do you know for certain that this guy killed Horn?"

"No, but all the evidence points his way. He had access to the mine facility through the back door. Walker was holding kids in the lower levels until it was time to ship them out."

"He was pumping the children through and some of them crawled away," I said. "That's how come the superstitious types were claiming that they were seeing people from the center of the earth.''

''We think Walker used one of the children to lure Jenna York away after Horn's death,'' LaRue added

''So, is he responsible for both of their murders?''

We shook our heads. ''We don't know for sure. If the scenario played out like we figure, then he had an accomplice.''

''Who?''

I sat forward on the couch. ''Myra Fontaine.''

Gibson got that wild-eyed squint the moment I told him. ''How do you think it came down?''

''Nurse York may have noticed the child and asked Walker to finish the procedure on Horn while she went to check. Having studied to be a doctor, Walker did have the knowledge and understanding to perform a spinal tap.''

Gibson grunted. ''What understanding? He stabbed him and popped the top on the syringe. What happened to the nurse?''

''It appears that she found the child and attempted to take him or her back to the lower levels, where she was attacked and killed.''

''And Myra did this?''

''Myra is a doctor, Gibson. We did a quick check when things started coming together and discovered that she had a degree in chiropractic service.''

''That's mandatory for every physician.''

''Then you see how she could have done it.''

He thought hard about what we were asking of him. ''What if your plan doesn't come together? I'm stew meat.''

''That's the chance.''

In the end Gibson's customary greed got in the way of his altruism and he gave in with a warning. ''I better get my clinic and patients back along with some lifetime assurances by tomorrow morning, or I'm not going to be the bouquet garni for this chili. Got it?''

I nodded at his big words and let him go on believing he had a stinking choice in the first place.

SIXTY-TWO

I balk at LaRue's mojo, but once in a while it comes in handy, especially with an uncooperative citizen. At that moment the citizen was Silvio Valinari. The maestro was playing musical chairs with the truth and so it was time to play Valinari by using Conchita Reuben's talents to the bitter end.

We'd had the good sense to toss the maestro into the dingiest lockup we had. Having cooled his rotors with the rats and the fleas, we figured he'd be ready to break if we pushed just the right pressure points. Our idea panned out almost immediately.

Upon seeing Reuben enter, Valinari came alive, sitting up on the bunk to rub his eyes when we hit the light switch. "What's going on?"

"We're here to talk," I said, pulling up to the small table. "This is Ms. Reuben. She called us tonight, very excited."

"About what?"

"About you, Mr. Valinari. You see, Ms. Reuben is an intuitive psychic that occasionally works with the Marshals Office to solve cases. She's been getting brain flashes lately. You know the kind—she sees the killer making his move in her head. It plays out scene by scene." Pulling back a chair, I motioned for him to sit in it. "Come here."

LaRue fetched a rickety seat for Reuben and the two faced off at the table. She then pulled out her tarot cards from a soft, linen bag, and as she shuffled she dove into her mystical act. "I keep seeing your face, sir."

Valinari wiped the back of his hand against his beard stubble, and from his expression, I could tell he'd started praying in between the syllables of his answer. "I haven't harmed anyone."

"But you know Purceval Walker killed Bernard Horn," I barked.

"No," he whined. "That's not true."

I moved around the table until I was behind him. Leaning over his shoulder, I spoke in a low, menacing voice. "You know it to be true. You also know where he is at this very moment."

"No!" He fumbled at his shirt collar and glanced nervously between us before settling his stare on the cards. "This is insane. Magic! You can't convict me on that!"

I stepped away and strolled around the table, coming to a stop beside Reuben. "You know he killed Bernard Horn and you know where he is. This nice lady is going to prove it to you and us." I pointed toward her. "If you would be so kind as to begin."

She nodded and jumped into the bullshit again. "I call upon the power of my guides and guardians to show us only truth and light." Taking a deep breath, she lifted her attention to me. "We are ready. Ask your first question."

I looked at Valinari while I challenged the oracle of the tarot. "What role did Valinari play in the scam involving the abduction of legally registered children?"

She flipped the cards. "Ten of wands. Oppression. Suppression of secrets; suppression of freedoms."

I chalked on a frown. "Now, isn't that interesting?"

"I swear to you, I don't know anything about Purceval Walker," he cried. "Honestly. What Bernard did was his business."

"But you knew what was going on," I said. "You convinced Betty Reseda to talk him into joining the Sparkers." Before he could answer, I flipped a look at Reuben. "Tell us, please, where Valinari aligns his political views.''

She complied, shuffling the stack and turning over the answer. ''Arcanum 18—the moon. This is the principle of choice. The moon represents the desire to remain genuine to ourselves, but at the same time donning the mask that hides our true motives.''

''Is that so?'' I said, adding a hint of incredulity to my voice. ''Tarot, tarot—tell me true. What is the connection between Valinari and the SoC?''

Reuben tipped up the card. ''Knight of swords. This card represents intention supported by pure feeling.''

''Imagine that? It sounds like you are up to your ears in the SoC, Silvio. It's time to crack the egg and tell us what's going on.''

''You can't scare me,'' he husked. ''You haven't said anything that would prove I knew about Walker.''

''Really?'' I pointed to the deck. ''Ms. Reuben, please tell us what sterling fact Valinari is hiding about Purceval Walker.''

She nodded and did as I asked. ''Arcanum 15—the devil.''

''No,'' he said on the exhale. ''No, you can't believe I had anything to do with him murdering Horn.''

I stared at him for a minute before he tried to explain without getting himself deeper. ''Yes, I'm involved in the SoC. Is that what you want to know? I couldn't talk Bernard into it, though.''

''But Betty Reseda could. You introduced her to the Sparkers and she took it from there.''

''You don't understand,'' he said. ''Bernard's talent needed nurturing. It needed freedom. The government chokes out any possibility of that, but he just wouldn't believe me. When he finally saw for himself, he changed. He understood.''

''Unfortunately, Walker didn't like what he was hearing.''

Valinari clammed up once more. ''I don't know.''

''You don't? Let's ask the cards just in case your memory needs jogging.'' Glancing at the ceiling, I said: ''Tell us, discarnate friends. Does Valinari know the whereabouts of Purceval Walker?''

Reuben turned up the card. ''Three of wands—virtue.'' She

leaned forward to speak to him. ''Virtue is another way of indicating a big, fat affirmative.''

Valinari's mouth dropped open, but I filled in the sound. ''Where is Purceval Walker as we speak, O metaphysical ones?''

Another card. ''Three of disks,'' Reuben reported. ''It represents the works.''

If I'd thought I was going to have to reel in Valinari by beefing up the answer, I was in for a nice surprise. The maestro abruptly started blubbering.

''Where is he?'' I demanded.

''There, right there,'' he said, jabbing toward the three of disks. ''He's hiding out at the District Glass Works.''

SIXTY-THREE

My partner and I took Valinari's word as gospel and we immediately ordered the ward cop on duty in that sector to unlock the side entrance to the factory. As it turns out, we shouldn't have embarrassed ourselves by rushing off on the word of this madman.

The streets were crammed with pedestrians, party goers, and work crews who were busy spiffing up the district for the celebration. By the time we reached the glass works, the ward cop had come and gone, preferring unruly drunks to a possible shoot-out. It was up to us, as usual.

The factory was dark, taken off-line in an effort to save money associated with the cost of recycling glass bottles. After a half hour of stumbling around, LaRue and I found the door half-hidden by an overflowing Dumpster. We yanked it open and climbed inside, but the moment my tail was in the building, the wind came up and slammed the door shut. Freezing to the spot, we waited in the darkness, letting our eyes adjust. I listened, hoping my lycanthropic hearing would pick up the whispers of children or the curses of adults. Nothing. It was silent, save for the scuttling of rats.

We drew our side arms and flicked on our service lanterns so we wouldn't fall into one of the giant pulverizers or trip over wires leading to the silent conveyor belts. There was trash lying all over the floor—heaps of old food, paper diapers, and soiled rags.

LaRue had an answer for what we saw. "The district had to run out a bunch of squatters after that hurricane we had."

I grunted, heading for the stairs leading to the basement. We padded down the steel steps quietly, but the metal clicked and clacked under our combined weight. Finally, we reached the bottom landing, and clinging to the walls with weapons at the ready, we held our breath and listened once more. I still heard no voices, but I did detect a gentle tapping and glanced at LaRue. He nodded, and we paused to snap our flashlights to our belts, giving us the freedom to use both hands.

The tapping continued, rhythmic and soft. On the telepathic count of three, we dove from our hiding place, and hitting the floor, we rolled apart, thereby splitting the field should we come across an assailant with a gun. We needn't have worried. The place was empty, and the rapping was nothing more than an air-handling fan at the far end of the room, cranking painfully against a bent coil as the breeze traveled down the shaft.

It was time to sink a foot in Valinari's ass. LaRue and I stalked back to the office and stormed into his dismal cell, grabbing him forcibly from his cot to slam him against the stone wall. The old maestro sang like he'd never sung before.

I kept smacking him across the jaw to make my point. He crescendoed, decrescendoed, and arpeggioed until his words were nothing more than a burble of blood.

"Where is Purceval Walker?" I barked.

"I thought he was at the glass works," he wailed. "That's where the card said he would be. I thought the witch was telling me where he was. I thought that's what you wanted to hear."

Crap. We'd taken the show a bit too far. Valinari believed in the cards so much that whatever they said, the answer was there and he would have agreed with it. Bamboozled by our own bamboozle. Upon realizing this, I lost all my fire and let LaRue have a go at him. I made myself comfortable in a greasy chair.

The strength my partner has in his fingers is enough to

crush a man's larynx. Combined with his verbal facility, LaRue proves time and again how much gumption he has. In fact, when it comes to dirtying a prisoner, he's a master; so for this crucial interrogation, he placed his right hand on the man's throat, massaged his Adam's apple, and gave Valinari his opinions on the opera.

"Horn was a no-talent, low-rent version of Antonio Gattali. He wasn't worth a plug nickel to you alive, and that's why you had no trouble teaming up with Myra Fontaine."

"I'm innocent," he whispered.

LaRue had him gurgling for air in a moment. "If you don't drop the routine, you will never be able to talk again, much less teach others to sing."

It took Valinari only a second to comply. LaRue released him, took a step back, and held out his hands to accept his explanation. The maestro hesitated to clear his throat and wipe at the blood weeping from the gash I'd given him.

"I didn't kill Bernard. He was everything to me. He risked his reputation for me."

"Why?"

"Because I'm a stupid man." Valinari shuffled back to the bunk, flopped down, and leaned against the wall. The minute his back contacted the cold stone, he sighed. "Several years ago I'd gotten into a bit of a bind. My first marriage was in the toilet; the government had abolished my job as a grounds-keeper for the School of Arts and Humanities. I needed employment and a place to live."

"Why not live with Horn if he was so special to you?"

Valinari frowned. "I have my pride, Marshal. Whatever you might think."

"So, in walks Myra Fontaine."

"No, in walks her father, Sydney."

LaRue glanced at me and I shrugged.

"Sydney had bucks," Valinari said. "Lots of them. He was a high-placed official, you see. Sydney licked the top of the boot instead of the bottom. Anyway, he hired me to help Myra through a required music course she was taking through the university."

I couldn't help finding that amusing. "She was tone-deaf, right?"

Valinari nodded. "They say that there is no such thing. Well, they've never met Myra."

"That squeaky voice started to drive you crazy, huh?"

"No, on the contrary. I found her delightful."

I was starting to get an ugly mental picture. "Let me guess. You partook of the cool springs in this fountain of youth."

"I fell in love with her," he snapped.

"And got her pregnant," LaRue said.

Valinari heaved another sigh. "Yes. Her father was a powerful man. If he'd known it was me, he would have had me erased, along with my family unit. Bernard came to my rescue."

"Being an orphan, he didn't have anybody to worry about," I said.

"That's right. Plus, he had his age and exuberance. Myra figured her father would make her marry him, if nothing else than to give the baby a last name and a legitimate family unit."

"But Papa fooled everybody," LaRue said.

"That he did. Instead of a marriage, he made Myra give up the child to the government."

SIXTY-FOUR

Valinari simply couldn't cough up the whereabouts of either Purceval Walker or Myra Fontaine, and the bloodier his lip got, the more forgetful he became. After nearly scaring the maestro to death with threats of violence, we were forced to call a halt to the brutality until the next morning, and so, LaRue and I joined Gibson and Baba back at my flat.

I have to admit that I was glad to get out of the car and away from my partner's lecture about synchronicity, tarot cards, and how beautiful Conchita Reuben looked while fortune-telling in a string bikini. LaRue's discourse followed me up the stairs, but upon seeing my roommate sitting in the middle of the floor counting the booty we'd scraped out of Pigeon's warehouse, he changed gears to talk about the fleeting nature of abundance. In Baba, he knew he had a captive audience and he squatted down to help her lift a couple of cast-iron pans out of a box while running on about the miracle of cosmic receiving.

Gibson gazed out of our dirty bay window, his expression shining with characteristic intensity. I joined him and he slipped his arm around my waist to pull me close. "I talked to the Osrics. They said they'd help with the sting if we can roll this guy. I promised them they wouldn't get shot."

In his career, Gibson has spent more time with freaks and outcasts than most people ever do. He's studied the brain-power of geeky geniuses, pinheaded telepaths, and weirdos who purposely pound nails into their nostrils. If we were going to con Walker out into the open, we needed help from these garden-styled schizos. "I'm sorry we're dangling you as the bait and I'm sorry we don't have a timetable for you yet. We lost the bubble tonight."

He shrugged. "I keep thinking about what the government has been doing to us all these years."

"And they'll keep doing it, Gibson. Don't fool yourself. If the Sparkers win, then they'll start their own abuses."

"It's too bad we can't be sure what's going on," LaRue said.

That was the basic problem, wasn't it? We were trying to see through a fog bank with a microscope. Our job seemed pretty petty compared to the weight of the world.

I sat down beside Baba and picked through a box, quietly inspecting this treasure trove. Gibson turned his attention to the revelry in the street, and LaRue actually shut up for a minute. It was then that I had a stretch.

I flopped around like a seal before Gibson came to my rescue. The pain rang through my chest, causing both of my arms to go numb, and I grappled with the air already captured in my lungs. No matter what I did, I couldn't breathe—in or out. Gibson pumped on my diaphragm, cursed me, demanded that I suck in the smelly atmosphere. For a good two minutes I was unable to do anything accept dive toward unconsciousness, and then, finally, something clicked inside me. I heard the lovely tones once more. When their crystal sounds faded into nothingness, I found that I had entered diamond mind.

I hovered over myself, satisfied that I was breathing on my own again, and the most amazing thing happened. My physical self realized the concern my astral body expressed and glanced directly at it. The shock was so much that I was unable to hold this state of clarity and went clattering back into my body, signaling my return with a gasp and a groan. My chest hurt like someone had shot me through the heart, and thankfully, I passed out.

Since Gibson's meddling in my noodle, I've gained a few real worries about my lycanthropic stretches, one of which is a predisposition to aphasia, a condition whereby the language centers in my brain just stop communicating. I end up speaking gibberish, and worse than that, I'm cut off from other people because I'm unable to understand their words and their meanings. So, when I woke up on the couch a few hours later, I panicked because LaRue was talking and I had no idea what he was saying. It was not until I calmed myself that I discovered I could understand his sentences; it was the subject matter that didn't make any sense.

I played possum and lay there with my eyes closed, listening to his thoughts on establishing a personal baseline for creativity while I reviewed the events of my stretch. First, I cataloged my physical changes and found out I was buffed to the max. My muscles strained, making my skin hurt; the inside-out fur was itching me to tears; and the vibration of lycanthropic vitality strummed through me.

Taking a long, slow pull of air, I attempted to review the feeling I'd had when I'd been wafting around my flat. Somehow, I had been aware on two levels, but only the thoughts in diamond mind had registered. It was as though my physical self had its own life free of my will, but my ethereal self held the reins of dominion. Whether this occurred with the help of the wolf, I cannot say, and to be honest? I didn't really want to know.

After ten minutes of listening to LaRue yammer on about meaningless shit, I raised my arm to check my watch and gathered everybody's concern.

"How do you feel?" Gibson asked, stepping over to check the pulse in my neck.

"Like new," I muttered. Pushing him away, I sat up, and did everything I could not to show the dizziness that swamped me. Finally, I managed to stand and walked into the other room to sit on the edge of my bed. I felt heavier than molasses, as though my mass was disproportionate to my size. With every bit of energy I had, I lay down, hoping for some solitude to consider the odd occurrences of my lycanthropy, but Gibson, ever the Saint Bernard with a healing draft of brandy, came to sit beside me. He studied me openly and then popped the question I knew was coming.

"What's happening to you?"

I sighed, then answered softly, "I didn't think it was that evident. Have I changed physically in ways I don't realize?"

He allowed his gaze to play over my body. "I don't know without closer inspection."

Before I could answer, he kissed me full on the lips and I threatened to leap into that comfort zone I desired so much. It took most of my strength to move past his power to speak. "In your opinion, have I been close to death during these last stretches?"

"Death? No. You've been having trouble getting your breath, but I think that may be from the presence of the radiodirium. As the bacteria dies you should return to your normal agony."

"My, what I have to look forward to."

He touched my hair with his fingertips. "What's wrong, Merrick?"

My entire life was wrong; that was the problem. "I've had a few out-of-body experiences."

Gibson's reaction was exactly what I thought it would be—he scowled, and then his expression grew intense and his gaze hooded. "Perhaps you need to tell me what's going on," he husked. "From the beginning."

"I'm experiencing awareness at two levels," I answered. "It's as if I break away from my body and I pause to hover over it. I even went flying across the tops of the buildings here in the district. At least, I think I did. It's hard to tell if it's a hallucination or if I've split in two."

"Astral projection?" he murmured. "The first time it happened was at Lizzie Borden's shack?"

I took a minute to stretch my tight muscles. "Is it possible?"

"Everything with you is possible." He slid off the bed and took a turn around the tiny room, pausing before our dresser to pick up a knickknack Baba had put there. He examined it carefully, but I could tell from the reflection in the mirror that his thoughts were galloping around the predicament I posed.

After replacing the trinket, he turned to face me.

"Intense pain has been known to produce out-of-body experiences, especially when they're linked to states of unconsciousness."

"And I passed out."

"Flat, like a flounder."

When I didn't reply, he went on, speaking with a soft, measured voice. "Neurologists haven't proven much about this phenomenon. So far, the experiments suggest that the brain is projecting the viewpoint back to the person, and from what science says, an OBE is nothing more than an illusion generated by a brain that is deprived of oxygen. We've had several classic cases of people with schizophrenia who have claimed this ability without the need for a life-threatening situation, but we're just not sure what causes the experience." He paused before demanding an answer. "What was your OBE like?"

I thought a moment. "I was filled with light, Gibson. What a wonderful feeling."

"You had feeling? From what? Your astral body or your physical body?"

I shook my head. "It didn't feel like I had a body at all when I was floating. There was no pain. No sensation except joy."

He must have read something in my expression. "Don't stop. Tell me more."

I smiled and slammed him with the truth. "I looked down at myself from the ceiling, and when I did, my physical body reacted. I looked up toward the place I was floating. I knew I was there."

SIXTY-FIVE

The next morning LaRue and I ordered a couple of ward cops to collect Engineer Zack from the train yard and install him in the cell right next to the comfy room housing Silvio Valinari. Upon entering this fine suite, we found that Zack had been shackled to the wall because he'd nearly killed one of the officers with that big torque wrench of his.

My lycanthropy makes me sensitive to changes in body temperature due to fluctuations in my metabolic rate, and feeling the dampness of this dungeon, I was forced to fight down a shiver. This symptom had been persistent lately, and as if to enhance my discomfort, it was the day before the full moon when I come down with a case of supernatural rabies. I could neither eat nor drink, and my mood had begun to deteriorate from the first moment that my saliva had dried up.

I smacked Zack's file folder on the table, but instead of sitting down, I pulled the chair out and propped my foot on it. Leaning my elbow on my knee, I studied the man while trying to work up enough spit to talk. His real name was Arthur Zack and he'd worked in that roundhouse for thirty years. He had a good work record and an interesting rap sheet.

"Says here in this file that you're the one who likes little girls," I husked. "You've been picked up and charged with sexual assault against minors four times.'' Zack yanked on his chains, but that was his only protest, so I continued. ''There is also one child who seems to be missing. Tell us where she is.''

He stared at me with a pair of cold eyes and I let him have that glare right back. ''You don't have nothin' on me.''

''We don't need anything,'' I answered. ''We could kill you now and no one would give a shit. In fact, I think that's what we're going to do.''

That got his attention, and his expression collapsed into a scowl. ''You're bluffing.''

To prove the point, LaRue flipped open a small switchblade and took a step toward Zack. The prisoner cowered and started whimpering.

''What are you going to do with that?'' he demanded.

LaRue pushed the calm-cool-cucumber package. ''This knife is an antique. It was used by my great-granddaddy to peel the skin off of cooked pig's feet. Yep, she's a beauty all right. Do you know that the blade is so sharp, it will slice the thinnest layers in the epidermis? It can take several minutes before we reach the muscle and hours until we strip away the muscle to reach the bone.''

''You wouldn't,'' Zack murmured, looking appropriately horrified.

LaRue paused to clean under his thumbnail with the tip of the blade and then took another step toward the prisoner. It was the only thing needed. Zack folded like a blanket.

''What do you want from me?'' he cried.

''Your cooperation,'' I replied evenly.

''I don't know anything.''

''Sure you do. Tell us where Purceval Walker is.''

''I don't know.''

LaRue shuffled his way and the answer jumped out of Zack's mouth. ''Okay, okay. I don't know where he is exactly, but I've got an emergency number where he can be reached.''

An hour later we'd convinced Zack to make that call for us, plugged the phone into the outlet in the cell, and then rehearsed him until he had the line down pat. We also gave him food and water along with a threat about poking the tip of the knife into his eyeballs if he double-crossed us. He assured us he wouldn't, but to make sure, LaRue hovered over him like a hawk with one lethal claw.

We put the phone on speaker and dialed the number. Purceval Walker answered after a couple of rings. "This is Turquoise," he said in a deep, rich voice.

"It's Zack."

There was a moment of silence before Walker hissed, "Zack. I told you not to call me unless it was a matter of life and death."

Zack glanced at LaRue. "It *is* a matter of life and death. Nichols and Carver have sold you out."

"What? How do you know that?"

"They told me. They found another person to make the roundup. You're going down, my man."

Walker's voice started to rise. "Why? I got a good load here. Lots of smart kids."

"Yeah, well, there's a doctor with his own ward clinic. He got wind of what was going on and he wanted in. He's playing a trump card, too."

"What kind?"

"He's got an alien baby."

"What?"

"That's right. And the moment the goose steppers heard that, they wanted this guy real bad."

"Well, what about my load?"

"What about it?"

"I nabbed some little, fucking geniuses. That's got to count for something."

"Against a kid from Mars? Are you nuts? This monster has a head twice the size of Venus. I saw it. The ETA is going to get hold of him and make clones. They got all the brilliant material they need." Zack stopped to take a deep breath before cocking the trigger on the shotgun. "There is a way you might save your ass, though."

Walker's tone swerved into petulance. "Oh, right. What would you suggest?"

Zack snorted. "I suggest you steal the brat."

SIXTY-SIX

I really wanted to get this game over before the full moon hit, and of course, my impatience and desire eventually conspired to be my undoing.

That night, LaRue and I met Gibson at his reopened clinic. There, he introduced us to Mr. and Mrs. Osric and their ten-year-old son, Jason. As I said, Gibson has treated a lot of freaks in his time, and the Osrics probably topped the list. They were a tiny, malformed family, and according to the good doctor, it was due to living in a district that ran along the sinkhole that was, until late last century, the Aral Sea in LaRue's beloved Soviet Union. What was once a big spot of water had disappeared completely and the people who lived around it had found themselves beset by a variety of plagues, cancers, and birth defects. I'm sure we broke most of the rules covered by the Disabilities Act and all of the rules of morality by asking for the Osrics' help, but we had little choice. Besides, we were paying them with my last red seven, a district coupon worth enough to buy food for a year. It had to be worth more than Jason and his oversized noggin.

I know it was wrong, but I couldn't stop staring at the kid's head. He looked like an alien with an overextended brow ridge and tiny eyes. It perched there above an impossibly skinny neck, balanced by his big, flaring ears.

"Did you explain everything to Mr. and Mrs. Osric?" I asked, nodding to the couple before glancing toward Gibson.

"Yes," he answered quietly.

"We're happy to help," Mrs. Osric peeped.

I looked in her direction and wondered where a woman who barely cleared three feet tall managed to find her clothes. "This will be dangerous," I said. "This man is a killer and will do anything to protect himself."

She smiled. "Dr. Gibson has faith in you and Marshal LaRue. He told us not to worry and we won't." With that, she turned to Jason. "Now, honey, you do everything the marshals tell you to do. Okay?"

"Yep," he whispered. "Not a prob. I'll help you catch this murderer."

He sounded like any smart-ass kid. I sure hoped he could run fast without that head of his tilting him off balance.

The parents left soon after and Gibson buttoned up the clinic, leaving a window open in one of his examining rooms. We pushed Jason into the cubicle, retired to the shadows, and waited for Walker to stop by for the extraterrestrial. It didn't take long.

About three A.M., he showed up and found the window. LaRue and I had been on guard duty right outside the examining room, and when Walker made a grunting noise, we chanced peeking through the crack in the doorway to check on the kid. Ambient red light from a flashing sign on the building next door lit up the room, showing me Walker's reflection in a nearby mirror. He was a big man with long, blond hair and a mustache. The bastard was none too gentle, either. He grabbed Jason by one of his slop-bucket ears and pasted his mouth shut with duct tape before pushing the child through the open window, not caring that the kid bumped his enormous head on the way out.

It was time to move. LaRue and I charged through the front entrance and started to track Walker. Our plan was to follow him back to his hiding place and hopefully find the children he'd nabbed already.

The streets were crammed with revelers—masks, costumes, dance contests, and impromptu parades. The district had rotated the electricity and the locality sparkled with strings of colored lights crisscrossing the thoroughfares. Music blared from gaily decorated apartment balconies. Horns tootled and honked. People screamed and laughed like it might be their last time to show open, spontaneous joy.

We kept several yards behind Walker as he hurried Jason through the crowd. LaRue and I fanned out, working both sides of the street in an effort to keep the killer in sight. We weaved our way toward the intersection of Duvalier Drive and Cathedral Boulevard, where a truck of chickens had overturned and had caused an impromptu barbecue. The fire department had a decrepit pumper at the scene, but the bonfire was more than the water hose could handle.

I lost LaRue in the noise, flame, and smoke, but managed to keep a close eye on Walker. He turned down Thirteenth Street and into an area of the district known as the fish factory. Here were the caterers of this precelebration—street peddlers, busy working in the garish blue light of fluorescent bulbs and neon signs, serving up fried squid, fish-head soup, and the occasional poisoned oyster.

I rushed through this throng of food merchants and whipped by a booth selling tuna noodle casserole. The smell was so good that my feet slowed down and I glanced back to look longingly at the food I could not have. My momentary weakness proved to be our undoing, because when I turned back to follow Walker, he was gone.

SIXTY-SEVEN

When we told Gibson what had happened, his face turned the color of a strawberry and the look in his eyes reminded me of a cartoon bad guy just before he starts shooting swords from the center of his pupils. In fact, he was so angry about our bungling that his voice stuck in his throat and it took him a couple of tries until he started screaming.

"I can't believe you let this happen!" he bellowed. "How fast could the bastard have been traveling with a kid like Jason?"

"The district streets are jammed, Doc," LaRue barked. "He took a turn down a dark, crowded alley and we lost him."

"That's no excuse. You two are supposed to know what you're doing. You sure as hell can come up with the scams, but in the end everyone else pays." He paused to stare at me like the wild man of Borneo and then he purposely pooped on the playing field. "Merrick, you're a curse on my life!"

I was feeling pretty low and angry at myself up to that point, but the moment he made that statement I turned my rage outward and slapped him hard across the face. My blow was enough to knock him backward a couple of steps and he stood there, silent and stunned. We faced off in the middle of the reception area for a good minute before the phone rang.

We all glanced toward the desk. "Answer it," I ordered. "And turn on the tape machine."

Gibson stalled a second more and then reached for the phone. "What?" he growled.

A moment later he fumbled for the speaker button to let us listen. The caller was Myra Fontaine.

"I assume Merrick and LaRue can hear me," she said.

I made a slashing motion across my neck and Gibson nodded. "No, Myra, it's just me. What do you want? I have big problems right now."

"Yes," she said. "You do. A problem with a missing child."

Gibson glanced at us before stringing her along. "How do you know about him?"

"Because he's here with me now. I also know this was a setup."

"It was no setup. That child was here for overnight observation. I came in to check on him and he was gone."

"Don't lie!" she screeched. "I know that Arthur Zack is in custody."

LaRue shook his head. We'd been sold out at a hundred different levels.

"I don't know who Arthur Zack is," Gibson said. "If you have Jason, please bring him back."

There were a few seconds of silence when a thrumming noise in the background bubbled through the machine. Squeezing my eyes shut, I focused on the sounds, but Fontaine screwed me up by laughing. "You must think I'm a complete fool, Lane. I wouldn't have expected that—not from you."

"Listen, Myra. The ETA and marshals want Walker. They know you're not involved in Bernard Horn's death."

She laughed again. "You were never a very good liar where I was concerned and you're still not. I'm up to my hips in this situation."

"What's that supposed to mean?" he asked. "Did you kill Horn?"

"I might as well have," she said. Fontaine paused and we counted down the seconds, hoping she would spit up a confession. She didn't.

Gibson pushed. "You and Walker have a load of kids ready to ship to the government, but now that Horn is out of the picture, you don't have anyone to mediate for you, do you? And let's see. I suspect the District Council has revoked your operating license and labor designation. Is that right?"

She didn't reply and again I found myself listening for background noise. I heard something, but it was faint and faraway.

Gibson continued to pound her. "The way I see it, they're trying to force you to come in off the street. You know too much about their scam. You've become a liability and we know what happens to people who are no more good to their government. Shoot 'em, burn 'em, mix in their ashes with a load of manure. The only choice you have is to bamboozle your way on the backdoor market. How long do you think you can keep that up?"

"I didn't call to talk about that," she mooed. "I want to know if you want this deformed brat back."

"Of course I do. He's innocent."

"He's a freak. The best thing to happen to him would be to die."

"Please, Myra, don't hurt him. He's had enough pain in his short life."

She sighed. "If you want him back, then you can have him. For a price."

What a cold, calculating bitch, and people said I was bad.

"What price?" Gibson murmured.

"Five thousand credits—cash," she answered. "I'll call you tomorrow night after the official start of carnival." With that, Myra Fontaine sealed her fate and broke the connection.

SIXTY-EIGHT

After being stonewalled by Myra Fontaine, we suddenly saw our hopes wash away like a drunk drowning his sorrows in moonshine. Gibson hung up the phone and started shouting again, so LaRue and I grabbed the tape and headed back to the office in hopes of fixing this disaster.

That damned shrink. Fontaine had gotten in my way a couple of times and had knowingly cast me to the Office of Intelligence so the creeps over there could keep stinking tabs on my lycanthropy. She'd betrayed me, but she had betrayed Gibson, too, and from what we could understand of this whole ETA mess, she'd sold out Horn as well.

For all intents and purposes, the carnival was under way. The streets were packed, and driving the Trabi through this crowd was like trying to run people before a charging bull. When we finally arrived at the office, it was seven in the morning. The shift was changing, and the moment we walked inside the homicide pen, we were greeted by Nichols and Carver. They sat at our desks, looking crisp, clean, and in control.

''Get out of my chair,'' I ordered.

Nichols glanced calmly at me and then rose with a liquid grace that I wished would congeal on her before she managed to stand up straight. Carver followed suit and LaRue and I took our rightful places.

"Did you find Walker, yet?" Nichols asked.

"Yes," I lied. "We're waiting for the right moment to spring the trap."

"I'll bet," she answered.

I glared at her, but her reply to my silent challenge was a smile. "You can see that we've kept our side of the bargain," she announced. "Dr. Gibson will find his paperwork in order this morning. He should be treating an overabundance of patients with alcohol poisoning by this evening."

"Where is Walker?" Carver said.

"Don't worry about where he is," I snapped. "We'll deliver him to you."

Nichols placed her hands on her hips and leaned slightly in my direction. "You'd better or you'll be frying."

I turned away to focus on my computer screen and dismissed them with my disinterest.

They grumbled, but left us to our work and our frustration. Though it was a small-scale victory, sending them away did a lot to boost my ego and I energetically attacked our problem. I slipped the telephone tape into my computer, brought up the electronic information on the screen, and tried to convert the sound into written language by playing it through a software package designed to track voice calls. The software wasn't powerful, but it did highlight the noises in a conversation and helped to identify the background sounds. Unfortunately, like everything else in our lives, this didn't work well and I came away empty-handed.

Cursing, I decided to set up the headphones, hoping to uncover Fontaine's whereabouts by using my lycanthropic talents for picking out the arias behind the noise. LaRue remained mercifully quiet and watched me while eating his breakfast. An hour slipped by, during which time I replayed the tape until I thought I was going to lose my mind from listening to Fontaine's squeaky words. I handed the earplugs over to my partner and he took a turn. In the end he came away without the answers, too. This activity went on for seven hours.

It was then, tired, annoyed, and hungry, that the wolf spilled the supernatural beans for me.

I took a piece of paper from the waste bin and began to doodle, translating the sentences I heard into the shapes they made me visualize. What I ended up with was a design that looked like the jagged scribble of a lie-detector pen. Above this meandering, I added the strange thumping noise by sketching in a bouncing ball. Below the zigzags, I added a ruffle design, brought forth by the gently rustling of what I was certain was Fontaine's classic silk blouse. I fell into an odd rhythm, not unlike the pace I set when beginning a self-hypnosis session. Perhaps I had relaxed enough, or maybe my lycanthropic brain helped me to deduce the answer, but at some point all the levels of sound were abruptly segregated.

It was then that I uncovered the voice in the background. I groped for LaRue to get his attention, yet squeezed my eyes shut and held a finger to my lips as I listened to the message for the hundredth time. The voice was barely there, but with the wolf forcing me to process the sound at a one-second delay, I clearly heard Nurse Addison.

SIXTY-NINE

When I realized Nurse Addison had talked when she should have kept silent, it took us about two minutes to get her home address and about three hours to get across district to her house. The Autumn Carnival was in full swing, with every street becoming a pedestrian detour.

After having to take the long way around Ward 23 to avoid a disabled truck carrying a float for the carnival parade, we finally found Nurse Addison's place—a small, concrete building, painted tropical pink. My patience had been bruised by the afternoon of dicey navigation and I hoped that Addison would prove to be her overbearing self so I would have a good excuse to manhandle her.

It took five minutes of pounding before she answered the door. The second we had entry, I bulled my way through, underestimating my supernatural strength and accidentally shoving the woman to the floor. She lay there, her bright red housedress hiked up around her black underwear. LaRue helped her sit up and straighten her clothes while I bit down hard on the reins in an attempt to be dangerous, but not lethal.

"You, Nurse Addison, are in a lot of trouble," I growled.

She pushed her glasses down on her nose and glared at me. "You are mistaken."

I took a step toward her and experienced a nig of satisfaction when she raised her arms to protect her face. "I'm not mistaken. In fact, I have your voice clearly identified in the background noise of a telephone call that Myra Fontaine made to us a few hours ago."

She scowled, staring at me as though her expression could change the truth. After I made her flinch a second time, she answered with alacrity. "I was held against my will."

"Why, then, did they let you go to come home?"

"Because I convinced them I would keep their secret."

"And you would have if we hadn't knocked down your door."

Addison tried to deflect the question. "Purceval Walker killed Bernard Horn."

"How do you know?"

She hesitated, grinding her teeth before spilling the salsa. "I saw him do it."

"Why didn't you stop him?" LaRue asked.

"You would have blamed me for the murder."

"Not doing anything is considered a felony accessory to murder, ma'am."

Addison blinked at us and then lost her composure. She sobbed uncontrollably, blubbering about having to do what the government tells her to do.

Finally, LaRue managed to calm her down with a glass of water after helping her to the sofa. When she could speak again, he pinned her bra to the sheets. "Tell us why you blame the government for your lack of ethics."

Addison wiped her fingers across her forehead and snorted. "Myra Fontaine told me that she would tell the ETA that I'd smothered several of the children they'd stolen from family units."

"Have you?"

"No," she wailed. "I tried to protect them from Walker and Horn."

"Why?"

"Because they used the children before delivering them."

"Used them how?" I said.

"Sexually. One little girl had just entered puberty and she

was made pregnant by one of those oafs.'' She grunted and glanced at her lap.

It was my turn to grunt. ''You didn't know who to trust.''

''That's right. I still don't. You two have got me dead to rights. I suppose I can't do much about it.''

''You can tell us where Fontaine, Walker, and the children are,'' LaRue said. ''That's something.''

Addison raised her gaze to study him intently. ''They're in the same place as before. Down in the mine.''

Bravo! For once, we were on the receiving end of some good news, but as usual, my celebration was cut short. Time must have gotten away from us and the moon must have been on the rise, because I exploded into a lunar stretch that left my awareness in two places at once.

SEVENTY

My full-moon stretches are never easy and I've suffered from a variety of problems, but a few things can be expected. Usually, I find myself phasing between reality and hallucination. One second, I've got a small hold on the events occurring around me; the next, I'm off in la-la land dancing the flimflam with some floozy from my imagination. I cycle between these two perspectives, yet, this time, it was as though I had adjusted my personal lens of understanding. The world had a finite focus viewed from the place where I floated above myself and there was not one bit of hesitation, confusion, or hallucination in the awareness of my physical body.

When I came around fully launched into this disposition, I saw my partner's face close to mine. I noticed the tiny laugh lines edging his eyes and how the lamplight caught the amber vein of color running through that mess he called hair. He spoke, but the words were lost to me, because the minute he opened his mouth, my gaze came to rest on the swath of his three-day-old beard. It was not until Nurse Addison screeched that I pulled out of his tight perspective and allowed my floating self to glance in her direction.

''What's wrong with her?'' she demanded. Before LaRue

could answer, she pushed herself to a stand and waddled for the telephone. "Go away!" she screamed.

My out-of-body partner tried to surge forward to prevent her from calling a neighbor with a shotgun, but it was useless. I'd abruptly found the parameters of my dual nature—my floating body couldn't move forward unless my physical one took the first step. Instead of the high-flying freedom induced by my unconscious states, my vantage point from above was secured squarely to ground. Somehow, I held this balloon on a short tether.

"Stop her, Andy," I croaked.

My partner frowned and whipped around. With a fluid motion, he smacked the receiver out of her hand and it clattered to the floor. "Let me make that call for you," he snarled, and yanking out his com-link, he did just that.

Fifty minutes later two ward cops showed up to haul Addison down to the Marshals Office. During that time I sat on the sofa, testing my flying ability, and found that I really couldn't go far without my solid half. What I couldn't figure out, though, had to do with the earlier diamond-mind experiences. The exhilaration and the joy had come with knowing the knowable, but shackled to my terrestrial perspective, I was somehow limited in what I understood. Had the laws of physics dented my metaphysical possibilities?

Thankfully, my skepticism got in the way and I decided that in the midst of the pain of a full moon, I didn't need to wander off on aimless reflection. I needed to catch a killer and give the ETA some more kids to screw up.

We hustled to the Trabi, and sliding inside, I found that my floating self preferred to hover over the roof.

"What's the matter?" LaRue asked, when he saw me trying to stare past the overhead upholstery.

"Nothing, Andy. It's just a weird stretch this time. I think I'm fine, though. Don't worry."

He gunned the car. "Worry is not in my vocabulary."

To be honest, a lot of other words were. My partner cursed for five minutes as our charge forward was limited to waiting patiently until the tail end of the carnival parade passed through an intersection. Once it tootled and banged down the street, LaRue pushed the Trabi engine until it whistled.

I was remarkably calm. A sting on the full moon would have normally squeezed adrenaline through my pores, but this time my alter ego seemed to be in control of my emotions. It harnessed them by feeding me a stream of images—I could literally see around the next corner and sense the collage of feelings wafting from the revelers. My flying perspective told me this carnival was a farce, both in the hearts and minds of the participants. Fear ruled, and for some reason, it was right it should. Man was fearful. That's what kept him strong. It's also what kept him from being honest, especially with himself.

I noticed how much brighter the district buildings were with their coats of whitewash, and the reflection of costumes created with sequins and layers of used tin foil enhanced the effect. My lycanthropic sight added to the brightness, making me catch myself in a question: what part of me processed this ability—my upper or lower body?

Flat on the heels of that thought, I found myself bombarded by an observation I could have lived without. I didn't have the fight in me necessary to take down a killer.

This panicked me and the passenger riding aloft started to weigh differently. Where before I floated along gently, I now had an invisible headwind bucking me. It wasn't the breeze kicked up by the Trabi, but instead, some force that opposed my essence. I lost hold of the diamond mind and this filled me with terror. Leaning forward in the seat, I tried to recover the euphoria by covering my eyes and breathing deeply.

"What's wrong, Ty?" LaRue demanded. "Are you going to be sick? If you are, let me pull over."

I shook my head, certain that I rattled my brain in the process. "Can you slow the car down just a little?"

He did as I asked and it helped to relieve the pressure my floating body felt. I forced the fear away bit by bit, telling myself that this emotion was nothing more than my usual encounter with the wolf.

"You said worry wasn't in your vocabulary, Andy," I said softly.

"It's not," he answered. "But prudence is. Do I take you to Gibson, or do we go through with this?"

I glanced at him. "Are you mad? We go through with this. Our butts are on the line and I'm not going to let the goddamned ETA win."

He grinned, and stepped on the gas pedal. I felt my astral self fly along once more, buoyed by resolve, and before I knew it, we arrived at the PHO Rehabilitation Facility. The place was manned by a single security guard who did nothing to prevent us from storming past him to the elevator. LaRue punched the down button savagely as we both drew our weapons. Guns, sick people, and kids. It was not a good combination.

The elevator dropped down to the rehab level. During the ride into the center of the earth, my lycanthropic resiliency came to bear and I found the strength and desire to flatten Purceval Walker. My astral body felt this power and rushed off to check the pathway ahead of us. How it all worked, I can't say, but I held the images sent to me in my mind's eye at the same time as I communicated with LaRue.

"This joint is packed," he whispered.

"Stay in the shadows, Andy. We don't want anyone alerting Walker to our presence."

The lights were dimmed in the corridors and most of the cubicles were buttoned up, but turning the corner, we came to an unmarked intersection and heard the gay laughter of people celebrating. To the right, we found the solarium, brightly lit and crowded with those arthritics who wanted to share in the festivities. They danced and shuffled to a recording of Bernard Horn's voice. LaRue took a few steps to the left to go around this herd of cripples, but I stopped him. Sending out my astral bloodhound, I took several seconds to scout ahead. The hall dead-ended into a storage room. We had to go past the solarium to get to the corridor leading to the auxiliary entrance.

LaRue and I zipped past, rushing now to make up time and leave any curiosity seekers behind. Thirty yards ahead, we hit a stone wall. Literally. My floating self had goofed it up, so now it was back the other way.

After another few frustrating minutes, complete with having to duck a nurse and doctor, we finally edged past the party and found the right direction to our killer.

LaRue relied upon his service lantern to show him the way while I used my lycanthropic twin, hoping I wouldn't get my wires crossed again. We finally found the service elevator, and after fumbling with the keys, we chose the right one to start the car. The next ten minutes saw us unlocking the doors leading to the surface as though this mine was some sort of Pandora's box holding a prize of hope.

By the time we reached the transformer room, my flying body had expanded, the twofold awareness evolving to include sound. I stopped dead when the sensation hit me, because this latest communications link confused my interpretation of the simulcast that I was being fed. It was like a hose had been pushed inside my brain, and once there, it pumped the noise into a filling well behind my sinuses. I was suddenly overwhelmed by a fierce headache. A moment after the pounding started, I heard the children.

My astral self zoomed toward the sound and I rolled with it, pulling LaRue behind me. I prayed my topside body hadn't bungled it again by leading us into another tight spot, but before we knew it, we stumbled upon the evidence of life—the sour scent of urine mixed with milky vomit.

I stopped at a rusted door set deeply into the stone wall. LaRue nodded, tried the knob gently, but shook his head when it came up locked. We stopped again to listen and, yes, the kids were on the other side. LaRue made a punching motion with his fist. I nodded and we backed up. Like two superhero rejects from a B vid, we used our combined weight to batter down the door. Once inside, we were forced to blink against the bright overhead lights, but my etheric body spared me the moment of disorientation by revealing Purceval Walker to me. He was wedged in the middle of a congested space, surrounded by at least a hundred children, all begging for a handful of clumpy rice from an old, wooden bucket that he protected.

Duvalier's covenant with the citizens mandates that no man may serve time for a crime unless he's caught in the attempt. I have never liked to go against this rule, but the clarity of this strange diamond mind told me it was necessary.

Walker shouted when he saw us and flung the iron ladle

in our direction. We ducked and the spoon flew over our heads and through my astral body. The killer lumbered like a football player, but he managed to grab for the pistol he carried on his hip. "Stop bothering me!" he screamed.

LaRue was quicker than thought. He used his flashlight like a shot put, snatching it from the clip on his belt and heaving it at Walker. It grazed him on the head, deflected by the guy's noggin right into the bucket of sticky gruel. Walker bellowed, but I barked louder.

"You're under arrest for the murder of Bernard Horn and Jenna York. Drop your weapon now."

We faced off for a solid minute before I realized the wailing of the children had escalated. They fought to get out of the line of fire, and one little tyke decided to cling to my leg for protection. I tried to shake him away while keeping both sets of awareness on Walker.

"I didn't kill Bernard," he said. "I didn't do it."

"That's right, he didn't."

The abrupt intrusion of the squeaky voice made me shiver. Myra Fontaine. I glanced behind me and there she stood, holding a loaded shotgun on us. With her appearance, I wished like hell my astral self could smack her in the chops. LaRue and I separated but didn't give up our weapons and she didn't ask for them. Instead, she pointed her blaster at the crowd. The children backed away before their crying died to sniffles and tiny, tortured sounds. They watched, big-eyed, showing all the characteristic fear that would someday motivate their choices in life. Of course, that depended on whether they lived or not.

"What do you mean Walker didn't kill Horn?" I said.

"That's what I said," she answered. "Bubblebrain over there was trying to save him. It was a good thing I'd come to visit Bernard to try to convince him not to sell out the ETA program."

"From what we understand, you should have been with the Sparkers," LaRue said.

"Well, I'm not. I'm a loyal citizen. I do what I'm told."

"And you hate every minute of it," I added.

She glared at me and then smiled slowly, taking a moment to brush at a stain on her silk blouse.

"What are we going to do with them?" Walker demanded, pointing at us with his pistol.

Fontaine shook her head. "We aren't going to do anything with them." With that, she raised the rifle, and pumped the man with both barrels of buckshot.

He took the blast in the chest and it splattered him all over the kids. The screaming started in earnest as the blood dripped from the ceiling and got into the eyes of the children.

I used my lycanthropic speed to get the drop on her by taking a step her direction and knocking the gun from her hand. It flew into the crowd, where it was swallowed up by kids trying to race to the door, but LaRue outran the little beggars in time to keep them from escaping. I caught Fontaine by the shoulders, and once the melee peetered out, I asked her that question I couldn't avoid.

"Why did you do it?"

"I told you," she screeched. "I'm a loyal citizen."

SEVENTY-ONE

My awareness was still out there by the time the Marshals Office managed to send in a crime team. The moment Gibson got word that we had secured the area, he stopped by, grabbed Jason, and then left without a word to me. LaRue and I then chased the patients out of the solarium and into their cubicles, and here we waited for Julie and the troops. She arrived, stared coldly at my partner as he munched on a cookie, and then gathering me into her fishy gaze, she came to attention and gave us both a crisp salute before stalking off to confer with her deputy.

The watch commander had barely cleared the door when Nichols and Carver came goose-stepping into our lives. Nichols nodded curtly, assuming the role of spokeswoman for the ETA. ''You've been efficient. That is to be commended.''

Because of my floating personality, I heard this compliment from the perspective of diamond mind. I knew she could offer nothing more, and I understood her words to be an attempt at an apology. Unfortunately, my physical body was left saddled with outrage as well as a mouth that could sound off my displeasure. Instead of backing away, I took a step toward her and spoke, using the measured strain of words like a Zen monk intoned a mantra. "I can see the future, you know. And you don't have any."

Nichols moved away from me until she stood beside her partner. "Where are the children?"

I grunted. "They're gone."

"What do you mean?" she barked. "Walker must have had some children collected for delivery."

"He did." I paused, drawing out her anxiety. When it looked like she was going to climb out of her black boots, I continued. "There were over a hundred kids crowded into a very small room. The moment we opened the door, they ran like hell."

"It was a stampede," LaRue said.

"We tried rounding them up, but it was too late," I chimed. "Since we couldn't get backup on this operation, there were only two of us. We couldn't contain the whole bunch."

LaRue flitted into the conversation again. "It was a free-for-all."

Nichols screwed up her lips and stomped angrily. "Dammit! Now we have to round them up again."

She turned away and started down the corridor, dragging Carver by the sleeve.

The truth had not been far from our story. We'd purposely led the kids out the back door, where they dashed through the roundhouse and into the questionable safety of the night. It was the best we could do for now.

Frank Wilson walked in after our meeting with our ETA compatriots, sweating and stinking of garlic pickles. He pushed up to the buffet table and poured himself a cup of punch.

"Is everything okay, Frank?" LaRue asked. "You did find the body, didn't you?"

He slugged his drink before nodding. "Yes. Walker is as dead as dead can be."

"So why the waterfall splashing down over your forehead?"

Wilson grunted, reached up, and swiped the perspiration away. Glancing at us from the corner of his eye, he gave us the news. "I just received a report over the communications array. We've got wholesale looting up-district and several neighborhoods are engaging the riot police at this very moment.'' He paused to shake his head and whisper the real fate of the future. ''The revolution has begun.''